NG Rippel's interest in writing was driven by a misguided impression that his great-uncle was writing deep thoughts into the small Scripto notepad which was kept in his front shirt pocket. At age of six, Rippel started doing the same, and continued the practice, despite learning that what Uncle George was writing were lines of information on upcoming weddings and funerals where he might be able to pick up a free meal. However, Rippel has continued the practice of writing lines in notepads for the past 65+ years.

NG Rippel began writing words and being an observer of whatever surrounded him. At the age of 25, he became a realist and dedicated himself to increasing his understanding of reality. An effort which has continued ever since.
To learn more about NG Rippel, go to ngrippel.com.

For my ancestors, wife, children and grand-children.

NG Rippel

Abe's Place

Book 1 of Wannasea Tales

Austin Macauley Publishers
LONDON · CAMBRIDGE · NEW YORK · SHARJAH

Copyright © NG Rippel 2023

All rights reserved. No part of this publication may be reproduced, distributed, or transmitted in any form or by any means, including photocopying, recording, or other electronic or mechanical methods, without the prior written permission of the publisher, except in the case of brief quotations embodied in critical reviews and certain other non-commercial uses permitted by copyright law. For permission requests, write to the publisher.

Any person who commits any unauthorized act in relation to this publication may be liable to criminal prosecution and civil claims for damages.

This is a work of fiction. Names, characters, businesses, places, events, locales, and incidents are either the products of the author's imagination or used in a fictitious manner. Any resemblance to actual persons, living or dead, or actual events is purely coincidental.

Ordering Information
Quantity sales: Special discounts are available on quantity purchases by corporations, associations, and others. For details, contact the publisher at the address below.

Publisher's Cataloguing-in-Publication data
Rippel, NG
Abe's Place

ISBN 9781685620493 (Paperback)
ISBN 9781685620509 (ePub e-book)

Library of Congress Control Number: 2023906721

www.austinmacauley.com/us

First Published 2023
Austin Macauley Publishers LLC
40 Wall Street, 33rd Floor, Suite 3302
New York, NY 10005
USA

mail-usa@austinmacauley.com
+1 (646) 5125767

Thanks to the assistance with I have received from my wife and the rest of my family which allowed this work to move forward.

Table of Contents

Openers	11
The Kingdom of Wannasea	17
The Kingdom of Wannasea	20
A Walk up the Mountain	23
Hugo Flies	32
Hugh Visits	36
Don't Blame the Alcohol	40
Enter the Tillerman	43
Alice	52
The Morris Returns	57
Dark Ringlets	64
Reggie's Return	70
Coming to Terms	77
An Unexpected Slip	85
Piano Notes	94
The Jitters	98
Opening Night	104
Incorporation	112
Night Three	117
The Dedication	121

Reggie's Performance	129
Final Offer	137
An Unwelcome Discovery	144
Another Unwelcome Discovery	147
Not the Same	153
Losing Power	161
Mindy	165
Reggie Unsolicited	169
Different Direction	172
Results	180
Emma Receives a Visitor	184
Full Disclosure	193
Cha-ching	199
Explosions	205
Assessment	210
The News	216
An Ending	220
Light Blue Sailboat	222
The Party	229

Openers

"Shouting threats, pirates roamed the rocky shores. Dwelt in the hidden coves when the need arose. Wannasea had always been their island of escape." Abe writes before putting down the pen, closing his black journal and rising from the cushioned chair which sits on the large deck outside of his bedroom. A room which had once been the storage area for the bar and grill. Picking up the journal, he walks into his bedroom, his eyes immediately going to the clock on the wall which reads 5:15 PM.

Damn, Abe thinks, *I've done it again.*

Placing the journal on the desk, Abe walks into the bathroom, pulls the toothbrush from its holder, adds a healthy dab of baking powder-based toothpaste before beginning to brush.

Maybe I've gotten too old for this place, Abe thinks as he finishes the task. *Beth doesn't need to be putting up with this nonsense anymore.*

Abe rinses his mouth, spits it out and walks out of the bathroom, across the oak planked floor of his cluttered bedroom, then down the stairs and around the corner.

Passing the customer restroom area on his right which sits immediately below his room, Abe walks down the hallway leading from the rear entrance into the dining area.

"I'm late, aren't I?" Abe says to Sallie, the kitchen manager of 'The Place,' as she comes out of the heavy swinging doors from the kitchen carrying a tray of food.

"You're okay, Abe," Sallie said without looking. "They are just getting started."

Abe turns left, goes around the corner of the long oak bar into the coffee and tea preparation area. This establishment has been in his family's possession for as long as Abe can remember.

"Hey Grandpa," Beth his twenty-five year old granddaughter intones as she buzzes him on the cheek while pouring out two cups of Wannasea tea for a couple of fifty-something ladies. Abe thinks perhaps the ladies might be tourists, but with so many new people having moved to the island, he can't be sure.

"I can help do the tea," Abe suggests as he nods a greeting to the two ladies.

Beth frowns. Making tea or almost anything else which is constructed from other than words is not in her grandfather's skill set.

"Why don't you relieve Marie at the cash register?" Beth suggests as she delivers the tea to ladies before heading into the kitchen to pick up the rest of their order.

Abe dutifully heads toward the front portion of the bar and the old cash register which his mother had bought almost sixty years ago. He taps Marie on the shoulder.

"I'm your replacement," Abe tells Marie.

Marie smiles and slides off the stool, patting Abe on the arm as she goes by.

'The Place' is starting to get busy. Not really that unusual for a late Wednesday afternoon in the end days of September.

'The Place' had once been a bar and grill called the 'Lakeside Inn.' Abe's mother had renamed the facility 62 years ago after its purchase. 'The Place' had begun business serving alcohol and a modified version of pub food.

'The Place' had its ups and downs until Abe's wife, Janie and his daughter, Julia, disappeared while out sailing almost 24 years ago. Within 18 months after the disappearance, Abe slid headlong into self-medication through all available alcohol. As his mother tried to pretend Abe wasn't in the condition which she found him, Abe's drinking increased exponentially Despite noticing that baby Beth now cried almost every time she saw him, Abe couldn't stop. He took the better part of four years to reach rock bottom.

Gradually turning into a mostly absent vagrant, Abe staggered home on a late August morning and found his mother preparing Beth for her first day of elementary school. At almost 73, his mother was increasingly failing in her effort to raise Beth and run 'The Place.' Until Abe forced himself to recognize the tiredness on his mother's face and in her movements while experiencing the look of sorrow in his granddaughter's eyes, Abe had not realized how much sadness he was helping to bring. Beginning that morning, Abe swore to try to do what he could to break alcohol and sadness's grip on their lives.

Abe tried to go cold turkey. After that didn't work, Abe began a slow, long ongoing process of weaning himself away from using alcohol at the first tinge of remembrance. When Abe finally started down the path toward full-time sobriety, his mother made the decision to cease serving alcohol. She began the process of turning 'The Place' into a Wannasea-centric coffee house with a focus on specialty teas and coffees, live music plus the addition of poetry and selected historical readings about the island. During the remaining years of Rebecca's lifetime, the business had been able to do little more than keep itself solvent. Yet the business and Beth were what kept Abe and his mother going. Over the past five years thanks in large part to Beth's leadership plus an improved menu, 'The Place' had caught on with both locals and tourists.

Abe felt little remorse that he had used alcohol to self-medicate over the pain of losing his wife and daughter. Abe's remorse was that it had taken him almost four years to realize how much Beth and his mother needed him. Twenty years ago, when Abe had finally pulled himself together, his focus turned to trying to do the best for Beth and his mother, Abe strove to make work and writing the only remedies used when the pain of remembering became too much. Since his mother's passing ten years ago, Abe and Beth had jointly been making a go of 'The Place.' That making a go was what had now begun to worry Abe. Abe felt 'The Place' was what was now holding Beth back. As much of a success as Beth had been able to make of the business since she'd taken over its day-to-day operation six years back, Abe was increasingly certain the business had become a weighty anchor Beth didn't need.

"Here Gramps," Beth says as she sets a steaming cup of tea down on the non-business side of the old cash register which is now more cash box than register.

"Who's the band tonight?" Abe asks.

"The Riggers," Beth replies. "They ought to be here by 7."

Abe uses the bill/card scanner to take care of a pair customers. Though it was unnecessary, Abe marked "Pd" on the bill before placing it into the one of the slots which once had been used for paper currency.

"You reading tonight, Abe?" the second customer asks.

"Might if they ask me," Abe replies.

On Wednesday and Saturday nights, the customers usually requested that Abe read from the poems and lyrics, which along with the production of historical books, had been the core of his life's work before the disappearance.

Abe sips his tea. It was what 'The Place' calls Wannasea tea. An orange pekoe which was spiced with a mix of cardamon, nutmeg, exotic cinnamon plus orange and lemon peel. Other brands of tea plus a broad mix of steamed coffees, bottled drinks and juice mixes rounded out the liquid refreshments. Scones, a variety of hand-sized cookies, pies, sundry sandwiches, quiches and soups were what the kitchen produced in addition to clean dishes.

Marie brings Abe a stack of receipts which she had just collected.

"What do you think it will be tonight?" Marie asks as she places the receipts down.

"We'll have to wait and see," Abe replies as he begins writing on the collection papers. "How are your brothers working out?"

Josh, 19, is helping Sallie in the kitchen. Randy, 16, is busing tables.

"They are doing okay," Marie replied. "I actually think Josh may have a knack for baking. Where that came from, I've no idea."

"I think your granddad's brother was a baker over on the Mainland."

"Hmm," Marie replies before she picks up a tray to deliver a couple orders out to the floor.

The floor area of 'The Place,' rectangular in shape, is at least 1,500 square feet in size. A large stone fireplace, usually burning from late August on until late March, warms 'The Place.' A small stage containing an upright piano stands to the right of the massive fireplace. The counter and bar were solid examples of mahogany bars from over a century ago. Rubbing the wood makes Abe feel a connection to 'The Place.' The long mirror over the shelving behind the bar was just as old and beginning to dim from years of reflection. Abe often feels that that mirror and he have much in common.

'The Place' is comfortable. *Too comfortable*, Abe worries.

Abe notices that the crowd was starting to settle into place. A sign that the customers are hunkering down for a little Wannasea history via poetry and a folk band which will play until Abe's closes at 10. Abe's crowds are normally rather sedate. Originally customers had come for the song and the connection to local history. Since Sallie had taken over Abe's kitchen, they also had begun to come for the food.

Abe spots a few customers pulling out flasks to strengthen their tea or coffee. He has been told that good rum mixed with Beth's tea was hard to beat when the weather turned a little cool. Neither Beth nor the rest of the staff would complain as long as the customers were discreet about their alcohol use. The alcohol added a bit of Wannasea charm. With members of the local constabularies being some of 'The Place' regular customers, wasn't much of a risk of anything adverse resulting.

Abe glances at the wall clock. 6:28. Abe refuses to wear a watch. In his mind, time stopped on a that July 21st afternoon almost 24 years ago.

"Have received some new books which might be of interest to you," Ben, one of the village's three booksellers, walks up to the bar interrupts Abe's thoughts.

"I'll come down Monday or Tuesday to take a look," Abe replies. "Is Jake with you?"

"He'll be here in about 30 minutes. He's closing up shop."

Ben had been one of Abe's college pals fifty years back. Abe had genuine affection for Ben. Abe also had a desire that Jake might decide to try to form a relationship with his granddaughter. Jake, who was Ben's oldest grandson, always asked about Beth when Abe went into the book store. Unfortunately, Abe had little confidence that the young man, who had gone through the Wannasea school system with Beth, would ever work up the nerve to act on that interest.

"Heard Reggie is coming to the island in a couple weeks," Ben adds.

"You don't say," Abe says to the reference to his old college roommate and the singer of songs which he and his wife had written. "Haven't seen Reggie for almost 25 years."

"You mean that you aren't still making a few royalties off of the 'Reginald Renaissance'?" Ben asks in reference to the former 'The Place' singer having a key part in a now going on two year's running folk revival on the Mainland.

"Not as much as I'd like," Abe replies in reference to the income from the songs that he and Janie had written for Reggie.

"Reggie must be rolling in it. There is a rumor that he belongs to a group which is planning on building a five-star resort up at the old government center," Ben relates. "If they do, that's really going to change things up here."

"But they haven't even opened the new government center yet," Abe says raising an eyebrow.

"Supposed to happen within the next 3–4 weeks," Ben replies. "They ran into some type of problem with drainage at the new place but I'm told it's now under control. The old center is going to be sold off sometime in January."

"Do you know who else is in with Reggie to do this resort thing?" Abe asks. "Some people from over in Halifax," Ben relates. "I've been getting my information on the sale from the historical society. They are interested in making sure a museum goes into the castle area. Doubtful that will be happening if the old Reginald castle is turned into a resort. A fancy resort isn't going to want island riff-raff like us nosing around."

"I'm sure they will if we have money to spend," Abe replies. "If Reggie is involved, you can be sure that it will be about making as much money as possible."

"Have you given any thought to writing any new songs for Reggie?"

Abe laughs, "Reggie's not going to switch to the blues at this point in his career."

"Come over and sit with us after you're done," Ben suggests as he walks back toward the table which he and his wife have occupied.

"I'll do that."

Abe watches the band come in through the front door.

These kids just keep getting younger, Abe thinks.

The drummer, Abe can't remember his name, walks up to the register.

"Is it okay to set up now, Mr. Stolz?"

"Knock yourselves out, kid," Abe replies.

"Beth says that you need to eat this," Marie says as she sits down a plate holding a smoked turkey and avocado sandwich with a cup of split pea soup. "I'll mind the register while you eat."

Abe knows there is not much sense in arguing. Particularly in that he does feel a bit hunger now that the food is directly in front of him.

The sandwich was good. The split pea soup with bacon was magical.

At 7:20, Abe begins to hear customers making vocal rumblings about what they hoped to hear tonight. A few *Stuck in my mind* could be heard, along with a few other of Reggie's more popular later songs. A couple Hugo's were mixed in but the most prominent sound was "Wannasea."

A Kingdom of Wannasea night, it was going to be.

The Kingdom of Wannasea

Most Wannasea Islanders knew the story. The Reginalds or whatever they originally had been called, came to the island over two centuries ago after a successful career as minor south coast pirates. The Reginalds managed to acquire the upper portion of Wannasea Mountain where 'The Place' now sits. The mountain is a 2,200-foot-high extinct volcano practically in the center of the banana shaped island. The Reginalds valued the view. Not for beauty but for their own security against those from the Mainland seeking redress against their practice of running boats aground then looting them. A hundred and fifty years back, after claiming the high ground and chasing off any trying to settle on the top half of the mountain, the Reginalds constructed what was essentially a stone slab fort. The Reginald family used ill-gotten gains to eventually acquire 2/3rds of the mountain plus the two lakes on its east and west sides. Lakes which contained the island's only meaningful source of fresh water. The Reginalds then began their first legal enterprise on the island as purveyors of the water held in those lakes. Raising the rates high in times of drought. Constantly trying to push out any who dared to compete.

The Reginalds built huge restraining walls and a complex piping system at the lakes which sent water down the mountainside to the town and farms below. By the time the fourth leader of the Reginald clan on Wannasea Island came around, the clan had begun starting to quarry granite from the mountainside. Four built a castle and began referring to himself as the island's king. Five took it a step further and began requiring islanders to swear loyalty oaths to the Reginalds, while continuing to charge them increasingly steep rates for fresh water. By the time Nine came around, the islanders were almost in open revolt. Eight had begun using his proceeds from the water sales to acquire more and more mercenaries from the Mainland to serve as his personal army. Nine refined the practice to the point of destroying any cache basins the Reginalds happened upon. By the time of Nine, the clan was generally going about the island creating fear and loathing by driving to the Mainland any who dared contest their rule of the island. In violent fits and starts, Nine prospered on the island for the better part of thirty years. Approaching 60, Nine had hoped to turn over the Wannasea kingship to his first-born son, Theo. In addition to his violent streak, Theo had a temperament very similar to his father. A rather untimely accident at the west lake which caused a retaining wall to fall and kill his primary son, thwarted Nine's plan. Nine hastily revised the succession, reluctantly moving to naming his only other son, Hugo, his successor. Hugo would be on a much different track than what Nine had been planning for Theo.

In addition to growing hatred from the islanders, Nine had begun to get a lot of pushback from the Mainland. Too many sunken ships. Too much midnight pillaging. With Theo gone, Nine decided to move away from the plan of strengthening the Reginald's hold on the island. Nine's new plan became to move as much of his wealth as possible off the island, then gradually doing a cut-and-run after Hugo was seen as the leader of the Reginalds. Nine hoped that the Mainland and the islanders would make Hugo the new target of any retribution which they might choose to direct against the family.

The story was that Hugo's mind was in the clouds. Literally. Hugo was almost exclusively interested in flying machines. Their operation. Their maintenance. Their quirks. Their possibilities. The only other thing which Hugo was really interested in was an island firebrand named Alice Bailey. This didn't worry Nine all that much. As long as Hugo took over the crown and assumed responsibility for the Reginald's almost two centuries of bad acts, Nine had little interest in anything else Hugo did. When Hugo became Ten, Nine also planned to have the clan on the island secretly run by his malevolent Prime Minister and first cousin, Sylvester, for as long as the rest of the Reginald clan could hold on to their power and produce a little profit. Though Hugo would become Ten, Nine had hoped that at least for a short time, the profits of the kingship might still continue to flow his way. If Sylvester could not keep the islanders in line, then steps would be taken to make Ten the target of the islanders' displeasure. Once the clan could no longer control the islanders, Sylvester and his crew were planning to also escape south leaving Hugo holding the bag.

At 7:30 Beth walks to the small stage and turns on the house microphone. Two members of the band sit behind her on stools. One with a guitar. The other a violin.

"Welcome to 'The Place,' ladies and gentlemen," Beth says to the crowd. "Is *The Kingdom of Wannasea* what you'd like to hear to kick off the night?"

In general, the customers confirm the selection.

"Then with no further ado, I'll ask my grandfather to come up on this stage and read the words of the lyrics which he wrote almost fifty years ago, *The Kingdom of Wannasea*."

Abe pulls out one of the oldest of his green journals which are stored on the bottom shelf where the liquor which he used to consume had resided. Abe strolls to the stage as Beth returns to the counter.

Abe pulls up an aged wooden stool to the microphone, put both feet on its lowest rungs, opens his journal to the 6th page and begins.

Like Reggie's version, the guitar and violin begin quietly playing in the key of D at 82 tempo in 3/4 time.

The part of the crowd which knows the refrains chants or sings as Abe in his strong island accent begins.

The Kingdom of Wannasea

The Reginalds were a most devious lot
self-proclaimed kings and good-for-naughts
Nine the worst of that dastardly crew
charging dearly for water the islanders drew
menaced by mercenaries common and crude
pushing the populace into virtual servitude

Oh, Isle of Wannasea
ever may your skies be blue
ever may your worries be few
forever your people free

Nine's plans moved along nicely until Theo died
buried by a falling wall and resulting landslide
but no never mind, Hugo would suffice as Ten
with duplicitous Sylvester in control of Nine's men
On an island brimming with pent up hate
Nine sensed the time had come to abdicate

Hugo followed Nine in every islander's mind
to Nine's machinations remaining fully blind
Sylvester would gather what was to be collected
Hugo soon enough be whom the islanders rejected
No matter how distracted this sky-minded son
Nine would continue the profit from his thirty year run

Oh, Isle of Wannasea
ever may your skies be blue
ever may your worries be few
forever your people free

Hugo even with a head always in the clouds
sensed rising anger among within milling crowds
Alice, the love of young Hugo's life
spoke of a plan to end their island's strife
Hugo was indeed to follow Nine as Ten
but Wannasea no longer would be ruled by evil men

Oh, Isle of Wannasea
ever may your skies be blue
ever may your worries be few
forever your people free
with the downfall of kings on Wannasea

Hugo succeeded Nine as Wannasea's king
Soon began moving like he was on a string
believing Sylvester had Hugo under his thumb
Nine sailed off south with a magnificent sum
all while Alice filled Mainland agents' eyes
with documents and drawings Hugo supplied

Oh, Isle of Wannasea
ever may your skies be blue
ever may your worries be few
forever your people free
with the downfall of kings on Wannasea

In deepest dark, the second night Nine was gone
three large Mainland ships to the harbor were drawn
without one single shot being fired
Sylvester and his men were bound, gagged and retired
the battle turning into a struggle of nerves

'til the Mainlanders drained Nine's cash reserves

Praise be to the bright stars above
shining down on this island we so love
Praise be to Wannasea Mountain so high
where freedom must keep a watchful eye

Lakes and castle under civilian rule
Hugo and Alice, off the island they flew
Hugo to flight training at Mainland's largest base
Alice to attend college at a nearby place
Faced with the outcome, Nine's ire was legend
Alice and Hugo with vile acts were threatened

Oh, Isle of Wannasea
ever may your skies be blue
ever may your worries be few
forever your people free
after the downfall of kings on Wannasea

Praise be
for pure rain which falls
midst storms and summer squalls
Praise be
to this strange island known as Wannasea
where always and ever we long to be
Praise be
Freedom had come to Wannasea

Two more times, Abe and the musicians go through the last three refrains. Each time the crowd's vocalizing grows louder. At the end of the third repetition, Abe wipes his now sweating brow with his handkerchief, turns to the band and says, "I'm through boys. You can take it from here."
The band breaks into Reggie's musical version of the same island folk story.

A Walk up the Mountain

Abe puts down the book which he has been reading since after his lunch.

Time for a walk, Abe decides and begins looking around for Riley V. Normally the 4-year-old golden retriever is somewhere in the vicinity of Abe's feet. Even when Abe sleeps. There was no Riley to be seen.

Abe rises from the deck chair and walks into his bedroom thinking perhaps the dog is lying on his normal spot atop the rug beside his bed. Riley V wasn't there.

After Riley IV had died, Abe told Beth that he was too old to have another dog.

"He will just end up orphaned," Abe had told his granddaughter Three weeks later, Beth showed up with a 12-week-old Riley V.

"He's my dog, Abe," Beth had said, "but you can borrow him whenever you want."

Beth only called Abe, "Abe" when she told him something which was non-negotiable.

Riley V had attached himself to Abe from the start. Abe had plenty of time for head scratching, treat giving, stick throwing and the other good things in Riley V's life.

Abe glanced at the wall clock. 3:05.

Must have followed Beth up to the house, Abe figures as on Sunday, 'The Place' closes at 2.

Sticking two dog biscuits from a box atop his dresser into his pocket, Abe goes back out on the deck and then down the rear stairs to the outside seating area of 'The Place.' Crossing the bricked in surface, passes a couple empty picnic tables, Abe walks up the slight incline to the house where he and his wife had lived until she disappeared. Beth and seven of her workers live there now.

The house is an odd conglomeration. An artifact from 25 years back when Janie had treated it as her non-stop construction project. Janie had been bent upon turning the house into a safe place for girls at risk. It had been more of a continuously evolving compound than house. Janie had added structures when the mood suited her. Abe had to admit though, that the house was very functional as well as visually appealing. Using the upstairs area as a dormitory from workers. Turning the dormitory area into a mother-in-law suite where Becca had come to reside. Adding a wing to North which became first a playroom which Hugh and Julia had used, then a structure rebuilt almost completely from windows which came to be used as a music studio/Janie's office.

Abe stands within five feet of the house's front door and calls, "Riley." To his surprise, the dog doesn't come.

Abe is averse to going into the house. Had been since Janie and Julia were officially missing. Going in the house brought too many memories. Even now, twenty years on, the few times that he'd gone in the house in the past couple years, he'd found himself crying at the oddest of things. The weird painted mantle over the main living room's fireplace. The carved door which used to lead into their bedroom. Having had Beth catch him twice this year with tears in his eyes, Abe wouldn't go into the house unless it was a necessity.

Fortunately for Abe, Beth appears at the front door with Riley V at her heels.

"Going for a walk, Gramps?"

"Was hoping to."

"Mind if I tag along because I think there are some things that we need to discuss?"

Even though Beth hadn't added Abe at the end of her request, Abe knew it really wasn't negotiable.

"Sure, the more the merrier."

"Which way are we headed?"

"I usually let Riley decide," Abe says as he scratches the dog's head.

Abe knew that when it is left up to Riley V, they would be heading up the mountain. Going around the lake or down to the village was a decision Abe made, not Riley V.

They headed to the path alongside the narrow road which leads to what used to be the Reginald's castle and at least for the next few weeks serves as the island government building. It was about a mile to the castle and the path was somewhat steep.

"Did you and grandma argue much?"

The question catches Abe off-guard. Beth hardly ever asked anything about Janie or Julia. She had only been 20 months old when they disappeared.

Deciding to be honest, Abe said, "We had our differences."

"About what?"

"Usually about what your grandmother was doing with the house," Abe replied as they began the steepest ascent.

"What's the worse argument that you ever had with grandma?"

The question reverberated more than Abe expected.

"A couple days before the sailing incident, Janie and I had a big blow up over the Morris."

The Morris was a 1979 Morris Marina which sits in the garage of the supply shed. Abe still used the car regularly.

"Why over the Morris?"

"Janie bought it when I had plans to buy something else."

Beth looked at him quizzically. "What something else?"

"A Fiat Spider convertible."

"What?" Beth bursts out laughing.

"I had arrangements on the Mainland to buy a 1983 model. Before I could pick it up, Janie used the money that I had set aside for its purchase to buy the Morris from one of her second cousins."

"What color was this Fiat Spider?"

"Bright red."

Beth burst into another fit of laughter at the thought of Abe cruising around the eighty odd miles of island roadways in a red convertible with the top down.

"Why didn't grandma want you to have it?"

"To quote your grandmother, 'Only a pretentious asshole would ride around in that type of car.'"

"She didn't tell you that she was going to buy the Morris?"

"Nope."

"I want the full story," Beth demands as they reached the halfway point to the castle.

"I'd just gotten a rather sizeable royalty check from our songs on Tara Rose's album. Your grandmother had just built out her music studio. After paying for her construction costs, I decided I owed myself a convertible. My mistake was in letting your grandmother know what I was planning on buying it. She spent every cent that I had toward buying the convertible for the Morris."

"So how long did this fight go on?"

Abe couldn't tell Beth that it had never really ended. Abe had been genuinely mad at Janie over the incident which occurred three days before the sailing disaster. He had stopped talking to Janie over his anger about the Morris. Then Janie and Julia were gone.

"A couple days," Abe said as he once again becomes lost in the same old regret.

Abe had long blamed himself for Janie and Julia's disappearance. Abe believed that Janie had been dwelling on their feud over the Fiat convertible rather than paying attention to navigating through a storm.

The pair walk on for a few silent minutes before cresting the small rise which fronts the castle. Abe walks to a bench which resides in a little park area that the government workers used during the week and sits down. Beth walks into the woods to find a good stick to throw to Riley V, who now sits at Abe's feet. Abe gives Riley V one of the dog biscuits.

"How long were you a drunk, Abe?" Beth asks as she tosses the stick toward the wooded area so Riley will chase it.

This seemed to be Beth's day for asking hard questions. Abe had slid into alcohol after having spent three months combing the west end of the island where Janie and Julia were reportedly last seen. Roaming frantically. Hoping some sign of Janie's blue sailboat would turn up. It didn't. The third week of resorting to self-medication, Abe moved himself into the storage room which now served as his bedroom at the back of the bar and grill.

"Better part of four years."

"What kind of drunk were you?"

Abe thought for a few moments before answering. Beth had seen it herself between the ages of two and six what kind of drunk Abe was. Abe reckoned that Beth either didn't remember or didn't want to remember.

"The sullen, silent kind. The kind that goes to the end of bar, orders a double and doesn't want to talk to anyone or buys a bottle after the bars close and sits in a doorway to drink it."

"Which bars did you frequent?"

"Every bar in Wannasea and most of those on the Mainland near the ferry landing. I think that I'm still banned in most of them."

"Did you start fights?"

"Only with people who wouldn't leave me alone," Abe replies as he reaches down to retrieve the stick which Riley had brought back. He throws it back toward the woods. "Riley III used to follow me to almost every bar. Whether noon or 3 AM, that dog would sit outside and wait for me. Sometimes we slept on a street corner or in a shop doorway. I'm not very proud of it, Beth."

"Why did you stop drinking?"

"When you were starting kindergarten, I stumbled back from one of my three day long drinking binges over in Halifax. When I walked into 'The Place's' kitchen and saw my mother getting you ready, the blinders lifted. I realized how old Becca had become. She was three years older than I am now. Along with taking care of you, she was running the bar and grill without a lot of help. What help she had, were ripping her off. Business was dropping. Becca was mentally, physically and emotionally worn out from a lifetime of having to lose the people that she loved. Becca really needed my help. She was no longer capable of getting by without it. It finally dawned on me what a self-absorbed, selfish bastard I'd become."

"So you quit drinking right then and there?"

This was a legend which floated around the island, along with so many other exaggerations related to Julia and Janie's disappearance. The story was that Abe had started drinking right after Janie and Julia disappeared. Four years later, he stopped just like that. It wasn't true.

"No, it took the better part of four months to get myself headed in the right direction. After three false starts, decided that if I was going to beat the bottle, I had to do whatever was necessary to stop drinking completely."

"That's why Gramma Becca stopped selling alcohol?"

"That and she'd finally reached the point that she had very little tolerance for drunks. Too many of my good-time drinking pals were showing up out here."

"What about me?"

Abe knew full well what it had been about Beth.

"When I finally realized how much my mother aged, I also saw very clearly that you were afraid of me."

Beth looked straight into Abe's eyes.

"I have never in my life been afraid of you. I was afraid for you. There is a big difference."

Beth knew. Beth knew and that's what actually worried Abe. Abe was now the one afraid. Afraid of the past and afraid that Beth was wasting her life because of it.

Abe once again takes the stick from Riley's mouth and throws it toward the woods. Beth gets up from the bench and begins walking around the circular pathway fronting the government building.

Abe didn't want to think about being a drunk or what it had done to Becca and Beth. He studies the structure of the castle. Massive solid cut stone which had been taken from a huge quarry up the mountain about half a mile. The Reginald's castle was too boxy. Aside from giving them a good view out to sea from a turret in the front, the rest of this castle was like a bunch of storehouses which had been tossed on top of each together.

That is really no castle, Abe thinks as he shuffles his feet on the dry grass in front of the bench. *The Reginald's were only kidding themselves. They were always just a bunch of raggedy-assed pirates pretending to be kings.*

Beth and Riley V return.

"Still want to go up the mountain?" Beth asks.

"Yep," Abe replies as he pulls the stick from the dog's mouth, rises from the bench and begins walking toward the path leading toward the top of the mountain.

Beth hands Abe a small plastic bottle of water. One of two which she'd just purchased from the vending machine in front of the government building's entrance just to the right of the old turret.

Abe unscrews the top of the water bottle, takes a small sip, recaps the bottle and puts it into the large bottom front pocket of his sea green, lined windbreaker. Riley V now walks close by Abe's side. The dog knows better than to go wandering while they walk the trail up the mountain.

"Uncle Hugh is coming next week," Beth notes.

Hugh was Abe's only surviving child. Aside from shared interest in Wannasea history, Hugh had essentially been disconnected from the family since Becca had died. Not that Hugh had ever been all that connected after Julia and Janie were gone.

"That's what he wrote me in the letter he sent last week."

Hugh and Abe corresponded through the post office. Main focus of their long letters being asking questions or providing answers about Wannasea's history. Personal items were kept to the bare minimum. Usually when Abe wanted to know something about Hugh's life, he asked Beth.

"Why don't you use email, Abe?"

Hugh was now in his 26th year of service in the Mainland's Air Corps. Hugh was some kind of technology wiz or something. Abe thought Hugh was now a full bird colonel but wasn't completely clear on that point. Hugh had brought Abe a laptop three years back. Abe now basically uses it as a typewriter, though recently he'd taken to spending a day or two per week entering entries from his journal into the computer for safekeeping.

"Because I trust paper much more than electrons, Kitten."

Kitten being Abe's magic word to counter one of Beth's demands which he wasn't certain he was capable of fulfilling. Kitten had been working for Abe almost from the time that Beth had begun talking.

"Paper is full of electrons, Abe."

"Yeah, but they aren't moving around as much."

They pass a 40-something couple coming down the well-kept path leading up the mountain. In the summer, except in early morning, the path becomes so crowded one could barely use it. The path is a spiral. Winding round the mountain revealing beautiful vistas of the island and the sea on all sides. Abe and Riley use the path a couple times a week. Even after forty years of walking the constantly improving trail, Abe still marvels at the wonders the trail reveals.

"Are you thinking of selling 'The Place'?"

"Hadn't given it much thought," Abe replied. "I've been thinking that I should be more concerned about my smart, beautiful 25-year-old granddaughter getting on with her life instead of being a caretaker for a cantankerous old man, who is fully capable of taking care of himself."

"I am getting on with my life, Abe."

"You haven't finished college. The only relationship which you have is with 'The Place.'"

"I'm not interested in finishing college. When I need to learn something that helps with running my business, I take an online course. I'll also have you know that I am completely satisfied with all my current relationships, Abe."

Abe raised his eyebrows and rolls his eyes.

Beth put her hand on Abe's arm forcing him to stop their walk for a moment.

"I want a promise from you, Abe," Beth says. "If you sell 'The Place' the only person that you will sell it to is me."

Abe pursed his lips and is silent, returning to the walk. They pass the next two bends which revealed the rocky shores of the west side of island. The side were Janie and Julia had supposedly been sailing when they disappeared.

"You need to promise me, Abe."

"I'll think on it, Kitten."

They walk around another bend before Beth asked, "Why didn't Becca leave you any money?"

Abe's mother had passed away ten years ago. She had left Abe 'The Place' and nothing more. The rest of her considerable savings and family inherited wealth were split between Hugh and Beth. Beth receiving an educational trust fund plus another rather large trust which had just been released to her this past August on her 25th birthday.

For the past eight years, Beth had moved from running 'The Place's' dining and coffee bar area to overseeing the entire operation. After four years of wrangling with Beth over going to college, Abe had finally leased Beth the place for $3,000 a month plus Beth covering all the tax, insurance and business costs of the entire 4.5-acre property. Abe's thinking had been that Beth would soon tire of dedicating herself to running a business. Abe had been wrong. Beth not only dedicated herself to operating 'The Place,' for the past two years, Beth had been pushing to expand the business and its focus on helping at risk kids.

Becca had divided the property into two parcels right before Abe and Janie had gotten married 50 years ago. The business consisted of three acres. The house had 1.5. Becca had made the split so that she could give Abe the deed to the house as a present when Hugh had been born.

"Guess Becca wanted to be sure that I had some incentive to work," Abe replies knowing when he says it that it isn't accurate. The entire time that Beth had been on this Earth, Abe had enough money that he really didn't need to operate 'The Place' for profit or do much of anything else that he didn't feel like doing. The royalties from his and Janie's years as songwriters are still normally $25 to 40K per quarter. Even four years of being an out-of-control raging drunk had not put much of dent in that financial cushion. Truth was that 'The Place' was Abe's rock. The foundation upon which he'd based his being.

From six months after the time of his father's death, he'd lived on 'The Place.' 'The Place' was where he and Janie had fallen in love. After serving as bartender/waitress for three years, Janie had come to run the customer facing part of the business. Becca, Janie and Julia were still part of 'The Place' in Abe's mind. Abe had no intention of leaving 'The Place.' Abe's focus is trying to get Beth to separate herself from the place. Abe doesn't want Beth going down the same path which he has been on for the past 20 years.

"Your work has never been operating 'The Place.' Making 'The Place' somewhere people wanted to come for entertainment, maybe. Making 'The Place' a focal point of the history of Wannasea, sure. Operating 'The Place' for a profit, never."

They walk around another bend, now being less than ¼ mile from the top.

"If you go off and finish your education, maybe work a couple years in the field you choose, then want to come back to Wannasea, I'll give you 'The Place,'" Abe offers.

"You aren't getting it, Abe," Beth says shaking her head. "'The Place' and this island are my future. 'The Place' and Wannasea are my work. Just as you have always been about this island's past, Abe, I am about its present and future."

In silence they walked around the next three bends to the summit. It was a clear day and the entire island as well as the sea far out to the horizon could be seen. Sail and power boats were in view on the water. There were a few whitecaps and a steady western breeze.

Abe sits down on a boulder at the edge of trail's end and hands Riley V the other dog biscuit as Beth says, "You need to promise me, Abe."

Hugo Flies

7 PM on Saturday. 'The Place' is packed. Inside and out. Beth and the staff are struggling to keep up. Abe had even been allowed to help with the coffee and tea making process. Something Beth had essentially banned him from a couple years back.

As the band, this time a threesome of 50-somethings known as the Wannasea Boys, sets up. Abe keeps his ear toward the dining floor. Seems *Hugo* is this night's favorite.

As Beth delivers a handful of receipts to Abe, Abe says, "You need to get more help, Kitten. At least from Thursday through Saturday."

"I'm working on it, Abe."

"Can you afford to pay them? If you can't, I'll help out."

Beth narrows her eyes and scowls at her grandfather.

"Believe me, I can afford it."

Beth scoots off to the small stage and turns on the microphone.

"Great to see everyone tonight. Welcome to 'The Place.' If you haven't been here before, we'll start out the night with a little poetry reading from Abe. That is if Abe has enough time to spare from the time and efficiency study that he's been working on tonight."

Beth stares out at her grandfather, who puts up his hands in an I-give-up gesture.

"Seems most of you would like to hear *Hugo Flies*. Have I gotten that right?"

The crowd responds affirmatively.

"Then with no further ado, my grandfather will read the words of the poem leading to the lyrics of the song which became Reggie Reginald's first hit."

Abe strolls to the stage. Careful not to cross Beth's path.

"My most wonderful, beautiful granddaughter, folks," Abe said gesturing toward Beth.

The crowd responded with a round of polite applause.

Abe nods to the band, adjusts the microphone and begins reading the poem which had not only become the genesis of Reggie Reginald, but also of Abe's and his wife's songwriting careers.

Hugo Flies (Reggie style at a tempo of 116 in the key of C Major in 4/4 time)

what came after Nine were Hugo and Alice
a tall thin cool drink of water, a lady quite capable of malice
Hugo, head in the clouds and sights on the stars
Alice, more interested in making history than reading memoirs

mind in the clouds
flying straight toward the sun
Hugo had only just begun

making the most of his aerial desires
Hugo went from trainee to the highest of fliers
Alice focused on studies and raising a daughter
As the planet's first great war grew ever hotter

mind in the clouds
flying straight toward the sun
Hugo had only just begun

what came after Nine were Hugo and Alice
tall thin cool drink of water, elegant lady quite capable of malice
war moved Hugo across the continent
where the Allies worked to establish air dominance
in six short months, Hugo became an ace
the best fighter pilot in hostile airspace

Hugo wrote to Alice every chance that he had
expressing his longings in words loving and sad
Each mission becoming ever more gory
As Hugo covered himself in honors and glory

mind in the clouds
flying straight toward the sun
Hugo had only just begun

With the Allies planning a last major push
Hugo and squadron plotted an aerial ambush
In hope of reducing the number of corpses
a plan was made to distract the Kaiser's forces

what came after Nine were Hugo and Alice
tall thin cool drink of water, elegant lady quite capable of malice

Hugo led the assault on the Kaiser's back lines
hand releasing two bombs per their plan's designs
dropping low to explode an ammunition shack
thus aiding the Allies rapidly advancing attack

the Kaiser's air fighters came at ten o'clock
non-stop anti-aircraft fire, a much greater shock
Hugo pointed his Vickers DH2 toward the sky
avoiding a Fokker's fire by the blink of an eye

Hugo watched an artillery shell whiz by his propeller
thinking perhaps once again he was one very lucky fella
but the secondary explosion meant he was done
Hugo had flown himself straight into the sun

what came after Hugo were Rebecca and peace
creating a pain in Alice's heart which was never to cease
of Alice's victory celebration, there was none
Alice began to do what had to be done
after Hugo had flown himself straight into the sun

the Kaiser's air fighters came at ten o'clock
non-stop anti-aircraft fire, a much greater shock
Hugo pointed his Vickers DH2 toward the sky

avoiding a Fokker's fire by the blink of an eye

Hugo watched an artillery shell whiz by his propeller
thinking perhaps once again he was one very lucky fella
but the secondary explosion meant he was done
Hugo had flown himself straight into the sun

what came after Hugo were Rebecca and peace
creating a pain in Alice's heart which was never to cease
mind in the clouds, flying straight toward the sun
ended what Hugo had only just begun
mind in the clouds, flying straight toward the sun
ended what Hugo had only just begun

    Abe did the reading once more before heading back to the stool behind the cash register.

Hugh Visits

Abe has the laptop out. He is working on typing in entries which are gleaned from an open black journal. Abe's journal filing system consisting of black journals for historical work, green journals for poems and lyrics.

"You know, Pop," the tall, lanky slightly graying man dressed in a dark blue NATO uniform with a colonel's insignia on the shoulders says, "you can scan the pages in your journal into the laptop and save yourself a lot of work."

"How would I edit them then, Hugh?"

"There are scanning programs with character recognition which can help you with that."

Abe rises from the table and takes what looks to be two very old books which were being offered to him from his son's right hand.

"I think these books might be able to help you solve the mystery of how our west end pirate ancestors were so successful back in the late 18th and 19th century."

Abe sets the book on his table and after thinking about it for a moment gives his slightly taller son a hug.

"What brings you out here?"

Normally whenever Hugh visited, he doesn't stay long. Usually all of Hugh's time with Abe is spent discussing island and family history. Abe still isn't sure if that was simply how Hugh was wired or whether that might be Hugh's way of dealing with a past, which like Abe, he'd much sooner not remember.

Before Hugh left for college then the Mainland military, he and Abe had been close but even back then most of what they did focused upon had been historical exploration of one sort or another.

"I have a few things that I want to talk over with you, Dad."

"About the Reginalds or Wannasea?"

"That will have to wait. First there is some news you need to hear which might impact both of our futures."

"Do you want to sit?" Abe says pointing toward the couch against the back wall.

Hugh gracefully sits himself down and fidgets a little bit before saying, "I'm retiring in six weeks."

This news catches Abe somewhat off-guard. Abe had always felt that Hugh was on a path to the general staff.

"What's brought this on?"

"A couple service buddies of mine have started up an electronic surveillance equipment operation at Swansea and have talked me into not only being a principle investor but running the production and business operation for them so they can focus on R&D."

"You think it's a better opportunity than going for generalship?"

"I don't think a generalship is in the cards, Dad. You almost have to be a military academy graduate for that these days," Hugh says placing his garrison cap on the table. "Doesn't upset me though, as I would have thrown in with these guys even if I had a real shot at making brigadier."

"It's the money?"

"No," Hugh replies, "it's the opportunity to help grow something pretty much from scratch while I still have time to do it."

"Kind of runs in our family, I guess," Abe replies as he begins to wonder what this has to with him.

"Helen and I are looking to buy a place around Swansea and were wondering if you'd like us to try to find something with a nice in-law suite so that you could come live with us?"

Hugh and Helen had been married since a year before Janie died. They were childless. Abe wasn't a big fan of Helen. She was even more of stickler for protocol than Hugh.

"Thanks son, but I'm not so sure that I can survive off this island."

"It would give both of us more time to do Wannasea historical research. There's a lot more information on the Mainland than you are ever going to lay hands on out here You also could probably do some work with Swansea University."

"I'm beginning to discover the benefits of that computer which you gave me. Anything that I could find over there, I can reach from here."

"Health permitting Pop."

"Health permitting Son."

"Why don't you think about it a bit. If you change your mind over the next couple weeks just let me know. If it's something you want to consider later, I'll try to find a property with enough land that we could build something out for you."

Beth arrives carrying a tray loaded with three steaming cups of tea and a selection of goodies. After setting the tray down, distributing cups of tea to Abe and her uncle, she pulls out the only other chair and sits down.

"I take it that Abe isn't much interested in going to Swansea," Beth directs toward her uncle.

"Doesn't seem so, but things have a way of changing. I just want to make sure that Dad knows that he has options," Hugh replies.

Abe picks up his cup and takes a small sip.

"Would you have any problem if Abe sold me 'The Place'?" Beth asks.

"None at all," Hugh replies. "The only question is where Abe would live after."

"Abe can stay on right here if he wants," Beth offers. "Although, I'd probably insist that he move out of this safety hazard. The island's building inspector has informed me on his last two visits, this room is out of code as a storage and part-time office area. If that inspector knew Abe is actually living here, we might have a problem."

Abe sees an opportunity.

"Hugh, do you think a bright young lady like Beth should be tying her future to a rundown place like this?" Abe asks. "She could move over to Swansea near you and finish her schooling?"

Beth scowls at Abe.

"Beth can do whatever Beth wants to do," Hugh says. "Beth has 'The Place' thriving. More than mom or Becca were ever able to accomplish."

Beth sticks out her tongue at Abe.

"Did you know Abe intended to buy a bright red Fiat Spider convertible just a little before our moms disappeared?" Beth says to Hugh with a laugh.

"First I've heard of it," Hugh says raising his right eyebrow.

"Grandma put a stop to it," Beth added.

"Mom was always very good at getting what she wanted," Hugh relates.

They trio sips tea for a few moments before Hugh picks up an orange cranberry scone.

"How upset were Becca, grandma and you guys about my mom getting pregnant out of wedlock?" Beth asks suddenly.

Julia, Beth's mother, had gotten pregnant at 17. Julia had Beth, one month before she turned 18. Julia never disclosed the name of the father. Julia was insistent from the moment that she knew that she was pregnant that she was going to keep the baby. Abe had always suspected that the other party was a fiddle player in one of the local bands called 'The Tillers.' A fiddler, who had seemed to be paying a lot attention to Julia around that time. That fiddle player had been married to one of Julia's best friends and had a child with his wife on the way.

"I was in school and honestly didn't know how anybody else in the family felt about it," Hugh offers. "I was sort of upset that Julia wasn't going to go college immediately but then Julia was always really close to mom, so I'm not sure that she would have gone away to college anyway."

"Gramps?"

Abe studies Beth for a long moment.

"Becca was a little upset for a month or so for the same reasons as Hugh. I honestly think your Grandma Becca didn't much mind. I was a little sad that Julia was tying herself down at such a young age but truth be told, it meant one of her offspring was going to stay on the island."

"So, it was important to you then that one of your kids stayed on the island, but it's not important now?" Beth posits, her eyes fully on Abe.

"Damn, Beth," Abe laughs, "I really think you are making a huge mistake by not going over to the Mainland and taking up lawyering."

"Just like you, Abe," Beth smiles, "My leaving this island is non-negotiable."

Don't Blame the Alcohol

Tuesday night. A little past 7 PM. The Wannasea Boys are setting up. Abe is sitting at a nearby table with Hugh drinking a new fruit concoction which Marie had brought to them.

"From what I've been able to determine," Hugh says, "the west end pirates were very adept at putting out the light in the lighthouse in the middle night then lighting a big bonfire about 3/4s of a mile back toward the mountain. They would wait until a passing ship mistook the bonfire for the lighthouse and ran aground out by Carter's Rocks. Then they would then climb into their skiffs, row out to the grounded ship and drag off everything that they could carry. They would do away with any who tried to stand in their way."

"An interesting business model," Abe says with a laugh. "The Mainland Navy let them get away with this?"

"The Navy wouldn't mind if it wasn't a ship which belonged to them or an ally. If it was, the Mainland usually would raid the island within the next week. The Navy would rough up anyone on the island that they could get their hands on. Meanwhile the west end pirates hid out in caves on the south side of the island."

"Were any of those pirates our lot?" Abe asks.

"They were mainly our lot."

Beth comes on to the stage.

"Good evening, ladies and gentlemen," she begins. "As the regulars know, this is a night for one of my grandfather's readings. Since my Uncle Hugh is here tonight, I'm going to stray from usual protocol of doing lyrics from Reggie Reginald's songs and ask Abe to do *Don't Blame the Alcohol*. Without any further ado, here is Abe."

Abe isn't happy with Beth's selection. This a song which not only is not a part of Reggie's repertoire, Abe had never done it before an audience. It is a set of lyrics which Abe had written about five months after he started drinking.

To complement his self-medication effort, Abe had gotten into writing poetry on sleepless nights. After everyone had cleared out of 'The Place,' Abe would drag a chair up on the stage and read the poetry which he had written aloud. It had seemed to Abe almost as if he could go back to the days when he and Janie had been a songwriting pair. Abe had almost been able to converse with Janie when he read the words. This particular poem, more than any other. He had no idea how or where Beth had heard or come to know of this poem's existence.

Abe slowly walks to the stage and adjusts the microphone. He turns to the band and whispers, "Could you play something similar to *Whiskey Lullaby*?"

"I think we can do something close," the trio's leader replies.

"Go ahead and start," Abe says, "I'll jump in after the first stanza."

Abe waits to adjust to the rhythm of the band before starting to read:

Don't blame the alcohol a tempo of 74 BPM in the key D in 4/4 time

woke up not remembering if that empty bottle in my bed
did anything at all to lift the overwhelming dread
of trying not to relive what I'm trying to forget
in hope of overcoming remorse which hasn't arrived yet

Please don't blame the alcohol
mixing draft beer with double shots of bourbon
temporarily numbs the mind decreasing the burden
bourbon and beer didn't start the fall
please don't blame it on the alcohol

stumbling down the stairs in search of replenishment
living life in an emotionless low-rent tenement
is the only way I have of telling you
I'm not so sure I can see this through

Please don't blame the alcohol
mixing draft beer with double shots of bourbon
temporarily numbs the mind decreasing the burden
bourbon and beer didn't start the fall
don't blame it on the alcohol

a full bottle of Kentucky mash from the bottom shelf
may be just enough to forget myself
until the next white-hot memory comes sailing in
reminding me of what should not have been

woke up not remembering if that empty bottle in my bed
did anything at all to lift the overwhelming dread
of trying not to relive what I'm trying to forget
in hope of overcoming remorse which hasn't arrived yet

don't blame the alcohol
mixing draft beer with double shots of bourbon
temporarily numbs the mind decreasing the burden
bourbon and beer didn't start my fall
don't blame it on the alcohol
bourbon and beer didn't start my fall
don't blame it on the alcohol

    Abe repeats the lyrics only once, even though the crowd had grown more responsive with each stanza. Abe wonders how long he could have gone on with it but neither the growing weariness in his heart nor his voice will allow it.

    "Sorry, folks that's all I'm up to," Abe says walking away from the microphone then off the stage and out the back hallway.

Enter the Tillerman

Abe drives the Morris through the gate of the Halifax car repair shop just a couple blocks east of the ferry drop on the Mainland. With such very limited use, the Morris is in excellent shape but lately the car had not seemed to be running quite as well as Abe thought it should. Abe had made arrangements to drop the Morris off on Monday morning to have it serviced.

Abe fingers the cell phone in his windbreaker pocket. He'd had the device for less than a week now. He been coerced into buying it by Hugh. Cell phones had not been much use until recently on Wannasea Island, so Abe hadn't bothered to get one. If someone wanted to talk to Abe, they could always come out to 'The Place' or call the business number and leave him a message. A method that had been working for Abe the past 40 something years now.

Hugh had caught wind that a cell tower was being installed on the backside of the Reginald's castle. Abe wasn't sure how the technology behind the towers which Hugh had described to him actually worked. Abe only knew the use of cellular devices which were all over the Mainland had suddenly arrived on the island.

Abe opens the device and calls Beth, who has driven into Halifax to pick him up.

"Am at the car repair," Abe says into the phone.

"Be there in a couple of minutes, Gramps," Beth responds.

Beth had begun to be in a much less contentious mood the last couple days after Hugh had completed his four-day visit.

Abe walks into the office, fills out the paperwork and turns over keys before walking back through the gate. He stands on the sidewalk to wait for Beth.

It was only a few moments before her VW Beetle came into sight. Beth drives Beetles. This particular Bug is a brooding shade of jet black. With low-profile tires, large round shining chrome hubcaps, this Bug rides a bit lower than her earlier Beetles. The car was also deceptively fast.

Before this particular Beetle, Beth had a couple much tamer models. The last one before this brooding little beast had been a light-yellow convertible with a ridiculous flower holder in the middle of the dash into which Beth had placed a carved wooden hand with an upraised middle finger. This latest bug suited Beth perfectly, Abe decided.

Beth pushes open the passenger door, Abe folds himself in. They drive to the ferry dock to catch the 12:15 ferry back to Wannasea.

"Why don't you go up on the deck while I'm parking in the car hold?" Beth suggests.

Abe obliges, going up the ramp and on to the deck. Being a Monday afternoon in late October, there are not all that many passengers. Maybe 30 or so. Abe finds an unoccupied bench in front of the ferry's rear railing and sets down. He contents himself with watching the coming and goings near the boat and dock until Beth arrives and sits down beside him.

"Now I've got a favor that I need from you, Abe," Beth begins. "We're going to grab fish and chips back in Wannasea at Archies and will meet someone there. It's a guy that I'm thinking of hiring for 'The Place.' He's the brother of a good friend. He's got a reputation as a decent bartender and a great bouncer but he's also as a musician. His sister says that he is wasting his time where he is now."

"But we don't serve alcohol, Beth."

"I don't think that matters to Ralph; he's more interested in expanding the music portion of his career. The place where he is now working is a weekend drinking hole in Halifax for dock workers. They let Ralph play on Tuesdays and Thursdays but he thinks they only keep him around as their primary problem resolver and bouncer."

"Okay, but why do you want me to pass judgement on him?"

"First of all, Ralph is a bit of a fan of yours. Beyond bringing him on as counter and kitchen help, he's a solo act that I'm thinking about starting out on Tuesday through Thursday nights. He doesn't do Reggie and if I give him Wednesday that means that he's going to have to do your background music. Ralph is also hopeful that you'll help him with his songwriting."

"You've piqued my interest a little," Abe replies. "I think 'The Place' is long overdue for an upgrade in its music."

"We'll take him out to 'The Place' for an audition after we have our fish and chips, if you're game."

"I'm fine with that."

The ferry began slowly moving away from the dock for the 30-minute journey over to Wannasea.

"Why did you stop songwriting after grandma and mom were gone?"

"The musical part of the song writing just wasn't possible. When all you got is words, there isn't a song."

From the time that Abe had been a senior in high school, he'd had a world class crush on the twenty months older and half a lifetime wiser Janie. Janie was then attending Wannasea extension part-time, working as a bartender at his mother's bar and occasionally performing on 'The Place's' stage.

Abe had begun writing song lyrics to get Janie's attention. Abe and Janie had evolved as a pair through that song writing. Jane was a capable musician on guitar and piano. Abe basically won her heart through writing lyrics for her. Janie had neither a unique nor perfect voice. Janie sang passably well. When Janie had played at 'The Place,' most came to see the strikingly pretty and graceful young woman dressed up much like Joan Baez, rather than to actually pay attention to her attempts at Joan Baez style music.

Abe had gone off to college in Swansea and was assigned Alf Cox as roommate. Alf, who would later evolve into "Reggie Reginald," was more interested in becoming a recording star than attending a school of higher learning. Once Alf, who was at that time the lead singer in a Beatles knock-off band, had learned about 'The Place,' he pushed Abe toward thinking they might become a duo. Reggie then arranged for the pair to take guitar and piano lessons from Janie. Abe never got the hang of either musical instrument but Janie had managed to teach Reggie the rudiments of playing the guitar. Janie developed an interest in Abe's writings. Janie encouraged Abe to show her more of his poetry about the island. She began writing melodies to the poems, having Abe adjust words as necessary. Janie began performing the songs at 'The Place' which would eventually evolve into Reggie Reginald's first album, *The Kingdom of Wannasea*.

Reggie, ever the opportunist, had seen the possibilities in using Abe and Janie as his songwriters and the use of 'The Place' as a springboard for his musical ambitions. Four months after Reggie started Janie's lessons, Reggie dropped out of his Beatles band and switched to folk music. First casting himself as Cruisoe and began doing mediocre Dylan plus Chad and Jeremy. After Reggie caught wind of the Wannasea Island songs which Janie was then performing, he begged Abe to let him use them. Reggie Reginald was born. Reggie not only appropriated Abe and Janie's songs, Reggie appropriated Abe's family history through taking the Reginald name. Reggie often told people that he was Hugo's illegitimate child.

Reggie wasn't much on the guitar but he could sing. Reggie also had the look. Reggie got himself a guitar player, a bass/fiddle player and a drummer/keyboard man. A Mainland producer heard Reggie do *Hugo Flies* at 'The Place.' Reginald's 'Kings of Wannasea' album was put together with 12 songs written by Abe and Janie. Ten months later, *Hugo Flies* took off. Reggie had been at the right place at the right time. Reggie was soon gone from Abe's, except for oddly spaced visits focused on Abe and Janie producing songs for two more albums at reduced royalty rates. Janie and Abe had also had three of their songs put on a rather popular album by Tara Rose. Up until the Reggie revival started two years ago, Abe had actually been getting more royalties from the Rose songs than Reggie's.

Abe looks out across the rather calm sea back toward the Mainland.

"When your grandmother went, as far as I was concerned, she took the music with her."

The pair are silent for the next few minutes as the ferry glides across the strait toward the island of Wannasea "Grandma Becca had a very tough life, didn't she?" Beth observes.

"Extremely."

Abe's mother had lost her father in the first great war, her mother and her husband in a car bombing during a terror spree which still wasn't forgotten on Wannasea Island or the Mainland, then her daughter and granddaughter were lost at sea. Beth and Abe had been all Rebecca had left.

"How was she able to stand losing so many of the people which she loved?" Beth asks.

Abe shakes his head, "I've no idea. Most people would have curled into a ball and died after Alice and my dad."

"Lucky for us, she didn't."

The ferry approaches the pier and loading dock at Wannasea.

"I'll go down and get the car and meet you at Archies," Beth tells Abe.

The weather was starting to turn a little chillier, so Abe briskly walks off the ferry, up the ramp and to the roundabout which is sheltered from the wind by the Post Office on the right side and Phillip's Restaurant on the left. Abe turns right and walks toward the entrance to 'Archies.'

Beth turns her Beetle east down Wannasea's main street. Two blocks down, she turns left into the village's parking garage. After parking the car, she walks across the street to 'Archies.' About five feet from where Abe is waiting, a slight, strikingly handsome, dark-haired young man, who looks to be about Beth's age stands in front of the restaurant, a guitar case strapped on his back.

"Abe," Beth says as she gestures toward the young man, "this is Ralph Jones."

Turning toward Ralph, Beth continues, "Ralph, this is my grandfather, Abe Stolz."

Abe shakes hands with the young man as he takes stock of him.

Nice looking kid, Abe thinks. *Maybe there's more going on here than just hiring a new musician/counter person.*

The trio go into 'Archie's' and sit at a table in the near corner. All three place an order for fish and chips which is the main feature at 'Archie's.'

As Beth and Ralph exchange small talk until their orders come, Abe occasionally inserts himself to ask Ralph questions about his living situation. Ralph is the brother of one of Beth's friends. Ralph has been working at Dave's in Halifax for almost a year now. Seems Ralph is two years younger than Beth and lives in his grandmother's house in the Village of Wannasea about eight blocks west of where they now sit. His parents currently reside on the northside of Halifax but are in the process of moving back to the island. From what Abe can tell, Ralph seems like a nice enough kid.

Abe being hungry, wolfs down the battered cod and wedges of potatoes. He sits crunching on ice from his water glass while the younger pair finishes their meal.

"My dad used to play out at your place with the band that he was in," Ralph comments.

"That so?"

"He played in a band called 'The Tillers,'" Ralph offers.

The Tillers. Jones. Local family. Abe has serious difficulty keeping himself from spewing out the ice in his mouth. This kid may well be Beth's half-brother.

Suddenly Abe has a completely new perspective on completing the DNA test which Hugh had been pushing him to take in order to try to establish whether or not Hugo had actually been a Reginald. Hugh had this theory that Hugo's mother, who was the third of Nine's four wives, had an affair with a Naval officer from Swansea which resulted in Hugo. Abe now decides that not only was he going to take that DNA test, so was Beth and her new employee.

Fish and chips down, the trio return to the parking garage and squeeze themselves into Beth's Bug. Even though Ralph is slight and two inches shorter than Abe, he has to place his legs sideways to fit into the rear seat. Fortunately, it is less than five minutes up the road toward the mountain to 'The Place.' Beth drops them at the front door.

Marie opens the heavy wooden entrance door and holds it open allowing Abe and Ralph to enter.

"Getting windy out here," Marie comments. "You doing okay, Ralph?"

"Never better, Marie,"

"Why don't you get yourself set up on the stage while we wait for Beth to get back?" Marie suggests.

Ralph and his guitar go off to the stage. Abe walks toward a table as far removed from the counter and stage in the east corner of the building as possible. Whether Ralph knew it or not, he would be auditioning without the sound system. An audition practice which had been in place since Janie ran the dining room and stage.

Beth comes hustling back in and sits down beside Abe. In a moment Marie brings over a tray with three teas and sets them down as well. This catches Abe a little off guard. No question Marie is a valued employee at 'The Place.' She'd been here five years, but Abe wasn't sure how this audition tied into her job duties.

"Any time you are ready, Ralph," Beth requests.

"Should I turn on the microphone?" Ralph asks.

"Let's try it without it first," Beth responds.

Ralph adjusts his guitar and breaks into his version of *Hard Headed Woman* by Cat Stevens.

The kid has tons of projection. Abe raises his eyebrows. Ralph could sing as well as play. He had talent. When the song ends even Abe joins Beth and Marie in applauding.

"Why don't you turn the microphone on now?" Beth suggests.

Ralph then launches into *Operator* (That's not the way it feels) by Jim Croce. It is even better.

After they again applaud, Beth asks, "What do you think, Gramps?"

"He's a keeper, if we can figure out the best way to fit him into what passes for the folk nostalgia craze these days."

"Marie," Beth requests, "why don't you take Ralph on a tour while Abe and I talk over how to try to fit Ralph in."

Marie rises, goes up to the stage and begins showing Ralph around 'The Place.'

"Originally I was thinking that maybe you could teach him enough Reggie songs to appease the masses," Beth says, "but that stuff we just heard makes Reggie's songs seem like pretty weak sauce."

"Cat Stevens and Jim Croce didn't start out in Wannasea," Abe reminds Beth. "Lots of the tourists come in for the full Reggie Reginald Kingdom of Wannasea experience. Let's see if I can teach him enough of Reggie's songs so that we can get away with sliding in whatever other stuff he does best."

"You'll have the time to teach him?"

"I'll make the time," Abe offers, hoping the time that he spends with Ralph can also be used to get him to take a DNA test.

As they wait for Marie and Ralph's return from the kitchen, Abe explains Hugh's suggestion about DNA tests to Beth.

"I really think that we should both get them to give us the broadest range for figuring out who Hugo's father was," Abe suggests.

"I'm okay with taking one," Beth replies disinterestedly.

Marie and Ralph are now halfway across the dining area to their table.

"Sit down Ralph and let's see what we can work out," Beth instructs as Ralph takes a chair. "I'm good with you starting by doing Tuesday through Thursdays if you can pick up a couple of Reggie songs so you can back Abe up on Wednesday nights. You already know what the pay is for the counter work. The tips can be pretty good on the weekends or when the tourists are in. As far as the music, like all the other bands, you will get $75 a night during weekdays. Plus you can put out your guitar case for tips and take everything the audience gives you. Sometime down the road, if we schedule you on weekends, you'll get $125 for Friday and $200 for Saturday. If you really catch on, we'll start doing a cover charge on Fridays and Saturdays with you getting 75%."

"I've learned that hard rock, grunge and punk don't work for me," Ralph says. "I'll try my best learning whatever songs you'd like that fit the folk vibe that you have going here. Usually don't have a lot of trouble learning new songs. Don't have a problem being able to read music. Will have to give the guys down at 'Dave's' two weeks' notice though, before I start. I'm willing to come in on weekday mornings to work with Mr. Stolz to learn whatever songs you want me to play so that I'll be ready to play my first week. That's if it's okay with Mr. Stolz."

"Sounds good to me," Abe replies. "I'll try to get all the Reggie sheet music together to give to you the next time we get together."

"I'll be here tomorrow morning at 8. Should be able to stick around until 11 or so. I'm off on Wednesdays, so we can do the whole day then if you want," Ralph suggested. "I'm just so thrilled to have a chance to work with you, Mr. Stolz."

"One question," Abe interjects, "what's the name of your act?"

Ralph looks puzzled, "Ralph Jones, why?"

"I'm not sure that Ralph Jones is a good name for a musical act," Abe replies.

"Hadn't ever thought about calling myself anything but Ralph Jones," Ralph answers. "Do you have any ideas?"

Abe thinks for a long moment, before suggesting, "How about Zack Tillerman?"

"Tillerman," Ralph muses with a broad smile. "Like the Cat Stevens song and 'the Tillers' my dad's old band?"

"Exactly," Abe says with a smile as he holds out his hand. "Do we have us a deal Zack Tillerman?"

Huge grin still intact, Ralph shakes Abe's hand then Beth's before heading to the stage to collect his guitar and case.

"You might not want to make any long-term musical commitments on weekends after the next six weeks," Abe suggests to Beth. "If this guy can produce anything close to the performance, he just gave us, this Ralph guy very well may be 'The Place's musical future."

Ralph, his guitar once again strapped to his back, returns to the table.

"I'm going to run Ralph down to his grandma's," Beth said as she rises from the table.

Ralph shakes Abe's hand once again after the old man stands up.

"You know I've got ulterior motives for wanting to sing here," Ralph says to Abe.

Abe smiles back almost as broadly as Ralph as he thinks to himself, *Don't we all, kid.*

As the pair leaves, Abe exits the dining area, goes through the back door and up the stairs as quickly as possible. He sits down at the desk in his bedroom in front of the laptop. Abe spends the next 40 minutes figuring out how to order three DNA test kits from the leading DNA research company's website.

Just have to figure out how to get Ralph to make use of one of them.

Alice

Wednesday night just before 7. Abe's sitting on the stool behind the cash register. Abe had spent three hours on Tuesday morning and most of this day going over songs with Zack. After the two sessions, Abe had decided that Ralph would now be Zack to him. The kid looked and played like a Zack. Zack having Wednesday off, was seated beside him looking through Abe's green journals.

Beth had forced Abe to break his edict against going into the house. She demanded Abe use Janie's old studio to mentor Zack.

"Otherwise you are going to distract everyone at 'The Place,'" Beth reasoned.

Abe hates to admit that he was beginning to enjoy being in the bright open space of the studio despite much of what Janie had put into it, including her grand piano, still residing there. It was a good room for music just as his wife intended. Zack was having no problem making the best of it.

Zack was a quick study. His audition songs were no accident. Abe didn't quite understand why Zack hadn't caught on at the place that he'd been working. Zack said that he'd been a folk musician playing in front of a punk/grunge crowd. *Whatever the hell that meant,* Abe thought.

Abe liked how well Zack was progressing that he had brought out the lyrics for *Don't blame the alcohol* and two other songs after getting sober songs to see if Zack could do anything with them. It had taken Zack a few hours to come up with the melody but after he had, Abe liked what Zack had done.

Much as he didn't want to, Abe was starting to like this kid.

Abe wasn't picking up much of vibe as to what the audience might want him to read as the Wannasea Boys began setting up.

Abe decides he would do the lyrics that he liked the most, 'Alice's rule.' The song had been a secondary hit from Reggie's first album despite the producers having complained that it was "too damned political."

Abe walks over to Beth and says, "I want to do Alice."

Beth nods her head and returns to filling orders.

Abe's grandmother had returned from the Mainland after Nine had finally died. Nine, the last royal Reginald, had thrown himself in with fascists of both Italy and Germany. Autocrats always seeming to find a way of making good use of each other. Nine had spent his last days living in Porto-Vecchio, Corsica at the urging of the Italian Military. Many said that Corsica had been the original home of the pirates, who became known as the Reginalds.

Before his death, Nine had badly wanted to put an end to Alice. The focus of his eight years of exile had been trying to extract revenge upon her. Until the day that Nine died, the former Wannasea king been working the Axis spy services to try to undermine the government on Wannasea in hopes of discovering where Alice was hiding. Nine's men had come to make it a habit of setting off bombs in the harbor or in the streets of Wannasea and Halifax, Nine died ruing that his remaining henchmen had not been able to find and take out Alice Bailey. Nine blamed the failure on his most experienced henchman, his first cousin Sylvester, still rotting away in the Swansea prison with 17 years left on a 25-year sentence.

Alice and her daughter had been living in Edmonton, Alberta under the assumed name Teresa Rossi. Alice worked supporting the logistics operation at the nearby CFB. The base security service in conjunction with NATO kept a close eye on Alice's welfare.

By the time Nine passed, Mainland Security Services had felt it was safe to allow Alice to come out of hiding. Over three months, Alice and Becca moved back to Wannasea. The Mainland feeling that Alice could be of real service to them as the second great war approached.

Becca had been 14 when Nine died and she began the return journey to Wannasea. She helped her mom move into a nice little flat in the heart of the village of Wannasea. Alice had little concern over what the flat cost. In addition to the lifelong pension which Alice continued to receive from Hugo's military service and death, Alice had just been given a sum of over $11.7 million of Reginald funds which had been frozen when Hugo abdicated.

The island welcomed Alice back as a venerated hero. Alice's first action was to establish a new political party. In the first election following her return, she was chosen the island's governor. An extraordinary feat considering that even on the Mainland, few women were then being elected to public office.

Alice dove right into revamping both the island's inefficient government and support for the Mainland's effort against fascism.

Alice had been the most popular politician during the island's experiment with democracy. Nine was a far distant thought in 1953 when Sylvester was released from prison. Sylvester had neither forgotten nor forgiven Alice however. After his release, Sylvester's first move was a trip to Berlin and a discussion with East German security services about whether they might be interested helping to extract Nine's revenge in exchange for certain Mainland secrets which the remaining Reginalds had managed to acquire. Becca had married the lawyer Nathan Stolz by this time. Her only child, Abraham, then being eight.

Beth walked to the stage, turned on the microphone and said, "Good evening, ladies and gentlemen. Welcome to another night at 'The Place.' Abe has chosen to do 'Alice's rule' for you tonight. Please enjoy."

Abe ambled to the stage, nodding to the Wannasea's Boys lead. After adjusting the microphone, Abe got right into it:

Alice's Rule (Done in Reggie's version in the key of G Major, tempo of 88BPM in 3/4 time)

Hugo and Alice were island legends
saved Wannasea without using weapons
defeated tyranny with a well laid plan
overthrowing the rule of the Reginald clan

Wannasea's governor wrote Nine had died
Alice's time to turn homeward finally arrived
With daughter in tow, she set out for Wannasea
their heart, their home and their shared destiny

Hugo and Alice were island legends
saved Wannasea without firing weapons
pushing for stronger, fairer and better rules
Alice soon proved to be nobody's fool

to the post of governor Alice was elected
then to work mending a government which had long been neglected

for eighteen years Alice made improvements
to the island's roads, schools and political movements
with guile, compassion and vision Alice had governed
changed even the minds of the island's most stubborn

there will always be an angry malevolent force
more than willing to help evil run its full course
Sylvester, consumed by Nine's continuing feud
plotted revenge against Alice in manner most crude
a bomb was ignited in the boot of Alice's car
the explosive extinguished Alice's bright star
yet her legacy triumphed over the terror Sylvester intended
what had been started was not to be ended

Hugo and Alice were island legends
saved Wannasea without using weapons
defeated tyranny with a well laid plan
overthrowing the rule of the Reginald clan

Hugo and Alice were Wannasea legends
saved the island without using weapons

for eighteen years Alice made improvements
to the island's roads, schools and political movements
with guile, compassion and vision Alice had governed
changed even the minds of the island's most stubborn

Hugo and Alice were Wannasea legends
saved the island without using weapons
Pushing for stronger, fairer and better rules
Alice proved to be nobody's fool
overcome by the terror Sylvester intended
what the pair had started was not to be ended
what Hugo and Alice start was not to be ended

Abe did his reading twice before the Boys kept it going by doing their own rendition of 'Alice's rule' another two times.

It was a mainly Wannasea crowd which had quickly gotten into repeating and singing the "Hugo and Alice" stanzas.

Seems Grandma Alice was still a hero to many on Wannasea Island.

The Morris Returns

The Morris hadn't been ready for pickup until the Friday after Abe's first session with Zack. Ordered parts had finally been received and the car hadn't been finished until late last evening. Abe was now seated in the front seat of 'The Place's' delivery van which Sallie normally used to pick up fresh produce and the other necessities for her kitchen. Sallie had offered to drop Abe and Zack, who still had a little more than a week to fill out on his old job, off in Halifax. Abe was in the passenger's seat. Zack was seated on an overturned large plastic container which Sallie used for produce. His always present guitar beside him. Zack's position was definitely not a Wannasea Island Motor Vehicle Department approved seating arrangement.

Sallie was now instructing Jack and a couple of the other kitchen helpers on what needed to be done in her absence. There were usually anywhere from 7–15 high school through college age kids working part-time at 'The Place' depending on day of the week and time of the season. Now in late October there were eight. Two in the kitchen. Six working out front. Abe thought that at least a quarter of the island's school kids had worked out at the 'The Place' over the years.

Sallie had been at Abe's since five years before Becca died. Abe wasn't all that clear on Sallie's age. He knew that she had come to 'The Place' after some type of a blow up in her marriage. Sallie had almost immediately begun to assume Becca's kitchen role right down to tending everything which grew in Becca's garden just off the south wing of the house. Sallie was also one of Beth's housemates.

Sallie slid into the front seat and turned on the ignition as Zack continues telling Abe about his reaction to Wednesday night's session.

"Didn't realize how powerful a reaction you can get from a crowd," Zack observed. "Down at Dave's they mostly talk over or ignore me."

"That was one of the better sets, Zack," Abe stated. "The crowd isn't always that into it."

"I've seen a little of that kind of crowd enthusiasm when I used to go listen to my dad play with 'The Tillers' but I never saw anything the level of last night."

Sallie shifts the panel van into gear and they are off to the ferry dock.

"Can you hear the band playing the music in the kitchen?" Zack asked Sallie.

"Usually," Sallie replied. "Sometimes we prop open the kitchen doors and listen. If it's not too busy, we'll slip out and stand at the kitchen end of the bar."

"What did you think of Wednesday night?" Zack asked.

"It was powerful," Sallie said thoughtfully, "but like Abe said it doesn't always work out that way."

The van continues down the slope toward the village. There are barely any homes near 'The Place.' Historically the area by the lakes had been used to provide water and electricity. Most of the island also preferred to live as close to the village or the sea as possible.

The island was shaped something like a banana with the two curled up ends pointing south and out to sea. There was a total of about 38 square miles of land mass, which includes five small scattered islands just off the south seaward shore. The village of Wannasea sits slightly toward the east end facing back toward the Mainland. There are approximately 72,000 full-time residents on the island. During tourist season, there might be as many as 500,000 on the island. Lately though people had begun moving out from the Mainland to retire resulting in houses in places Abe could not remember seeing houses before.

They arrived at the queue for the ferry.

"See you tomorrow," Zack said to Sallie as he went out the side door.

Sallie preferred to stay in the van during the ferry trip.

"I'll drop you off at 'Dave's' if you want?" Sallie offers.

"Thanks, but I've got to run into the music store just down from dock and pick up some new strings that I need."

Abe and Zack made their way up the ramp, use their ferry cards to get through the turnstiles and take seats in Abe's preferred spot near the rear of the ferry where the spray and noise were always less.

"I'm thinking of buying a motorcycle," Zack says unprompted.

"Are you sure that's a good idea? This island is not really a very safe place to be operating a motorcycle. Take a spill, mess up your hands, you might still be able to tend bar but your guitar playing days would be over."

The thought causes Zack to pause for a few moments before saying, "A motorcycle is really all that I can afford at this point."

"Tell you what," Abe offers, "I'm willing to be your lender if you switch to buying a car. You can pay me back from your performance tips."

Zack looks at the old man quizzically, "You're serious?"

Abe nods.

It was a very pleasant day for this time of year. October weather could be stormy but this was an almost perfect day to be out on the bay.

Janie would have loved a day like this, Abe thinks as he rises from the bench and walks to the back rail of the ferry.

Abe watches the island gradually disappear. He could almost envision Janie's sailboat gliding past the western horizon.

It had been a different kind of day the last time when he had last seen Janie and Julia. A day in late July. Although they hadn't been talking, Abe had known that Janie was going out by the west end to practice for a sailboat race coming up in late August. It was a day which had been much warmer and more overcast. More breeze coming from out of the west. Abe had been on the ferry that day, but he'd been under the deck in the Morris with Becca and Beth. Headed to Halifax to pick up supplies and to allow Becca to buy Beth a new pair of shoes meant to help her walk a little better. Beth was 18 months then and still stuck in a teetering, tottering walk which led to too many falls down the slope from the house to the business. Abe remembers that trip all too well. It had been the last time in his life that he was not be aware that his wife and daughter, like his grandparents and father, were not going to be there anymore.

Abe stands at the rail with his thoughts until the ferry slows down and pulls into the Halifax dock.

"See you tomorrow, Mr. Stolz," Abe hears Zack call out to him.

He waves toward the young man before quickly walking to the stairs which leads to the car. Abe reaches the van before a queue of cars has started to move.

"Nice guy that Ralph," Sallie says as she waits to start up the van. "Marie says that she thinks he has a lot of potential."

"He certainly does as a musician," Abe replies, "We will have to wait to see how he works out behind the counter."

Sallie starts the engine and the van moves slowly out of the ferry, up the ramp and onto the streets of Halifax.

It is only three blocks to repair shop. Sallie drops him off at the front gate.

"Thanks."

"See you back at 'The Place,' Abe."

Abe goes into the shop pays the $855 bill with his infrequently used credit/debit card, then climbs into the Morris and heads straight back to the ferry. Usually, Abe would use a ferry trip like this to do some shopping or just a little driving around the Mainland but Abe wants to get back to island in hopes the DNA kits have arrived.

Those DNA tests have now become one of the big drivers for Abe to be able to determine his future. If Zack did indeed turn out to be Beth's half-brother, Abe was beginning to lean toward selling the business. If it was negative, he would work on legally transferring 'The Place' to Beth. All other considerations seemed as if they would flow from the DNA results.

Abe switches on the Morris, noting that the car now sounds much better. He drives straight to the ferry just in time to be motioned aboard for the Wannasea leg of the trip he'd just come in on. Abe, like Sally, usually stayed in the vehicle during the trip but it was such a nice day, he decides to go back up on deck.

Abe is able to set down upon the same bench which he and Zack had been sitting on thirty minutes previously. Abe had barely made himself comfortable when a portly fifty-something walks up to him and says, "Abe Stolz?"

Abe thinks he recognizes the man from the island. Maybe he is one of the Wannasea Boys but Abe can't be certain.

"In person," Abe says cautiously.

"I'm Stanley Goode, the Development Assistant to the Governor," the man announces. "Mind if I sit down with you for a minute?"

Abe gestures toward the bench beside him trying to figure out why on earth a Wannasea government official has any interest in talking with him.

"We sent you and invitation to the dedication of the new government building two weeks from tomorrow but haven't gotten a reply from you as yet. As we are naming the building after your grandmother, we were hoping that you will say a few words about Alice Reginald for the event."

Abe turns sheepish. He had seen something that looked like an official Wannasea government envelope in the mail which Beth had handed over to him on Monday. Since it wasn't the DNA kit which he was looking for, he'd ignored it. Abe knew exactly where it was laying on the top of his desk.

"Sorry," Abe says with chagrin, "I was meaning to answer but have gotten so tied up mentoring a new guy, who is coming on at 'The Place' that it completely slipped my mind."

"We'd really like you to speak."

"I'll be there," Abe promises. "Will have to see if Beth can make it but I will definitely come. I could do 'Alice's rule' if you like?"

The official smiles as he rises from the bench, "Sounds good."

"What's going to happen to the old government building and property?" Abe asks.

The property, soon to be former government center, abuts both of Abe's properties.

"We are planning on selling them next year," the official replies. "We are hoping to work something out with the historical society to turn at least part of the castle into a museum."

Another thing to worry about, Abe thinks.

"What's the official name of your new building going to be?"

"The Alice B. Reginald Government Center," the official replies. "Now if you don't mind, I've got to get back over to the group my staff and I will be showing around the island. Maybe we'll even bring them out to your place. See you on 10th."

"Thanks, see you then."

Alice B. Reginald Government Center. Abe knew that his grandmother would much prefer the Alice Bailey Government Center in honor of her given name. Alice didn't much like anything about the Reginald name other than the fact that it had also been Hugo's last name.

What the hell's the difference though, Abe conjectures. *People have already formed their own images of the people from his family's past. I, for one, have done as much as any to provide them those images.*

Abe is able to remember quite a bit about his grandmother which is outside the public image of Alice B. Reginald. His grandmother had always been a true force of nature. A personification of competence. When Alice set her mind to something, it got done. Alice wasn't your cheek kissing, baking cookies style grandmother. Alice was a kick ass and take names type of grandmother. He remembered walking behind her as she inspected some new construction at the castle. He could also remember how Alice had often browbeaten his father when he'd screwed up some negotiation or other.

Nathan Stolz, Abe's lawyer father, was more lawyer in the figurative sense than the literal. Nathan believed in the concept of the law more than its actual structure. Nathan had only become a lawyer because that was what his father and older brother were. There was still a Stolz Law firm in the Wannasea village. Now run by the son of Abe's cousin, Herbert.

Thinking of his father made Abe smile. His father had always been able to make Abe smile. Nathan seemed to believe that life was an opportunity to manufacture smiles.

Grandma Alice as the island governor with his father as her legal advisor had always been quite the adventure. At least when Abe had been around them.

Abe could still remember something of Becca before the explosion. Becca had been almost as fun loving as her father. Alice was constantly badgering Becca to work on an advanced degree but Becca was perfectly content teaching Kindergarten at Wannasea Elementary and enjoying Nathan, her son and the island.

Wonder if that's why Becca married my dad? Abe suddenly thinks. *Had Nathan been Becca's opportunity to subvert Alice's rule?*

The thought vanishes from Abe's mind almost instantly. Abe well knew that his mother had doted on Nathan Stolz. His mother had never been the same after Nathan was gone from her life.

Everything had changed after Alice and Nathan were assassinated. Becca stopped smiling and had little interest in having any sort of fun. Becca resigned from her job at the school, bought the Lakeside Inn and moved out of the village. Becca concentrated on cooking in 'The Place' kitchen, growing her garden and raising Abe. When Becca bought the Inn, she hired all the former staff and basically allowed them to manage all customer facing aspects. After Janie and Julia disappeared, Becca became even more nose-to-the grindstone. Abe was unable to remember his mother even once smiling after Janie and Julia were gone.

"Sir, you are going to have to exit the ferry." Abe hears one of the attendants tell him.

"Shit!" Abe exclaims, more to himself than the attendant. "I've got my car downstairs."

Lucky for Abe, he had been the last car on the ferry so there was not now a whole line of very angry ferry users waiting to curse him out when he reached the Morris. Most of the cars are already out of the hold as Abe cranks up the Morris and heads toward the exit.

Dark Ringlets

Abe sits behind the cash register running a finger over a page in one his older green journals Abe's mind drifts back to almost fifty years previous.

In Reggie's second month of performing as Cruisoe at 'The Place,' he decided that Janie ought to be his muse. On Janie's part that idea lasted about ten hot seconds. Three days into Reggie trying to woo Janie, the pair were on the stage with Janie trying to teach Reggie how to play piano. To this day, Abe wasn't certain what Reggie did or said, but Janie had punched him on the chin so hard Reggie went backward over the back of the piano bench and ended up laying on the stage floor looking dumbstruck.

"You ever do anything like that again, you miserable little cretin," Janie had shouted to Reggie "and you'll not only be back down on this floor, you'll be lucky if you'll ever be able to get up again."

This being back in the days when 'The Place' was still essentially more bar than grill, there had been a rumor floating around at Abe's since Janie started working there as a waitress that she carried a knife inside her skirts. Reggie had heard the rumor and took Janie's threat to heart. Abe had been married to Janie for almost a year before she revealed to him that she had planted that rumor purposefully when she first started working at 'Abe's.'

"Made the local Romeo's stop and think twice before they came on to me," Janie informed him.

"Didn't stop me," Abe had replied.

Janie had laughed, "I hit on you, Abe. You didn't hit on me. Took you almost two damned years and a hit album before you figured out that I liked you."

The "piano bench incident" had been essentially the end of any direct working relationship between Reggie and Janie. After that almost everything went through Abe.

Which in the end, Abe thinks, *worked out pretty well for me.*

Abe then moves to looking over songs which had been written for Reggie's second album. A time when things had begun to turn sour between Reggie and the Wannasea songwriting duo.

Reggie's first album had been exceptionally well received, not only on the Mainland, but throughout most of Europe and North America. Reggie had rushed Abe and Janie into producing songs for a second album. At the time, Janie and Abe had begun putting together a group of songs with they thought would fit nicely into Reggie's historically inclined folk style. Reggie had wanted nothing to do with it. Reggie was adamant that he was going to move into what he called romantic folk. Reggie wanted songs which he thought would be capable of turning him into the next folk heartthrob. Abe and Janie had ended up giving Reggie reworked songs which Abe had written for Janie to perform early on. Abe always felt the best of that lot was *Dark Ringlets*, which basically only took changing the gender in the song's last line to make it suitable for Reggie. The lyrics were from a poem Abe had written when he first realized how hard he'd fallen for Janie. It had taken Abe months for Abe to show it to Janie.

Although the song went on the second album, Reggie had not done the song justice.

Fifteen years after Reggie's second album had met with lukewarm success, Tara Rose's manager called Janie and asked for permission to record the song. The song had done rather well.

Earlier in the day, Zack and Reggie had played around with *Dark Ringlets*. For Abe, there really wasn't much tweaking that he could do to the lyrics. Zack had played around for half an hour or so before putting a slight reggaeton twist on the melody. Abe felt that twist was the way the song should always have been played. The pair had decided the song would be added to Zack's repertoire for his opening week.

Abe had also decided that to get Abe's patrons used to moving a little further away from their 'Kingdom of Wannasea' fixation, he'd try it out tonight, a little more than ten days before Zack's opening.

Over the past few days, Abe had become more appreciative of Zack's musical potential. So much so that he had begun to think of steps which might be able to be taken to rework some other "Janie songs" and have Zack record them.

Beth walks up to Abe and sets down a cup of tea.

"I want to do *Dark Ringlets* tonight," Abe informs Beth.

She gives him a quizzical look before asking, "Have you ever done that song in here before?"

"Nope, but I want to see how the crowd responds to it."

"You are getting adventurous in your old age, Abe," Beth comments before asking, "Didn't Tara Rose have a hit with *Dark Ringlets*?"

"She did okay with it, but I'll read it the way I wrote it for Reggie's 2nd album. Had Zack do it up today and I think he just might be able to do something even better, so I want to get the crowd used to it."

"Okay," Beth says in a way that made Abe think maybe she wasn't actually okay with that line of reasoning. "While you are redoing old hits, is there any chance that you might have time to decide whether or not you are going to sell me this place?"

"How much money do you have?" Abe asked hoping that might cool Beth's interest in buying the place.

The second trust fund which Becca had set up for Beth had just been released last month. Abe wasn't certain how his mother had structured the trust and whether Beth now had full access to all the funds in it.

"I figure that if you are going to charge me full market rate for this place, I might have to pay around $1.5 million. I can certainly handle that, but I am hoping for the sweetest granddaughter on the island discount."

Abe laughs before saying, "I've still got a couple things to figure out before I think of selling the place. I will however promise you that those things should be worked out no later than the end of January. As soon as I've figured it out, you will be the first to know and we'll go from there. Until then, I'm not selling to anyone else."

"I've got your word on that?"

"You have."

Abe processes a handful of receipts collected from the dining area and manages to finish his tea before Beth walks on to the stage. The Rumrunners were up tonight. Abe hands the band's lead three copies of sheet music then asks whether he and they know the song. They didn't, though they'd heard of it and thought they could pull it off.

"Welcome to 'The Place' ladies and gentlemen. Tonight we are going to kick things off with a reading of *Dark Ringlets*. Hope you enjoy it."

After Abe adjusts the microphone, he turns to the crowd and says, "Hope you'll bear with me tonight as we are going to try something a little different. I'm going to read the lyrics of one of the songs from Reggie's second album called *Dark Ringlets*. Tara Rose also had a hit with song about twenty years back. This song has a special place in my heart as I originally wrote it for my wife, who would have been 72 this week."

What the hell am I doing? Abe thinks before he turns to the band to get them to slide into the opening melody.

"Janie, wherever you are, I hope you appreciate this," Abe says in a whisper.

Dark Ringlets – Reggie's 2nd album done in key of C, tempo of 135BPM in 4/4 time

dark ringlets flowing down
fingers dance on piano keys
notes spinning my head around
you've cast a spell on me

dark ringlets reflecting soft light
soft voice flowing free
takes over the day and the night
weaving a spell over me

where wandering mind goes
your presence now comes with me
this spell's hold over me grows
doubt I will ever break free

dark ringlets fill my day
racing over the sea
you sailed my fears away
and make a man of me

invading all my dreams
no longer able to tell
how to plan my schemes
or just how hard I fell

dark ringlets flowing down
fingers dance on piano keys
notes spinning my head around
you've cast a spell on me

where wandering mind goes
your presence follows me
your hold on my heart grows
so tight I can't break free

dark ringlets fill my day
as we race across the sea
you've swept my fears away
and made a man of me

dark ringlets flowing down
fingers dancing on piano keys
notes spinning my head around
you have cast a spell on me

where wandering mind goes
your presence comes with me
your hold over me grows
so tight I'll not break free

dark ringlets fill my day
as we race across the sea
you've swept my fears away
and made a man of me

Abe got through the first reading without much problem and was a little surprised that by the second time into the last stanza some in the crowd were singing it.

Abe did it once more with a few more joining in on the stanzas each time.

As Abe ended and nodded for the Boys to take over the microphone, the group breaks into their version of 'Roll the old Chariot Along.'

Reggie's Return

Abe is entering the village of Wannasea in the Morris. Zack/Ralph was in the passenger's seat. Abe had finally received the DNA test kits and was on this way to the Post Office to send the completed test kits out. On the way, he would drop Zack off at his grandmother/s house in west side of the village.

After having finalized his own test tube and getting Beth to do the same, Abe hadn't had any trouble getting Zack to take the last DNA test. He'd told Zack that as part of his continuing historical research on Wannasea Island, he'd like to study Zack's family roots. Zack's grandmother's family had been on the island living in this exact area as long as any could remember. Abe used the excuse of wanting to figure out where that family had originated for his historical research. Although Abe would very likely add Zack's family DNA information to the volumes of information which are now contained in his black journals, the real purpose of Zack's test remained determining if he is Beth's half-brother.

Abe was certain that he could have asked Zack to take the DNA test without any explanation and Zack would have complied. At this point, Abe was fairly certain that he could ask Zack to do almost anything short of doing physical harm to someone and Zack would do it.

Abe steers the Morris west on main street, drives six blocks through the center of town before bearing left toward the Black Smoke Hill area. Abe drives two more blocks before Zack says, "Take a right here."

Abe complies, going another two blocks before pulling up in front of a long row of narrow town houses. It was now almost 11:30 AM on the Tuesday of Zack's last week working at 'Dave's' over on the Mainland. Abe had learned that Zack's hours there were from 3:30 PM through whenever the bar decided to close. Considering Zack usually showed up at 'The Place' about 8:30 for his Reggie Revival music lessons, Abe wasn't sure when or if Zack slept.

"Just pull up to the curb anywhere here," Zack instructs Abe.

Abe has learned from Zack that he spent the time between leaving Abe's and going to job on the Mainland taking care of the grandmother, who has Alzheimer's disease. There was something of an overlapping care arrangement between Zack, his sister, who worked at the bank they had just passed when turning off Main Street and Zack's mother. Zack's mother worked night shifts at one of the resorts down at the island's far west end. Zack's stint with his grandmother gave his mother a chance to grab some food, catch a nap or just go into an empty room and decompress from the stress of having dealt with her husband's mother all morning. Once Zack left, his mom would put in two more hour before Zack's sister Saanvi picked up the care after finishing at the bank. Zack's grandmother was now in year three of her decline. From the little bit of information which Zack had provided, it sounded as if she was becoming more detached from reality by the day.

Zack reaches over the seat and pulls his guitar from the back.

"Are there any more of Reggie's songs that you think I should try to learn before next week?" Zack asks.

Zack now had Reggie's songs which were common at 'The Place,' down pat. Abe has changed his mind during the last week from wanting Zack to have almost a complete Reggie repertoire to thinking too much Reggie wasn't going to help Zack's career or expand Abe's audience in the long run. Wasn't that Zack couldn't do Reggie. Abe honestly thought that Zack could outdo Reggie but Reggie's songs weren't what Zack did best. Based on the past ten days, Abe thought Zack's wheelhouse was a folksier sort or blues. Most of the past morning had been spent playing around trying to put a few of Abe's darker writings into musical form. From Abe's perspective, those types of songs were likely going to drive Zack's musical future.

"What you've got of Reggie's is more than enough," Abe says. "I'm actually beginning to think that once you've established yourself at the place for a month or so, you may end up dumping them."

"Whatever you think, Mr. Stolz," Zack replies as he opens the passenger door, climbs out and then says, "Don't forget I won't be out tomorrow until 4 or 5."

Abe nods his head, knowing that Zack is going car shopping tomorrow. Abe has promised Zack that he will make him a loan on the purchase of a car up to $20K. Zack has about six grand which he was planning to use to buy a motorcycle. Zack getting in an accident on the motorcycle genuinely worried Abe. If he were being honest with himself however, his purpose in giving Zack the loan had been to make certain getting the DNA sample from Zack was easier to obtain.

"When you find the car which you want, give me a call and we'll work out how it's paid for," Abe says.

Zack closes the door, walks over the small cement stoop of the second town house from the end and disappears inside.

Abe circles the block, before heading to the other end of the island and the Post Office.

Abe gets lucky and finds an open space in the limited parking area in front of the cement block building. Abe pulls the DNA packets from where he had stashed them by the parking brake in the area between the Marina's two front leather bucket seats. Climbing out of the car, Abe goes into the building and waits in a line behind two other customers before paying the fees to have the tests sent out by the fastest method, express mail. Too much of Abe's life was now pending the outcome of these tests to not want them back as quickly as possible.

Mission complete, Abe drives back toward 'The Place.' Now almost noon, Abe had a 12:15 meeting with Alfred Cox for which he did not want to be late. The same Alfred Cox which the rest of the world knew as Reggie Reginald.

Abe has no idea when the last time was that Reggie had been on Wannasea Island. Abe had not laid eyes on Alfred Cox since just before Beth was born. This being between the time of fall of Reggie's folk star power and his revival which was now entering the third year.

Three years after the release of their *The Kingdom of Wannasea* album, Reggie's fall from popularity had been hard. Abe and Janie had written all the songs for Reggie's two follow up albums. Both had been met with increasingly tepid response. In typical Reggie fashion, Reggie blamed Abe and Janie's songwriting for the failure of those two albums. Reggie had a fourth album produced with songs by a couple of the Mainland's supposed hottest song writers. That album was DOA. Within eight months, Reggie, who was always a big spender, was back to performing at lesser venues and not being heard on the airwaves. Reggie moved from lesser venue to lesser venue. Fifteen years on, Reggie ended up right back where he had started, having persuaded Abe to let him do one weekend a month at 'The Place.' One of the few times in 'The

Place' history that a cover charge for two straight days had been the order of the evening.

At the time, Reggie was also playing clubs over on the Mainland near Halifax and Swansea. Most of those clubs were run by the remaining Reginald clan. Really more mob than clan if truth be told. Other than Sylvester, who spent 20+ years in Mainland prison, most of the rest of Nine's family henchmen served anywhere from a one to five years. When they got out, they settled in the outskirts of Halifax and gravitated toward gun running, protection schemes, loans, strongarming, illegal substances of all types and running a variety of "clubs." Reggie being Reggie and the Reginalds being the Reginalds, Reggie soon fell in with sons and grandsons of Nine's scoundrels. Reggie had also fallen into being a user of a variety of the Reginald's illegal substances.

When Janie and Becca had operated 'The Place' as a bar and grill, they had essentially developed a look-the-other-way attitude toward staff or customer use of weed. As long as marijuana use didn't impact their work or was blatantly open, the pair would ignore it. Blow, psychedelic chemicals or anything injected was out-of-bounds. If the pair caught someone using those particular mood modifiers, they were given a warning. The second time one of the two usually went to the Wannasea Constabulary to discuss what had been witnessed.

About a year after Beth had been born, Abe could no longer overlook that not only was Reggie using cocaine but that a lot of people around Reggie were also using. When it became too much, Abe told Reggie that he either stopped or the gig was over. Reggie had tried to glad hand Abe by insisting that every performer at his level used a little. Janie and Becca weren't having it. After finding Reggie and two of his backup players snorting coke under the stairs during their break, Janie, who didn't really like Reggie much to begin with, put her foot down. For the first time in his life, Abe had told Alf that he had to go. Abe hadn't seen him since.

Abe pulls into the parking lot noticing the sleek, blue Mercedes coupe parked in the handicap slot by the main entrance. Rather than driving the Morris back to the garage attached to the storage shed, Abe parks in an empty spot in the second row.

Abe had been somewhat surprised when Reggie had called him on Sunday afternoon and asked for this meeting. Reggie had been vague about the meeting's purpose, saying only that he wanted to talk over a business opportunity. The only business opportunity in which Abe could imagine that Reggie having an interest is the purchase of Abe and Janie's songwriting catalogue.

After Reggie's flop in his fourth year, Janie and Abe had become more than a little surprised that a not insignificant amount of royalties continued to flow in from their Reggie songwriting. *The Kingdom of Wannasea* plus the two succeeding albums had, it seemed, a strong and loyal following in Eastern Europe, as well as Korea and Japan. The royalties, though nowhere close to what had been generated during Reggie's first heyday, continued right up to the Revival. A bigger and bigger portion of those royalties coming from artists covering the songs in those nations. A practice which put money in Janie and Abe's pockets not Reggie's.

Abe turns off the Morris, sits back in the car's seat for a few minutes trying to put thoughts of Janie out of his head. Abe exits the Morris, crosses the parking lot and walks through the main entrance of 'The Place.'

Reggie is holding court at the kitchen entrance end of the counter. Reggie seems to have two security people with him. He is surrounded by Marie, a few of the wait staff and a small line of customers, who seem to be asking for autographs. Abe notices that Reggie seems to be hitting on Marie.

Same old Reggie, Abe thinks as he moves closer.

Alfred/Reggie was six months older than Abe. Abe studies his old college roommate as he watches him from the front counter of the old bar. Reggie now has the deep sort of tan that seems to go with being part of the leisure class. Reggie, also seems to have had a lot of work done on his face. Reggie even seems to have thicker and even more luxurious hair than when he'd had starting out. Hair worn in the same old page boy manner which was now blond rather than dark brown.

Reggie hands the pen back to a couple of ladies, who seem to be close to his own real age, walks up to Abe and pats him on the back, "My old songwriting partner," Reggie announces.

The closest Reggie ever came to writing a song was telling Janie and Abe that he didn't like something they'd produced. Reggie hadn't suggested how they fix it. Reggie had just demanded that it be fixed.

"Alf," Abe says nodding his head, "you're looking chipper."

"I'm as chipper as they come these days, Abe. Is there anywhere we can go to have our little discussion?"

Abe nods his head and points toward the back area.

"Sorry folks, business to discuss," Reggie says to those who are gathered around him. "Maybe I will stop back by after Abe and I have our little talk."

Reggie follows Abe through the kitchen, out the rear entrance then up the stairs to Abe's room.

"A long time since I've been in this place," Reggie says, "brings back lots of memories."

After Reggie had given up on college in their second year, he'd begun his run as Cruisoe, playing at Abe's four nights a week, Reggie had been the first to take up residence in this room. At the time, it had been used for liquor storage and bookkeeping. There had been a day bed in the corner at that time where Reggie had slept.

"Abe motions Reggie to sit down on the small couch which sat against the back wall. Abe pulls the swivel chair from his desk out, turns it toward Reggie and sits down in it."

"What's on your mind, Alf?"

Reggie fingers the pocket of his blue blazer, "You know we go back a long way, Abe."

"Can it Alf," Abe says with a frown. "Cut to the chase."

Reggie adjusts his position on the couch to make himself a little more comfortable before saying, "I want to buy this place from you, Abe."

Abe is caught off-guard.

"I'm in the process of moving back on to the island," Reggie continues. "Having a house built out on the east end near the Caves Resort. Since I'm not getting any younger and it's getting harder for me to tour, I thought that it is now time for Reggie's fans to come to Reggie rather than the other way around. As you've just seen, this seems to be a good place to get that started."

Moving back to the island? Abe thinks, *Reggie's never been on this island a hot minute longer than it took him to find his way off it.*

"You want to buy 'The Place'?"

"Not just Abe's, I want to buy the whole property," Reggie continues. "Have some expansions which I'd like to make."

Abe had not given any consideration to selling the house and its accompanying acreage. Abe had only been considering selling the business in hopes of incentivizing Beth to stop trying to keep Becca alive through 'The Place.'

"It's not really for sale at the moment, Alf."

"I'm willing to pay good money, Abe. Let's start at three million."

3 million was close to 150% of what this place was probably worth but thinking of selling had not been about the money. Abe had more money than he needs at this point of his life. With his current lifestyle, Abe was still saving money. Abe didn't need money. He was also fairly certain that Beth didn't either.

Abe shook his head, "Can't say that I haven't given some thought to selling 'The Place,' but it's only the business that I've considered selling. There are some things that I'd have to work out first before I'd begin to consider selling it. It's probably going to be the first of the year before I'm certain where I stand. The house property simply isn't going to be sold."

Reggie frowns, "I was hoping to get moving on something sooner than that but guess if I have to, I could wait until earlier next year."

"Didn't say that I was going to sell it then, Alf. Only said that I would know then if I will be selling."

Reggie thinks for a long moment before continuing, "Abe, you know I'm no good at making deals. Why don't you talk with my people, who deal with this sort of thing? That $3million is just the starting point."

"Can't commit to anything before January."

"Just talk to my guy. Let him give you an idea of what we can do."

"He can talk all he wants but I'm not selling the house."

"At least listen to what we're offering, Abe."

Abe was not going to sell the house. That would be pulling out the entire foundation of Beth's being from under her.

"Have him give me a call," Abe finally says after a long pause.

"Now you're talking," Reggie says rising from the couch. "You want to take a spin with me in that new Mercedes of mine? It would be like old times."

"Sorry Alf," Abe lies, "I've got another meeting coming up soon."

Coming to Terms

Abe is sitting at the table in the most remote corner of 'The Place.' At this time of day, Abe usually sits here with Beth to have dinner. Now at 4:20 PM on Wednesday, Abe is seated with Ralph/Zack and Phil Marchand, owner of the car lot in Halifax from whom Zack has decided to purchase a three-year-old VW Beetle. A car, which although not nearly as menacing as Beth's, bore many striking resemblances. Dark Blue, same huge chrome hubcaps. More practical and a little slower than Beth's.

These kids have a penchant for purchasing cars that fit their personalities, Abe thinks.

Abe had expected to have to go into Halifax or his Wannasea bank to get the dealer the funds. He'd been surprised when during the phone call which Zack had made to disclose his purchase, the car lot owner requested coming out to the island to meet Abe. Abe guessed the car dealer was either very leery of what Zack was telling him or he was a fan of Reggie. After it started raining as they had been looking over the vehicle, the trio had come into 'The Place' to finish the transaction.

After signing the last document with the dealer, Zack goes over to Molly, who helps Beth with 'The Place's' accounting, to have the loan agreement printed out for Abe.

"Seems like a nice enough kid," says the car dealer, who Abe judges to be pushing sixty.

"He does," Abe replies before adding, "I hear you are a fan of Reggie's."

"Not really," Phil Marchand says quickly, "he's a little too smarmy for my tastes."

Abe raises his eyebrows, "So you have met Reggie?"

"Sold Reggie a car about fifteen years back. He still hasn't bothered to finish paying for it." the dealer relates. "He told me that I should be paying him for driving the vehicle around and providing advertisement for my car lot."

"Zack said something about you being a fan."

"I'm your fan," Phil says with a sheepish grin.

This is beginning to be the strangest week of my life, Abe thinks.

"You like the songwriting my wife and I did?" Abe asks.

"I like the songs you did about Wannasea well enough," Phil replies, "but I'm a real fan of those history books that you put out with Brad Meacham."

Thirty-five years ago Abe had co-authored two volumes of local maritime history with Professor Meacham. Abe had done the heavy lifting on historical research and writing, his old mentor had designed the book structure and provided beautifully crafted photographs. It had been years since anyone had spoken to Abe about them, much less paid him a complement.

"I wish you would do some more," Phil adds.

Brad Meacham had been dead for fifteen years now. Although most of his time was still spent doing historical research, Abe had closed the historical book writing chapter of his life more than twenty years ago.

From the time of the first Reggie phenomenon, Abe had remained enrolled at the university in Swansea, though at a lesser pace due to songwriting and family demands. Abe usually went to the university two days a week. Abe had mixed a degree in literature with one on maritime history. He'd basically stayed in school over 15 years through two graduate degrees and lots of research work. If it had not been for Reggie's break out, Abe was certain that his future would have been at Swansea University.

That had all been before Janie and Julia's disappearance and his efforts to drink enough so he wouldn't remember it.

"Not really sure I am up to it now that Brad is gone," Abe responds with a half-truth.

Abe knew that he was not nearly adept as Brad at putting the right information in the right order and adding photos as Brad had been. Abe also knew that he had filled at least five journals with enough other island information to fill at least two new books if he set his mind to it. Abe had been secretly hoping that he could coerce Hugh into a collaboration when he retired from the Air Corps. A prospect which now seemed dead in the water.

"Do you still do research?" Phil asks.

"On and off," Abe replied, which was more or less true, if the on part was 30+ hours a week.

"Have you thought about writing articles for the local historical society on your research?" Phil asks.

"Not really, I'm not all that sure I have anything which would be of interest to them as my focus has been mainly tied to my family's history."

"You ought to get in touch with them," Phil suggests. "I think there are quite a few folks like me, who would have a real interest in what you've discovered."

"I'll give it some thought," Abe responds absently as Zack returns with the printed loan agreement.

After Zack signs and Abe counter signs, Zack hands Abe a check for $5,228.64 to cover the reminder of $12,000 Abe is loaning him for the car.

"Why don't you take the afternoon off and give that new car of yours a tour of the island," Abe suggests. "You could pick up Sandy at the bank and give her a ride before you go back to your grandmother's?"

"Saanvi," Zack says almost automatically in reference to his older sister, "it's a name from Northern India."

"I'm really sorry, Zack," Abe apologizes. "I didn't realize it was Saanvi."

"Don't worry, everybody does it."

"Why did your family name you Ralph?" Abe suddenly says impulsively.

"Dads get to pick their son's names. Mom's get to pick their daughters. It's an old custom in my mom's family," Zack relates. "Dad named me after his great-grandfather."

Phil Marchand rises from the table.

"I really have to be getting back to Halifax," the car dealer says. "You can't believe what an honor it has been meeting you, Abe."

"I'll drop you at the ferry," Zack offers.

Abe watches the pair go out the front door. It wasn't all that busy this Wednesday afternoon. Business probably would pick up a little afterward but with the rain, you never knew. Rain came with late fall and stayed around in varying degrees until May. It might spit a little snow once in a blue moon, but the snow never stuck.

Northern India, Abe thinks searching his memory where he'd made this Sandy, Saanvi mistake before.'

About six-seven years back, there had been a just out of high school, olive-skinned, rather pretty girl named Saanvi who had worked the tables and counter for the better part of three years.

Has to be Zack's sister, Abe thinks. *Might also turn out to be Beth's half-sister.*

Beth had followed in the footsteps of her grandmother and mother. When a local girl needed to earn some money or for whatever reason, living at home was no longer an option, they came to "Abe's.' If they needed shelter in addition to a job, they would usually end up at the house. The housing needs had fashioned most of Janie's construction efforts up there. The house was really more of a compound built around the old central house with a lot of small rooms attached on the outside in a block C shape. It had made for a wonderful open tiled courtyard, now that Abe thought about."

Beth arrives and sets down a tray with duplicate soup, salads and teas.

"Do you remember a girl named Saanvi, who worked out here a few years back?" Abe asks his granddaughter as she distributes the food.

"Sure," Beth replies without much thought, "that's Ralph's sister. She's Prisha's daughter. Saanvi is one of my best and oldest friend."

The name Prisha brings another memory into Abe's mind. A memory which involves Julia. Memories of Julia usually bring pain with them, so Abe is in the habit of trying to avoid them.

"Prisha was my mom's best friend," Beth says.

Abe had no earthly idea how Beth knew this as she had only been 18 months old when her mother disappeared.

"You learned this how?"

"Grandma Becca told me. She told me everything that she could remember about my mom and grandma."

Abe found this a little odd. Becca and Janie hadn't always been on the same page or friendliest terms after Abe and Janie gotten married. Janie had lived through quite a lot before Abe had met her. Janie had been one of Becca's projects. Just like so many other girls, who had cycled through 'The Place' over the years. Janie had been Becca's favorite until things between Abe and Janie became serious, Becca had then came to see Janie as the older woman, who made off with her unworldly son, even though Janie had only been 20 months older than Abe.

"You remember Prisha?"

Abe thinks for a moment. The image of a slight, dark-skinned girl with the brightest eyes that he had ever seen comes into his mind. She had worked in the kitchen. Julia hung out with her most of the time. Having made a point of helping Becca out in the kitchen because Prisha was there. Neither Prisha, nor Saanvi, had ever been residents at the house.

"She worked in the kitchen with Becca and was the best tea maker this place has seen," Abe replies, unsure what recess of his brain this information is pouring from. "I think that she may have been the real inventor of Wannasea tea."

"Same thing Becca told me," Beth says as she begins eating her soup.

"Getting any closer to coming to a decision about selling this place, Abe?" Beth asks.

"I should know in 4–6 weeks."

"Does that conversation you had with Reggie yesterday have anything to do with it?"

"Honestly, I'm still not sure what that conversation I had with Alf was all about," Abe replies. "I figured that he came out here looking to buy up our songwriter catalog. Now I'm not sure what he is up to."

"Reggie asked me if he could use 'The Place' to hold a benefit next Saturday night in conjunction with the opening of the new government center," Beth says offhandedly but she is keenly aware that it has perked up Abe's interest in the conversation. "Reggie wants to play two 45-minute sets."

"Benefit?" Abe asks quizzically. "Alf only does things which benefit Alf. Who is this benefit supposed to benefit?"

"The Wannasea Hurricane Relief Fund."

"Are you going to do it?"

"I'm leaning toward it," Beth says. "I have the Wannasea Boys scheduled those two nights but if Reggie will agree to use them as his front band for the evening, I think it will work."

"There will be a cover charge?"

"Fifty dollars. The money will go to a good cause, though."

Abe whistles at the price which is twice as much as 'The Place' has ever charged for any event.

What the hell is Reggie up to? Abe wonders as he works on finishing his dinner.

"What are you planning on saying at the government center building dedication?" Beth asks.

"Thought I'd do 'Alice's rules' and not say another word."

Beth ponders the thought for a few moments before responding, "I like it."

The pair complete their dinner in relative silence before turning to the still steaming tea.

"Beth," Abe starts, "outside of continuing what your grandmother and mother started out here, what are you really getting out of this place?"

Abe could see that his question had raised a little ire in Beth.

"Why on earth would anyone want to get anything more out of this place than Grandma Janie and Becca did?"

"Sometimes I think you use this place to make up for losing them and this is your way to try to keep them alive," Abe blurts out then immediately regrets having said it.

Beth puts down her tea and sighs, "I am proud of continuing Becca and Grandma Jane's tradition but I'm working on doing it my own way. I think we give our customer's their money's worth but more importantly I think we give a whole lot of young people on this island a real chance to find a footing in this world before they figure out where they are headed."

"Fair enough."

"Now let me ask you something," Beth says, her eyes flashing angrily. "Since you stopped trying to drink yourself to death and began helping Grandma Becca out, what have you accomplished, Abe?"

Abe was stunned to silence. He knew better than to say that he had helped to raise Beth.

"I see it this way," Beth continues, "we have both had more taken away from us than most people can usually stand. The flip side of that was that we both have been given more materially than almost any two other people on this island. I chose to use what I have been given to give back. Just like Grandma Becca did. Just like Grandma Jane did. What are you giving back, Abe?"

Abe knew the only thing that he had actually given back over the past 20 years was just being here. Being a living fragment of what he used to be before Janie and Julia disappeared. Semi-existing. There wasn't all that much beyond it.

Like a guilty schoolboy, Abe's face reddens as he rises from his chair.

"I'm going to go feed Riley."

Abe walks across the dining area, through the kitchen and out the back door. Riley V was waiting for him.

Dog at his heels, Abe moves to the area under the stairs which led up to his room, opens the supply closet and pulls out a bag of dog food. He measures out the usual portion into Riley's food dish before picking up the 1/4 full water bowl. Walking to the outside spigot near the kitchen entrance, Abe empties the bowl before filling it with water and returning it to its place under the stairs.

After feeding Riley V, normally Abe would go back into the dining area and manage the cash register, not that the cash register really required any managing. Tonight he thought it might be a good idea to steer clear of Beth for an hour or so.

Abe walks up the steps, across the deck and into his room. Remembering the signed loan agreement and Zack's check which are in his inside pocket, Abe pulls them out as his cell phone begins to buzz. Abe pulls the phone from his outside pocket and holds it to his ear.

"Abe Stolz," he says into the device.

"Bernard Fuller here, Mr. Stolz," came from his phone's speaker. "I am the attorney for the group which Mr. Reginald was representing the other day when he asked about buying your property."

Abe sits down in the swivel chair.

"As I told Alf," Abe replies, "I won't be in a position to make a decision on selling the business before the first of the year and I have no interest in selling the property which the house sits on."

"I understand Mr. Stolz but I'd just like to make clear to you what we are suggesting. We would very much like to purchase both parcels. As Mr. Reginald stated, we are willing to start the negotiations for those properties at $3 million. If it is only the business that you are looking to sell, we'd start our offer at $2 million."

"Those are very generous offers, sir, but as I told Reggie, I will not be in any position to sell before next year."

"Sorry to hear that," the voice on the phone continues. "One other consideration which we may be able to work out prior to next year is the sale of your establishment's liquor license. We understand that you are not currently using the license. I'm in a position of being immediately able to offer you $250,000 for its purchase."

Liquor license, Abe thinks to himself. Abe knew that the business had never cancelled its liquor license after Becca had switched to being more of coffee shop/restaurant. The business had continued to pay the base licensing fee as far as he knew. *Why did these guys want 'The Place' liquor license?*

"I will need to discuss that with the people who manage the business," Abe replies after the pause. "Could I get back to you in a few days on it?"

"Certainly, but don't wait too long Mr. Stolz, we don't have unlimited time to close these transactions. The clients, who I represent, do not have unlimited patience."

With that the call ended.

An Unexpected Slip

Abe sets his cell phone down atop a stack of papers on the righthand side of his desk. He wants to go downstairs and ask Beth about the liquor license but thinks perhaps he should leave things well enough alone for the time being. Maybe Beth was going to be easier to talk with after tonight's performance. He'd decided he would do *The Kingdom of Wannasea* if the crowd wasn't calling for something different.

Abe opens his laptop. He considers doing a review of his historical research but after a few moments decides that he isn't into research this particular afternoon. Abe opens a blank Word file and begins work on a new poem to be used as a lyric.

Back in the day, Abe might produce 10–15 such writings in a week. Immediately after Janie and Julia disappeared, Abe had produced two green journals full of poems and lyrics over the first eight months. Since that time, Abe had produced a total of 12. Three of which have been written in the past week.

Over the next 90 minutes, Abe fashions this output:

Carried Away –

there'll come a day
the very next change carries me away
away from a life lived in disarray
when that change carries me away

away from strife and division
stumbling, falling, lost in indecision
avoiding the cost of emotional collision
and a future I'm unable to envision

there will come a day
the very next change carries me away
away from living life in disarray
when that change carries me away

away from all the heartache and pain
stumbling falling, making no gain
away from fighting, clawing, trying to explain
all those qualities I'll never obtain

there will come a day
the very next change carries me away
away from those I don't wish to betray
when that next change carries me away

away from those my heart holds close
away from those I need the most
from those in which my life's engrossed
becoming another memory with no host

there will come a day
that very next change carries me away
away from kindnesses I'll never repay
when that next change carries me away

there will come a day
that next change carries me away
away from living life in disarray
when that very next change carries me away
that very next change will carry me away

    Abe names the file *Carried Away*, closes the document and pushes his chair back from his desk. Riley V, who has been lying beside his chair, rises too. Abe strokes the dog on the top of his head.

    "Let's go see if the wrath of Beth has subsided," Abe says to the dog.

With the dog at his heels, Abe exits his room, walks through the continuing mist across the deck and begins going down the stairs, He gets to the fourth step from the bottom before his feet suddenly come out from under him as if he were on ice. Abe goes crashing against the steps, his right foot stopping the fall abruptly on the concrete patio. His back hurts from striking the steps behind him and his lower right leg is throbbing like mad. Abe manages to sit up despite an incredible bolt of pain shooting through his lower right leg.

Two kitchen workers, who had been standing by the side of stairs taking a break rush up to him.

"Are you okay, Mr. Stolz?" the red-headed boy, who Abe recognizes as Josh, says with concern.

Abe tries again to rise but the pain isn't going to let him.

"Would you mind going in and asking either Beth or Sallie to come out?" Abe instructs as calmly as he is able.

Randy, Josh's brother, runs to the kitchen door and disappears inside as Josh bends down and looks at Abe's right foot.

"I think we'd better pull off your shoe," the teen says.

Abe grimaces as the boy removes his right deck shoe.

Beth shows up with concern in her eyes. Without saying anything she bends down and looks at Abe's right foot.

"Josh," Beth instructs, "go back in the kitchen, get a couple big plastic bags full of ice and string and bring them back here."

The boy darts off.

"What happened, Gramps?"

"Slipped on the steps."

Beth shakes her head before saying, "We are going to have to get you over to the hospital in Halifax. I don't think the island clinic has the right tools to deal with this."

Beth strokes his hand until Sallie and Josh arrive with the ice.

Beth pulls off Abe's right sock, rolls up the corresponding trouser leg, before carefully placing Abe's right foot into the empty plastic bag and ties it off. She then takes the bag filled with ice and places over the first bag. Beth then apportions the ice around Abe's ankle area where the swelling is the worst. "She then ties off the top of the second plastic bag and inch above the rolled up trouser leg."

"Do you know if we have any ibuprofen in our medical kit?" Beth asks Sallie.

Sallie nods her head affirmatively and goes back into the kitchen to fetch the pain reliever.

Beth rises and instructs Josh, "Stay here with Abe while I go get the van."

Beth scurries off first to the kitchen for keys then around the other corner of the building where the van is parked.

Josh asked, "You doing okay, Mr. Stolz?"

"I've done better, Josh," the old man says with a grimace.

Sallie returns with a glass of water and three 250 mg pills.

"Take all of them, Abe."

Abe swallows the three pills as Sallie drives the van as close to the stairway as possible. She swings open the van's passenger door. With Sallie and Josh's help, Abe swings himself into the passenger seat without bringing on too much new pain.

"You know I'm on tonight," Abe informs Beth.

"No, you're not on tonight, Abe," Beth replies. Then turning to Sallie instructs her, "Please have Marie do the introductions tonight. Ask her to let the band know that Abe is inconvenienced."

"That's one way to put it, Kitten," Abe says as Beth walks around the front of van and climbs in. Sallie and Josh stand watching as she backs the van up then disappears toward the village.

"You are done living in that damned storeroom, Abe," Beth says forcefully. "I know you like to hang out on the deck when it's nice, but this is an accident which has just been waiting to happen."

Abe thought it might be better not to say anything, so the chances of Beth's edict evaporating were better after they got back from the hospital.

"You are moving into Becca's old place," Beth said firmly. "I'll begin to have it fixed up for you tomorrow."

"I thought that's where Sallie lives?"

"Sallie's been living with her boyfriend on the west side since August. I've actually been meaning to work out moving you into Becca's before this. I have also been wanting to turn the store room into a gift shop. We can have some 'The Place' tchotchkes as the tourists keep asking us for that sort of stuff."

Beth enters the queue for cars which will be boarding the ferry. There are only three cars ahead of her. Luckily the ferry has just pulled in and looks like it's almost ready to unload the cars, which are filled with workers returning from Halifax.

"Do we still have our liquor license?" Abe asks Beth.

His granddaughter gives him a rather quizzical look, before say, "Yes, it's still ours. Are you thinking of getting into liquor again?"

Abe laughs trying to ignore the throbbing in his back and leg.

"I got a call from Reggie's lawyer and they say they want to buy it," Abe stated. "They are offering $250,000 for it."

"That's insane," Beth said. "What on earth could they want with our liquor license and why would they offer so much?"

Abe shrugs his shoulders as Beth begins following the now slowly moving cars into the ferry hold.

"Last week one of the Governor's assistants mentioned to me that the island is looking to sell the castle and government center that they are closing down," Abe says as Beth stops the van and turns the engine off. "Maybe that has something to do with Alf's people wanting our liquor license?"

"Why wouldn't they just apply for a new liquor license if they are thinking of opening up something at the Castle?"

"Beats me," Abe replies.

"I think we need to find out, Abe," Beth says. "Mix that in with this benefit which Reggie was so hellbent on having and there is something strange going on."

"There's always something strange happening when Reggie is involved."

"How's that ankle?"

"Throbs like hell but I think I'm good until we make it to the hospital."

The Halifax Hospital is less than two miles from the ferry dock headed east toward Swansea.

Beth pulls out her phone from her jacket pocket and began texting as Abe drifts into a fitful upright sleep which lasts until they reached the Halifax dock.

The ache in Ben's back has now been added to the throb coming from his lower right leg. He winces as he tries to adjust his position in the van seat.

"Should be at the emergency room in about five minutes," Beth says as the ferry ramp descends and she starts up the van.

Abe manages his discomfort as Beth steers the van into gingerly exiting the ferry. They turn left at the roundabout and head toward Swansea and the hospital.

"Uncle Hugh says that he is going to come out for the dedication," Beth says off-handedly trying to distract Abe from the pain. "He's also going to talk to your cousin Herbert to see if he can tell him why anyone might be willing to pay $250K for our liquor license."

"Did Reggie also inquire about purchasing your song library?" Beth adds.

"Strangely enough, no," Abe replies, "Alf seemed more interested in making sure that I know he's moving to the island. Said he's in the process of having a house built out on the east end."

"Maybe he's looking to rekindle your friendship?" Beth suggests.

"Alf doesn't have friendships," Abe replies almost automatically. "Learned a long time back that Alf only has people around him, who can do something for Alf. When they no longer can do something for Alf, Alf dumps them."

"Guess Reggie thinks you can once again do something for him?" Beth posits.

Can't fool Beth, Abe thinks as the van pulls into the circular drive of the Halifax Hospital's emergency room.

"I'll be right back, gramps," Beth says, as she swings open the van's driver-side door. "Need to get someone to help me get you out and get you inside."

Beth disappears through the sliding glass doors. It is a full five minutes before she reappears with a burley emergency room attendant pushing a wheelchair. Abe opens the passenger door and makes a move to exit.

"Hold on there, Captain," the attendant bellows so loud in his Caribbean accent that Abe stops dead in his tracks.

"He's a stubborn old cuss," Beth informs emergency room attendant.

"Most of them his age are, Miss," the fellow says before parking the wheelchair about two feet back of the passenger door entrance, then moving in and picking Abe up under his shoulders, lifting him upward than out. Abe is seated in the wheelchair faster than he knew what had happened to him.

Before releasing the brake on Abe's chair, the attendant pulls out a horizontal leg support from on the right side and straps Abe's aching leg to it. Beth walking behind, the attendant then pushes Abe into the emergency room.

"You're lucky it's not a weekend," the hospital worker comments. "If it was, probably would be at least an hour before you would be admitted for treatment."

The burley fellow deposits Abe at the incoming counter. No one else is in the waiting area.

Abe thanks the attendant as the burley fellow disappears down the side hallway. Beth begins filling out the forms provided by the attendant behind the counter. Abe tries to reach into his back pocket for his wallet but the pain simply will not allow it. Beth manages to slide the beaten leather bifold out of his pocket and fishes out the required documents before placing the wallet into her jacket pocket.

Over the next three hours, Abe is provided a shot of morphine which immediately dulls his pain and soothes his mood, has a series of X-rays on his lower right foot area and his back, then the placement of a hard cast around his ankle and the lower part of the leg below the calf. The Physician notes that the bruising on his back will likely cause him pain for at least the next two weeks. Abe is given a prescription for a Percocet/Tylenol pain killer mix and instructions to make an appointment with the orthopedist over on the island as soon as possible to outline further care. Abe had been told in no uncertain terms that he needs to stay off his right foot until at least next Monday.

"Only use these tablets when you absolutely need them," the young female doctor advises after handing him a week's supply of Percocet. "As soon as you can tolerate the pain, switch to ibuprofen. If you let them, those pain killers will cause more trouble than your ankle."

As Beth disappears out the door to collect the van, the burley attendant reappears and pushes the wheelchair with Abe in it out to the driveway.

After depositing Abe back into the passenger seat, the attendant instructs Beth, "Get someone else to help you get him out of the van when you are back to your place. If you don't, there's a good chance that I will see both of you back here before my shift is done."

The pair laugh as Beth says, "Thanks," and Abe added, "You are a real prince."

"I am, aren't I?" the attendant says as he stashes the wheelchair into the cargo area of the van, slides the van door closed and pats it twice on the side to let them know they were ready to go.

"Wasn't that bad," Abe announces.

"Easy for you to say with a head full of morphine," Beth replies. "I like that guy but let's make sure not to do this again anytime soon."

"I've been thinking, Beth," Abe says, then after a pause through which Beth says nothing, "I need a personal attendant. Been thinking about it for a while now, I could really use somebody to help me get my journals and writings in order. Now that I'm going to be laid up with this leg issue, seems as if it would be a good time to start."

Beth doesn't say anything until they arrive at the queue for the ferry.

"There's a waitress out at our place named Molly Peters," Beth begins. "She waitresses tables and goes to university night classes at the island's extension. She helps me out with the accounting but there really isn't enough of that to take up more than a few hours on Saturdays. She's really bright. A whiz at technology. She'll finish up a business degree in May. At this point, it's a waste of Molly's talent to be waitressing. Molly might be just what you need."

Abe thinks for a few moments, *Molly Peters…small mousey-haired girl with big glasses. Pleasant enough. Always seemed busy.*

Abe was kind of surprised that she was old enough to be finishing up at the university.

"I'm willing to give her a try," Abe says as Beth pulls the van into the ferry.

"How much can you pay?" Beth asks.

Abe really had no idea. He hadn't been much involved in paying anyone for the past six years since Beth had taken over the operations at 'The Place.'

"What should I pay?"

"Fifteen an hour ought to be good for a start," Beth suggests. "How many hours would you want her to work?"

"As many as she wants up to 30 hours a week," Abe replies.

"I'll speak with her tomorrow to see if she's interested," Beth says.

The ferry gate closes behind them.

"I've already asked Marie to help arrange to have everything moved out of your old upstairs room at the business," Beth announces. "I'm going to have you hang out in Marie's room until I can get Becca's old in-law suite spruced up. Her room is also right next to the studio. Should make it easy to roll in there and work with Zack for the time being."

"I'm not in a position to make objections."

"Thought I would move your desk, one bookcase and all of your writings into the studio temporarily," Beth advises. "That will give you something to work on while you recover. Everything else that you want to keep, I'll try to store until Becca's suite is ready."

"Sounds okay."

"I'm going to throw out your bed, the couch and all that other stuff that your claim passes for furniture. They will be replaced by something from this century."

"Don't throw out Riley's rug," Abe demands.

"Riley's rug can stay."

As the ferry pulls out from the Halifax dock, Abe drifts into sleep.

Piano Notes

Abe's cell phone is buzzing atop the desk which had just arrived on Friday in Janie's old Studio. Abe, seated in his wheelchair with his right leg propped up, rolls himself over to the desk, picks up the phone, notices the call is coming from Alf's lawyer, Bernard Fuller.

"Mr. Fuller," Abe says into his cell phone, "could you give me minute to get situated?"

"Take your time," the lawyer responds.

Abe wheels himself to the entrance to the studio's bathroom, rolls himself inside and locks the bathroom door after closing it.

"Okay," Abe tells his caller, "I'm situated."

"Mr. Stolz, I had been hoping to hear back from you on the offer for your liquor license."

Abe quickly explains his present condition to the lawyer but immediately begins to understand this guy really had no interest in anything to do with Abe's personal situation.

"Have you been able to make a decision?" the lawyer demands.

Abe has not as yet received any guidance from Hugh about the liquor license.

"There are a few other parties involved in the ownership of Abe's," Abe lies. "We have decided that we want to hold on the liquor license until we decide whether or not to sell."

"Are you getting any closer to that decision?"

"The accident will probably cost me a week but I'm still confident that I will be able to give you a decision right after New Year."

"I really wish we could do something faster, Mr. Stolz," the lawyer says. "The people that I represent aren't very patient people."

"Right after the first of the year is the best that we can do," Abe says rather sternly.

"I will hold you to that," the lawyer replies. "If for any reason, you come to a decision sooner, please call me. I would really like to put this to rest for my clients."

"I'll do that," Abe says disconnecting the call.

Pushy SOB, Abe thinks as he unlocks the bathroom door and rolls himself over to the desk.

Abe picks up the new tablet/keyboard device which Molly had pushed him into acquiring. Molly had begun working with Abe on Thursday. Abe had spent the better part of that day showing Molly which journals contained what, what was on the laptop and what loose papers, he hoped to have entered for historical research, song writing and separately poetry.

After getting a grasp of the Abe's inventory and his storage methods, Molly had been absolutely horrified.

"Mr. Stolz, your entire life's work is at risk here," she'd said shaking her head. "Do you have copies of all these documents anywhere else?"

Abe had been working on putting copies into his laptop since Hugh had given him the laptop almost three years ago. He explained this to Molly.

"Mr. Stolz, if there is a fire or some kind of disaster out here, everything can be lost," Molly had said with genuine concern. "You need to get all of your work copied and backed up to cloud storage as soon as you possibly can."

"Do you have an email or cloud account somewhere?" she'd asked.

Abe replied that he had a Yahoo email account which Hugh had set up and he'd then never used. As far as a cloud account, Abe told her that he had no idea what cloud accounts were.

Molly had created a new Gmail account for Abe. Subscribing to oversize storage after judging that Abe had in excess of 40gb of possible material to upload.

The following day Molly was able to convince Abe of the urgency of the situation. She suggested that he turn the laptop over to her to speed up transfer of existing laptop documents to the new cloud storage area.

Abe had pushed back saying that he'd gotten by for 50 years without "backups" or "cloud storage."

"We live on island in the middle of the sea. Most years we have a couple bad storms. Some years we have a hurricane. How you've managed to go fifty years without ever losing anything is beyond me," Molly had retorted.

The truth was, Abe had lost quite a few things over the years. Alf had made off with a couple of his green journals at the time Abe turned him loose twenty-five years ago. He had also had some research journals badly damaged by water six years ago. It had taken Abe three months of work to rewrite those journals.

Abe relented and had Molly go to the local Wannasea office supply store and purchase the tablet, a flatbed scanner and a high-quality laser printer while he had visited at the orthopedist on Friday.

The orthopedist instructed Abe that he would need to be in the hard cast for three more weeks after which he would be fitted with a walking cast. Abe was to do no walking until Monday. He was then to come back to the orthopedist's office for a quick follow up. If all was judged to be well, Abe would receive a crutch and instructions how to use it.

Abe was beginning to like this tablet thingy. The device was light. Abe could move objects around on the screen and the swivel keyboard which flipped back when it was not in use, suited him. Molly had even transferred everything relevant Abe had on the laptop over to the new device. Abe still wasn't certain that he would make much use of the email account.

Abe is fiddling around writing a new poem on the tablet as Beth comes to the rear sliding door carrying a tray with Abe's lunch. Abe puts the tablet back on the desk, rolls the few feet to the sliding door and pulls it open for Beth. Beth carries the tray with a Jarlsberg, Swiss chard, bacon quiche and two cups of tea to the bench of her grandmother's piano.

The piano is an impressive, polished grand piano. Abe still had no idea how much it had cost Janie.

Beth sits on the bench and hands one of the cups of tea to her grandfather.
Beth belongs in front of a piano, Abe thinks.

Like her grandmother and mother before her, Beth could play. For the past eight years, Abe hadn't heard anything more than a few quick bars of things Beth played on this unit when he happened to be walking past the house on Sunday or Monday afternoons. Abe had also caught fragments of Beth's playing while lying on his bed at night in his old room. Beth sometimes played the upright model on the back of the stage after everyone else was gone. Abe hadn't listened to Beth play a full song since a recital when she was a senior in high school.

"Play something for me, Beth," Abe requests.

"I'm too rusty, Abe," Beth says shaking her head.

"Humor an old man," Abe pleads.

"What is it that you'd like me to play?"

"Why don't you do that Jim Croce song which Zack did during his audition."

Beth pulls out her phone and takes a few minutes to bring up the score for the song, before placing the device upon the piano's built in music stand. Beth plays the melody but doesn't sing.

Beth was into the second stanza when Zack walked through the sliding door. This was the first day after ending his final two weeks working on the Mainland. Zack had come in at seven to begin learning more about his non-musical duties. With Abe's having just closed at 2 PM, Zack had come over to work with Abe on preparing for his opening, now two days away.

Zack walks behind Beth and begins singing at the third stanza.

As Zack gets through that stanza, he motions for Beth to sing with him.

Beth frowns but Zack kept motioning to her so that when fourth stanza started, Beth was singing background to Zack.

This is pretty damned good, Abe thinks.

Abe knew that like Janie and Julia, Beth could play piano. What Abe hadn't known until this moment was that Beth could sing. Beth could sing very well.

The Jitters

Abe rubs his eyes. He is laying on the bed in Marie's room with his right foot propped up on a stack of pillows. Abe has just finished a two-hour long nap after his second trip to the orthopedist to check his recovery progress.

The stiffness and aching in Abe's back seemed to have worsened as the throbbing in his lower right leg subsided somewhat. The biggest problem with the leg at this point was a burning desire to scratch at the non-stop itch under the hard cast. Abe had decided that today, he would stop with the Percocet and rely strictly on ibuprofen. Though the Percocet dulled the pain and bettered Abe's mood, it also dulled his senses and was increasingly bringing on constipation.

On the side of his wheelchair is a sturdy wooden crutch which he'd been advised to begin using at gradually increasing intervals. Spend an hour or so walking over the rest of this week, then increase that by another hour next week with the hope that he would be up to three hours of walking by the time that the hard cast has been removed. If Abe reaches that milestone, he will then face the prospect of at least six weeks of physical therapy.

This bedroom certainly doesn't seem to have been in use before Beth deposited me here, Abe thinks as he slowly brings his leg down from the pillows, slides his lower body over the edge of the bed by the wheelchair then slowly and painfully raises himself into a sitting position. *Maybe Marie has something going on down in the village like Sallie?*

Following instructions, Abe uses his arms and good leg to swing into the wheelchair backward. Releasing the chair's brake, Abe spins himself around and heads to the bedroom door.

Abe can hear light traces of guitar and piano playing along with Zack singing from the studio. Zack has been in the studio since before the trip to the orthopedists.

The kid is nervous about tomorrow, Abe thinks as he swings the thick door open and the sounds from the studio became louder.

Abe can also hear the chatter of a few of the other residents coming from the kitchen. Along with Abe, Beth and Marie, there were at the moment, Molly and other five other girls living in the house. Marie had now moved to a daybed in Becca's suit which just today was beginning renovations. Aside from late Sunday afternoon, Abe hadn't really seen or heard much from his other house companions. They were usually down at 'The Place' or attending classes somewhere.

Swinging right on his exit from the bedroom, Abe hand-wheels the short distance down the hallway and through the open large wooden doors into the studio. Molly is busily at work behind his desk. Beth is at the piano as Zack was fiddling with the tuning of his acoustic guitar. This morning Zack had brought two other guitar cases into the studio with him and deposited them on the far side of the piano.

All three greeted Abe as he rolls across the tile floor toward the bathroom.

"Want to hear a new arrangement of *Orange*?" Zack asks.

"Let me get cleaned up a little first," Abe says as he swings open the bathroom door and disappears behind it.

This bathroom was one on Janie's best construction efforts. This particular bathroom had been built onto the back wall of the studio. Along with a huge shower in the rear which could probably hold four people, a double vanity with a seating area, what Abe liked most was the frosted glass sliding door which leads out to the patio. Janie had constructed the bathroom to be used upon return from sailing or the beach. Two years earlier, Beth had the bathroom updated to include a shower which now operated much like something NASA might produce to clean space capsules.

Abe brushed his teeth and gave himself a wipe down with a warm washrag. Although he had been instructed to steer clear of showers for the time being, Abe had decided that tomorrow he was going to wrap his lower right leg in one of the large plastic bags from the kitchen and make use of the shower.

After wetting and brushing his hair, Abe goes back out into the studio. Zack is still fiddling around with *Orange* asking an annoyed Beth to modify what she was playing and singing. Abe had begun to think that perhaps a romance was beginning to bubble between the two. If there wasn't, why else would Beth be sitting in this studio at the piano humoring Zack's case of nerves.

"Are you ready now?" Zack asks.

Abe rolls himself over by his desk and parks the chair before nodding his head in the affirmative.

Orange All Around was a weird song which Abe had helped create for Janie. The Mainland's Orangemen football team had been her favorite. The Orangemen had historically been one of the worst teams in all of football. Janie said she liked the team because one of her great uncles had played on it. On occasion, he and Janie would spend Saturday night through Monday afternoon over on the Mainland hanging out in the team's home city of Hanover and attending one of their home games. The lyrics for the song had been written by Abe as a zinger about Janie's poor choice in football teams. Abe had always supported the team from Swansea. Despite Abe's intent, Janie had actually liked the lyrics, set them to music and every once in while sang them at 'The Place' just to annoy Abe.

Abe had provided Zack with printouts of all the music which he and Janie produced. Zack was now going through them to see if there was anything which he might want to play. For whatever odd reason, Zack locked on to *Orange* song and began experimenting on playing it in different styles. Zack seemed more focused on how the words melded to the music than what the words meant. Zack had decided that Orange should be done in folk rock style. Abe was uncertain whether Zack had any interest in football or the Orangemen.

Zack is using an electric guitar attached to a small amplifier and speaker system which he had brought in with him this Monday morning. Zack nods to Beth.

Orange All Around – played in the key of Eb major at a tempo of 112BPM in 4/4 time

orange sun, orange sky, orange gown
orange leaves now turning brown
orange trees, orange spires
orange flames dance in bonfires

orange juice, orange soda, orange slices
orange mark down stickers fight rising prices
orange painted faces, orange flags abound
orange ball, Orange's strategy running aground

Orange is our team
'tis for the Orange we scream

Orange is our team
'tis for the Orange we scream

orange cups, orange plates, orange cheese
orange banners blowing in the breeze
orange figures dance in an orange dream
orange towels, orange socks, Orange is our team

orange hats, orange balloons
orange sherbet eaten with orange plastic spoons
orange kimonos, orange saris
orange car lets me go where I please

Orange is our team
'tis for the Orange we scream

Orange is our team
'tis for the Orange we scream

orange juice, orange soda, orange slices
orange mark down stickers fight rising prices
orange ball, orange strategy running aground
orange painted faces, orange all around

orange cups, orange plates, orange cheese
orange banners blowing in the breeze
orange figures dance in an orange dream
orange towels, orange socks, Orange is our team

Orange is our team
'tis for the Orange we scream

Beth joins in the vocals on the last line of each stanza.
It really isn't half bad, Abe thought, *but it's still a very strange song.*
"What do you think, Mr. Stolz?" Zack asks as he sets down his guitar.
"Let's ask Molly," Abe replies.
Molly, who had been scanning documents during the song's performance, hesitates for a moment before saying, "I think that it's quite good, actually."
"I think we need to get you something to eat, Abe," Beth says rising from the piano bench. "Soup or sandwich?"
"Whatever is easier," Abe replied.
"I'll whip up some soup," Beth says heading toward the house's kitchen. "Ralph, would you mind going over to 'The Place' and fixing one of your special smoothies for Abe?"
"No problem, boss," Zack says before heading out the sliding door to retrieve the fruit, yogurt, grain, no fat milk concoction which Sallie had helped him come up with to fight the effects of all the pain relievers which Abe was taking.
"You really think it's good, Molly?" Abe asks after the pair exited.
"I do," Molly replies with little hesitance.
"You know last Monday after class, some of the girls and I went over to 'Dave's' to hear Zack play?" Molly continues. "We didn't think he was all that good. We did think that he was awfully cute, though."
"Why didn't you think he was all that good?" Abe asks.
"Maybe it was the acoustics or the fact that he was playing grunge and punk rock songs and didn't seem all that into it," Molly replies. "Emily, who heard from Marie that he knocked her socks off during his audition out here, asked Zack during a break why he was playing that trash."
Girls are a cheeky lot these days, Abe thinks until it occurs to him that his own wife had been a very cheeky girl in her day.
"How did Zack respond?"
"He said that's the only thing that 'Dave's' wanted him to play," Molly replies. "Which is crazy because when Zack plays folk or blues, I think it may be some of the best stuff that I've ever heard."
"You are sure that it's not because he's cute?" Abe asks.

"Well that certainly helps," Molly says before returning to her scanning.

Beth returns with a bowl of soup on a tray. A few minutes after Zack comes in carrying one large carry-out cup of the special smoothie plus three smaller cups.

"I got carried away," Zack says sheepishly handing the large cup to Abe then a smaller one to Molly and Beth.

"Why don't we drag your stuff over to 'The Place' and check out the acoustics for tomorrow night?" Beth suggests.

"That's a terrific idea," Zack replies. "Mr. Stolz, do you want to go over there with us to critique."

"I think Abe needs to stay here and rest up for tomorrow night, Ralph," Beth says.

The pair began collecting Zack's equipment and putting it into his car for the short trip down to 'The Place.'

Opening Night

Zack fidgets as he stands by Abe's wheelchair which has just been rolled up to the table closest to the wall end of the stage. Abe has been over what Zack intends to play in his first set three times in the last thirty minutes. After Abe introduces Zack then reads 'Don't blame it on the alcohol.' Zack will follow it up with *The Kingdom of Wannasea, Hugo Flies, Dark Ringlets, The Alice's Rule,* Jim Croce's *Operator,* Cat Steven's *Hard Headed Woman* then end his first set with Dylan's *Hard Rain*. The plan was for Zack to then tell the audience that they could come up to the stage to make requests for folk/blues tunes Zack would play in his next set. Hopefully they will also place money in Zack's open guitar case.

Abe knew that beyond what had been the original task of mentoring Zack to learn the tunes of Reggie Reginald's revival, he was now filling both a songwriter and manager's role for Zack. Abe felt confident about Zack's musical abilities. Abe wasn't sure how he felt about his own entertainment management abilities.

"I'll be back in minute," Zack says moving toward the front of the counter area across the dining room.

Ten minutes to showtime. Abe is a little nervous himself. He is going to use his crutch to maneuver himself to a stool placed in front of the stage. A wireless microphone sits atop the stool which Abe will then use. Abe wasn't all that familiar or comfortable with wireless devices of any sort.

The arrangement of that particular stool being in front of the stage was per Beth's demand. The only way Beth was going to let Abe do the introduction and kick off Zack's set was if he didn't have to negotiate the 8" rise to the stage.

Zack returns to the stage with a man and woman, who appeared to be in their late forties.

"Mr. Stolz," Zack announces, "this is my mom and dad. Hank and Prisha."

A voice which Abe had not heard for more than twenty years went off in his brain, "You don't know, Abe. Until you know for certain, don't make an ass of yourself."

The voice was Janie's. The last time that Abe had heard Janie's voice this clearly had been in Becca's kitchen when Beth was getting ready for her first day in school.

Abe shook the pair's outstretched hands.

"Why don't you sit down at this table," Abe says pointing to the table beside which his wheelchair is parked.

Zack's mother takes the middle seat, Zack's father, the seat furthest away from Abe.

"You don't know how much this opportunity means to Ralph," the lady with the still flashing eyes says to Abe. "All that he talks about now is how much music he's learning out here."

Abe exchanges small talk with Zack's parents. First about how his recovery from the fall has been going, then after Abe mentions Zack's grandmother in Wannasea, the pair talk about her declining health and their pending return to living on the Island to assist with her care. Seems Zack's dad, who is an electrician, had managed to land a full-time opportunity with the Wannasea Electrical Co-op. This wasn't a trivial achievement as many on the island were forced to work and live on the Mainland because of the slim out-of-season work opportunities here. Zack's parents had just sold their North Halifax house and were in the process of moving everything into Zack's grandmother's.

"It will be easier having more helping hands take care of Emma," Zack's mom explains. "It's also why it's so great that Ralph is now working on the island."

Zack moves to the stage and begins getting himself ready. Abe excuses himself, picks up his crutch and carefully negotiates the open twelve feet to the stool in front of the stage. He picks up the microphone and props himself up on the stool before switching it on.

"Welcome to Abe's, ladies and gentlemen," Abe begins. "I think you are going to be in for a treat tonight. Making his first appearance of what we hope will be a long run, Zack Tillerman."

Abe nods toward Zack, who has his head down looking at his cell phone which is perched on a holder on the microphone stand. Zack begins playing the first bars of the tune to *Don't Blame It on the Alcohol*.

Kid needs some work on his stage presence, Abe thinks before beginning to recite the song's lyrics.

Abe likes the background music which Zack was providing for this reading. More like a whisper in the background rather than standard band volume. Abe reads the lyrics through a full first reading, then right after the second stanza of his second time through, nods to Zack, who begins gradually increasing the volume of his playing along with beginning to sing.

Zack owns this song; it is in his musical wheelhouse. It is also not a song any of the customers at Abe's had ever heard performed before. The audience doesn't chime in on the stanza but as Abe watches their reaction from his perch on the stool, they didn't seem displeased.

I don't think that they have caught on yet to what they are hearing yet, Abe thinks.

When Zack ends the song, Abe climbs off the stool, puts down the microphone and with the aid of his crutch goes back to his wheelchair.

Abe watches intently as Zack plays through the 'Reggie's' portion of his set. The customers sing along but Abe didn't sense they were getting much more out of it than when the Wannasea Boys or other groups performed the same songs.

When Zack broke into *Operator*, things began to change. The audience is beginning to feel it. Abe could see the damn-this-kid-is-good look in their eyes. Zack plays the song through two more times before the audience is satisfied. They roundly applauded when Zack finally ends and cuts into *Hard Headed Woman*.

Abe is beginning to understand that Zack gets into performing only when he is playing music which he likes. There is no banter between songs. At this stage of his career, Zack is a musician pure and simple. Whether Zack is ever going to become a performer is yet to be determined.

Abe gets a little surprise while waiting for Zack to start up *Hard Rain*. It wasn't *Hard Rain* which Zack was playing, it was the version of an obscure song that he had written for Janie called *Not the same*. Zack had been playing around with it on Sunday. There had been no mention by Zack that he was going to use it.

Abe's history with *Not the Same* was almost as strange as the song. Normally Janie would take poetry which Abe had written and build a melody around the words. *Not the Same* had not been constructed that way. During their work on Reggie's 3rd album, Janie had come up with a guitar melody which she really liked. She began badgering Abe to write some words for it. Abe procrastinated. They were having increasing problems with Reggie and making words for Janie's tune wasn't at the top of Abe's list of priorities. Janie kept badgering. The day after they had completed delivery of what Reggie finally accepted for his third album, Janie pinned Abe down.

"Why is it that you have no trouble completing stuff for that asshole Reggie and you cannot complete a simple set of lyrics for me?" Janie had demanded.

Using a cheap cassette tape recorder, Abe got Janie to record her tune. Once completed, Abe had gone into their studio, shut the doors and began playing and replaying the tape. It took him two hours to complete the first line. It took him five more minutes to complete the rest of the song. Janie had been annoyed with the results and Abe was fairly certain that Janie had played the song at 'The Place' a couple of times simply to poke fun at him.

Zack had turned Janie's melody completely around making it into something of a country rap song with the first line spoken and the following line sung.

Not the Same – in C Major with BPM of 86 in 2/2 time

not quite the same
isn't it a shame

wanting to know
is not the same as knowing
wanting to go
not the same as going

not really the same
who is to blame?

wanting to create
is not the same as creating

wanting to fight
not the same as fighting

not quite the same
isn't it a shame

wanting to stop
is not the same as stopping
wanting to be
not the same as being

wanting to wait
is not the same as waiting
wanting to scream
not the same as screaming

not really the same
who is to blame?

wanting to hide
is not the same as hiding
wanting to reject
not the same as rejecting

not quite the same
isn't it a shame

wanting to flee
is not the same as fleeing
wanting to be
not the same as being

not really the same
who is to blame?

wanting to do
does not get it done
wanting to do
means nothing's begun

Through the first two stanzas, the audience didn't seem to know what to make of it. Zack had geared them up to do sing along with old hits and this wasn't anyone's old hit. Not even Janie's.

Oddly, Abe was beginning to sense that the song as Zack was playing it seemed to attach itself to his brain. By the second time through the refrain, some of the audience was singing along with a few of the stanzas. More picked up on it as Zack went through the song a second time. By the end, most of the audience was either chanting or singing the lines.

"I need to take a little break now folks," Zack says into the microphone. "While I do, if you'd like to come up and make requests for me to do one of your favorites well known folk or blues tunes, I'll see if I can do it for you."

Zack sits down his guitar by the mic stand, then took a sip of water from a bottle which he pulled out his back pockets. A few people began moving toward the stage.

Abe looked up at the clock which hung above the bar area. 8:12 PM. Too long for a set. Abe also realized the refrain from the *Not the Same* song is now stuck in his brain.

"Wanting to do, gets nothing done. Wanting to do, means you've just begun."

"I think Ralph was rather good," Zack's mom comments.

"Indeed he was," Abe affirms as he watches Zack writing down the customer's requests on a small notepad.

Wish I had brought a notepad and pencil, Zack thinks as Beth walks over and sits down in the chair at the table facing away from the stage.

"Doing okay, Gramps?" Beth asks.

Abe nodded his head.

"Ralph really killed it," Beth says to Abe's parents. "You think there's any way we can spring Saanvi free to come out and see him?"

"Maybe Thursday night," Hank Jones replies. "I'm almost finished moving things out of the old house. By Thursday I think that I can watch mom so Saanvi can come out."

"I'd do it," Prisha says, "but I've already switched my days once this week to come out here tonight."

"Beth, would you happen to have a piece of paper and pencil I could borrow?" Abe asks. "I want to make some notes."

Beth fishes in her apron pocket before handing Abe an order paid and a pencil stub. After finishing the task, Beth rises from her chair.

Abe begins writing down his thought about Zack's first set.

"I'll be back to get you after this next set," Beth said to Abe. "I think that will be enough for one evening."

Having completed the request taking, Zack goes to the back of the stage and pulls his electric guitar from the case, attaches a cord from the amplifier system to it and returns to the microphone.

Abe writes "Needs help taking requests – 8:24" on the back or the order pad which Beth had given him.

Zack searches his cell phone then breaks into a version of Dylan's *Tangled up in Blue*.

Abe writes, "Tangled up in Blue – not great audience response but wonderful rendition."

Zack then does *Hard Rain's Gonna Fall*.

Abe writes, "Hard Rain – better audience – might be better if more bluesy."

Zack searches the cell phone then breaks into Neil Young's *Heart of Gold*.

Abe writes, "Heart of Gold – good audience response – original – repeats."

Zack puts down the electric guitar, picks up his acoustic and breaks into Cat Steven's *Peace Train*.

Abe writes, "Peace Train – crowd is into it – repeats 2nd stanza – keeper."

Zack searches his phone, then starts Gordon Lightfoot's *Sundown*.

Abe writes, "Sundown – crowd really likes this song – should have used electric? – repeats – another keeper."

After quick referral to his cell phone, Zack then goes into Simon and Garfunkel's *The Sound of Silence*.

Abe writes, "Sound of Silence – crowd seems more attentive – Good cover – 9:28 too long."

After Zack announces a short break and once again begins writing down the requests on his notepad, Beth arrives at the table.

"Time to go, Abe," Beth says to Abe releasing the wheelchair's brake.

Turning to Zack's parents, Beth adds, "I'll come back and set down with you just as soon as I get Abe over to the house."

"She's the boss," Abe says to Zack's parents as he waves good night to them.

Beth rolls Abe across the dining area, through the kitchen area, out the back doors then up the slight incline toward the house.

"What's your verdict, Gramps?"

"Damned good," Abe replies. "He's going to have to work on his stage presence and crowd interaction but when Zack gets into the right music he goes to a completely different level."

"I think you ought to see about getting him videoed and recorded," Beth says. "If it were me, he ought to be up on You Tube right now."

"You Tube?"

"Most aspiring artists post their music videos to You Tube these days. It's become the 20th century version of an audition tape."

"I don't know how to deal with any of that stuff," Abe replies.

"Talk with Molly," Beth suggests. "I'm fairly certain she can work something out."

Incorporation

Abe picks up his cell phone from the desk in the studio and calls Beth. Two rings occur before she answers, "Need something, Gramps?"

"Would you mind sending Zack up here with lunch when it's time for him to take his break?" Abe asks. "Molly has some ideas about recordings which we need to talk over with him. We might tie him up for an hour or so, so if he hasn't had lunch himself have him bring some for himself as well."

"Sure," Beth replies, "he should be up there by 1:30."

1:30 was twenty minutes away.

Abe puts down the cell phone and turns to Molly, who is seated in a newly acquired office chair in front of a small table which she has been commandeered from Becca's in-law suite.

"Good," Molly replies. "I'll work on making a list of discussion items."

Abe returns to reviewing his notes about Zack's first performance from the night before and using them to expand his entries into a notepad file via his tablet's keyboard.

"You like that tablet," Molly says without stopping her own typing, "don't you, Abe?"

"It's certainly growing on me," Abe responds. "Didn't have it with me last night. Won't make that mistake again tonight."

Fifteen minutes pass before Zack appears with a tray filled with sandwiches and drinks.

Molly motions for Zack to set it down on the table.

"Let's go outside instead?" Abe suggests. "It's nice out today and who knows how many days we will have like this for the next four months?"

Molly rises from her chair, opens the sliding glass door to the patio before moving behind Abe's wheelchair. Abe releases the brake, and Molly pushes the chair to the end of a large patio table where Zack has begun setting out the food.

Task complete, Zack says, "Beth says that you want to talk with me, Mr. Stolz?"

"We both want to talk with you, Zack," Abe replies. "We want to talk about possibly recording you and perhaps think about formalizing a business arrangement."

"Okay," Zack says somewhat uncertainly as Abe motions him to sit down in one the webbed aluminum chairs.

"We think it would be a good idea to have you recorded playing some of your songs," Abe begins. "The songs would be put up on the internet. What do you think?"

"I was actually trying to record a couple songs from my last set with my cell phone last night to put up on You Tube," Zack says. "What I ended up with was basically unwatchable."

"I think you ought to consider doing the recording a little more professionally," Molly said. "Also might not be a bad idea for you to have a website."

"I do have a website," Zack responds.

"What's it called?" Molly asks.

"ralphjshreds.com," Zack replies.

"I think it is time for a new website," Abe offers. "Let Molly tell you what we want to suggest."

"I know some AV guys down at the Wannasea Extension, who dabble in recording events," Molly begins. "They are pretty good in my view. I suggest that we get them here to record some of your sets at 'The Place' which we then put up on You Tube. We also have them record some songs in the studio which will go up on a new website to be called, 'ZackTillerman.com.' I've checked and that website is available."

Zack thinks for a moment, before saying, "That sounds good but what's it going to cost?"

"Probably around a thousand dollars for starters," Molly states.

Zack thinks for a second, "I'm not really sure I can come up with that kind of money right know. I need to pay back, Mr. Stolz for my car and I'm really hoping to be able to begin paying for someone to come in and help with my grandmother's care."

"That's where we have another idea," Molly says. "Abe."

"You've got talent, Zack," Abe begins. "More talent than I have ever seen out of anyone, who has performed at 'The Place.' More than Reggie. You have a bright musical future ahead of you if you catch a few breaks. A future which eventually is probably going to move beyond this place."

"I'm not sure that I want to move beyond this place," Zack says with concern showing in his voice. "It's taken me a long time to be able to work and live on this island. I'm not feeling like that's something that I'm going to want to give up."

"Fair enough," Abe says. "Let's forget about what your long-term future might be then, let's talk about the short term."

Zack nods his head in hesitant agreement.

"In addition to recording your songs and putting them on the internet, we have the issue of the joint new songs which you and I have created. Songs which by the way, need to be copyrighted. There is real potential to profit from selling those songs as well as the recordings of your performances. To make that money, care will need to be taken to try to effectively produce and protect the material, making sure what we provide is what we legally have the rights to provide, as well as managing the associated costs for doing these things. There is also a business aspect to this which will not handle itself. Due to those considerations, I feel that we should formalize the arrangement which we seem to have fallen into," Abe says. "Molly and I propose that the three of us form an LLC based around our song production and the income from the sale of the materials which is recorded. Molly would be the business manager of this LLC and receive 10% of the profits. You will be songwriter/performer receiving 60% of the profits. I will be the lyricist/creative advisor/financier and receive 30 percent. All songs which we create will be property of the corporation. Any business decisions which are made will require two out of the three of us to agree on their implementation."

"Sounds complicated," Zack offers. "I just kind of like to play the music and see where it goes."

"I know you do, " Abe says, "but you are not seeming to understand that if you want to have fun and make real money from your music that process isn't going to go anywhere unless it is done professionally."

"And legally," Molly interjects.

"Zack," Abe begins, "I can tell you from painful personal experience that if you don't protect yourself while abiding by the rules, the further your career goes, the more people are going to be coming after you trying to pull pieces of it away."

"Mr. Stolz," Zack says after thinking for a moment, "I'm not really good at these sorts of things. I like music. I have always been good with music, when put in right set of circumstances. I'm neither good nor much interested in the business aspect, but I trust you. If you think creating some form of business structure is in our best interests, then let's do it."

"We can structure that organization to be as flexible as possible," Molly suggests. "We can make part of our original organization a deal that after some period of time, if one of us wants out, it can be dissolved and distributed equitably."

Zack looks at her quizzically.

"Let's just agree that any of us can leave the corporation after 18 months," Abe states. "I'd also like to make clear that as financier, I will fund the startup of the corporation with $10,000. If the LLC never goes anywhere, you two will have no responsibility for repaying whatever money we spend. Molly what do you think it will cost us to get fully up and running?"

Molly goes through a list of incorporation, tax copyright and licensing fees then adds, "In addition to what it's going to cost for the recordings, I also like to have the website professionally built. I can make a website but I've never made one with this type of potential bandwidth, pay and security considerations. The guy, who I'd like to have do the videoing is also a good website developer, I'd like to talk with him today when I meet with them to also ask if he'd be interested in creating our website in addition to doing the recording."

"What do you think all this may cost, Molly?" Abe asks.

"Maybe $3,000."

"I am okay with that cost long as it not exceeded by more than five hundred dollars," Abe states. "How about you guys?"

Zack and Molly nod in agreement.

Abe fishes in his pocket and pulls out a check which he has written out for $10,000 earlier in the morning.

"Molly can use this to get us set up at the bank," Abe says.

"Before we officially agree to form Zack Tillerman LLC," Molly urges, "I suggest we each state a list of needs and goals for our organization. I will start, I want to make sure that our organization is fair, honest and legal."

"I'd like to make sure that we don't forget about the music and try to keep it as much fun as possible," Zack offers.

Abe thinks for a second before saying, "Seeing as how we are about to be business partners, my only request is that we call each other by our first names. No more Mr. Stolz, Okay with you, Zack?"

Before Zack can say anything, Molly interrupts, "His name is actually Ralph, sir."

"I'd prefer to be called Zack here," Ralph/Zack says after a brief silence. "I like the name. I feel like a Zack when I'm out here."

"Okay then Zack it is," Abe replies with smile. "Are we all in agreement about starting this LLC?"

Molly and Zack nod their heads.

Zack puts his fist in the middle of the table and the two join him in a fist bump.

"I'm really so glad to be your partner," Molly says with a broad smile.

Abe notes that Molly is looking directly at Zack when she says this.

Maybe Beth has some competition, Abe thinks before biting into his sandwich.

Night Three

Ten minutes before seven on the night of Zack's third performance, Abe is seated in his wheelchair which is once again parked in the corner by the stage. Abe is proud of himself. He has just managed to talk Beth into doing the reading of *The Alice's Rule* for the dedication of the island's new government center. All that it was cost Abe was to agree to wear a new suit which Beth had bought him for the occasion.

The two AV guys which Molly had contracted, are fiddling with their equipment at the far end of the stage. Zack is still dispensing beverages at the bar. Beth has disappeared toward the area of the entrance. Abe is somewhat surprised that the dining area is almost full. Usually in an out-of-tourist season Thursday night, being 2/3rds full is considered a success. Abe also notices that this is a different crowd from normal. Abe's local customer base has become the 45 and up crowd. At least half of tonight's customers appear to be in their twenties.

Abe pulls out his tablet from the wheelchair's side pocket, taps on it, then after entering the date of 11/10, types in "Is younger customer base just for Zack's performances?"

Beth comes through the crowd arm-in-arm with a slight, dark complexioned, bright-eyed girl with long, flowing black hair in tow.

"This is Saanvi, Gramps," Beth announces bring her up to the wheelchair.

As Abe starts to rise from his wheelchair, the girl says, "No need to get up, sir."

Abe holds out his hand while saying, "I remember you from a few years back. You girls were thick as thieves back then."

Saanvi laughs and places her small hand into Abe's and shakes it as Zack comes up behind his sister and buzzes her on the cheek.

"I'm going to do the standard opening set tonight, if you think it's okay, Abe," Zacks says.

"I'd suggest only one difference," Abe replies, "I'm not going to read the lyrics of your first song. I'll just introduce you and then you can get right to it."

"Okay," Zack says somewhat hesitantly. "If we are going to do it that way, I'd like to kick it off with *Dark Ringlets* instead of one of Reggie's big hits."

"Sounds like a plan, kid."

Beth and Saanvi had seated themselves at the table beside Abe. Saanvi in the middle, Beth on the outside. The pair are lost in conversations about their working mates from five or more years back.

Abe, who has not thought about the DNA tests for going on two days now, suddenly remembers their results may be coming to him as soon as two weeks from now.

As Abe studies Beth, lost in happy conversation with Saanvi, he begins to think that perhaps no matter what the results of those tests, Beth is not going to lose. Either Zack won't be her half-brother and the path is clear to anywhere their relationship may take them or Beth is going to have both a half-brother and sister for the rest of her life.

Abe shifts himself in his wheelchair. His back, though increasing less painful than it had been right after his fall is aching a bit to go with the constant throb in his lower right leg. Abe has been pushing himself a little too much this week. Riley V, who has been totally disoriented by Abe's relocation to the house, has become something of a pest to those working on the changes to the old storage room where Abe had lived. Each day, Beth has had to bring Riley up to the house with instructions for Abe to keep him at the house until after the work crews are done for the day. Abe had now gotten in the habit of taking Riley out on the patio and throwing him tennis balls for thirty or forty minutes at a time at least twice a day, in addition to letting Riley guide him and his wheelchair around a little piece of the lake path and back. Those efforts were now catching up with him.

Zack has finished getting himself set up on stage, Abe slowly rises from his wheelchair and hobbles over to the waiting stool in front of the stage. Picking up the mic, he switches it on.

"Welcome to Abe's, ladies and gentlemen," Abe begins. "I believe that you are going to be if for a real treat tonight. So, without further ado, here is Zack Tillerman."

The AV crew have positioned themselves and now give Zack a thumbs up.

Zack gradually breaks into *Dark Ringlets*.

After settling himself in the wheelchair and picking up his tablet, Abe begins taking notes.

The audience seems more intent on listening than singing along tonight.

"Ringlets is the only Reggie song which Zack does well. Don't bother with the others," Abe writes.

Zack only plays two other Reggie songs.

Croce's *Operator* and Dylan's *Hard Rain* have the crowd clapping. *Not the Same* has them calling for more.

As Zack ends his last, *means nothing has begun*, he tells the audience, "Before I take a short break and begin collecting your requests, I have a request of my own."

Zack puts down his acoustic guitar and picks up the electric before continuing, "I'd like to ask my boss to come up her on stage and help me out with a couple songs which I think you just might like. Beth?"

Beth scowls at Zacks and does not appear to be making any movement toward the stage.

"Beth Stolz, folks," Zack say pointing his outstretched hand out toward Beth.

The crowd applauds politely.

Grudgingly Beth rises from her chair and moves toward the stage, Zack hands her two printouts of sheet music as she moves past him on her way to the upright piano. Zack trails her and puts a second microphone stand in place beside her.

Zack breaks into *Orange All Around*, the song Abe had written for Janie so long ago. Two stanzas in the crowd have gotten into it with them.

"Orange – if this isn't a crowd of Orangemen fans Zack may actually be on to something," Abe enters.

"We're going to do one more before the break," Zack announces before jumping guitar first into Billy Joel's *We didn't start the Fire*.

"Wow," Abe says aloud twice.

Zack and Molly keep it going for a good ten minutes.

"8:32" Abe types into his tablet as Beth exits the stage and Zack after a big swig of water begins taking requests.

Two minutes later Abe has drifted off to sleep his finger still on the tablet's surface.

"I'm going to roll Abe back up to the house," Beth tells Saanvi as she moves behind Abe's wheelchair and releases the brake. "You want me to bring you anything on my way back?"

Saanvi shakes her head negatively.

Abe remains asleep most of the way through the dining area, before jolting awake and turning himself around a little.

"Where are we going Beth?" Abe asks.

"Up to the house. I think you've had enough for tonight."

They roll past the now extremely busy coffee bar and out the front door into the full parking lot.

"Zack's really good, Abe."

"So are you, Kitten. So are you."

The Dedication

Abe is seated in the passenger's seat of Hugh's large Mercedes headed toward Wannasea and the dedication of the new government center. Abe feels refreshed after being able to take only his second shower since his fall. He's also dressed in a new light gray suit which Beth had bought for him. Abe had forgone the shirt and tie which Beth had also purchased for a black turtleneck.

Hugh has come to the island for the dedication without his wife, who has been off visiting her sister in Antwerp after Hugh had officially retired from the Air Force on Tuesday. Hugh would be formally starting as the head of operations of 'Defense One Surveillance' in Swansea next Monday.

"Finally got a chance to talk with Herbert yesterday about the offer that Reggie's lawyer made for the liquor license," Hugh says as he guides his car away from the house. "Herb thinks that $50K might be the top end going rate for a normal liquor license."

Due to his increasing focus on the selection of songs and videos for Zack Tillerman LLC, Abe had almost forgotten about that offer and Reggie's lawyer.

"I take it we don't have a normal liquor license?"

"Herb says that for this side of the mountain, interior area of the island and the lakes, only one license is authorized," Hugh says. "Seem that's a decision which was made when the Island's Alcohol and Beverage Commission was set up. Herb also thinks that our license also entitles us to have on-premise gambling but he is still working to clarify that."

"There is no way to apply to have that stipulation on only one license on the mountain amended?" Abe asks.

"It would take the presence of a lot more people than are currently living around the north side of the mountain plus unanimous approval by the island council."

"Why do you think Reggie and crew want that license so badly?"

"After what Herb told me about the machinations going on over the sale of the castle and old government building," Herb replies. "I'd venture to guess that Reggie's group is planning on using the liquor license for something he plans to do there."

"But the old government center is not up for sale until late January, I was told."

"Seems Reggie's group has gotten permission to survey that property and develop some plans," Hugh says entering the traffic circle by the ferry dock.

"Who are Reggie's people?" Abe asks.

"Sylvester's grandsons and the rest of that lot," Hugh replies as he takes the third exit to head west. "Herb has heard that the governor wants to do everything in his power to keep the Sylvester Bros. from operating on this island."

"Hasn't this island had more than enough from that lot?" Abe asks.

"Apparently not, Dad."

"How did the Sylvester Bros. manage to get permission to do all this surveying and plan making?"

"They bought off the head of the island council and two other members it seems," Hugh replies.

"Hugh," Abe thinks for a long moment, before deciding on full disclosure with Hugh, "I haven't told you that Reggie also offered me three million for both of the parcels which we have up there."

Hugh raises his eyebrows, "That's a good deal more than they're worth."

Hugh turns right into the parking lot for the new center. The lot is about 2/3rds full. Hugh switches off the engine but remains seated.

"Are you thinking of selling?" Hugh asks.

"I was kind of playing around with selling or leasing out the business in hopes of forcing Beth to make a decision to go back to getting her education," Abe responds. "Lately however, I've come to realize that college isn't really going to help Beth do what she wants to do. In any case, selling the house was and is never going to be on the table."

"I thought that I had this liquor license thing figured out," Hugh says. "If they bought your business, wouldn't the license come with it?"

"Yes," Abe says.

"So why offer to buy the liquor license separately and what would they want with the house?"

"Your guess is as good as mine."

Hugh sits for another minute behind his steering wheel thinking.

"Beth doesn't know that Reggie and crew have made an offer," Abe says to Hugh. "I'd rather keep it that way for the time being."

"When are you planning on letting Beth know about it?" Hugh asks.

"As soon as those DNA test results come back," Abe says. "If the results determine who Beth's father is, I'll let Beth decided what happens to 'The Place?'"

Hugh looks at his father quizzically, "What if they don't determine who Beth's father is?"

"Haven't figured that part out yet," Abe says opening the passenger side door.

Hugh climbs out of the car and pulls Abe's wheelchair from the trunk. Abe with the help of his crutch has managed to move to the back of Hugh's car. Hugh unfolds the chair and waits for Abe to climb into it before heading to the ceremony area set up by the front entrance to the new building.

Beth and Marie are seated at the outside end of the first row of spectator chairs which have been lined up in front of a small dais set up to the right of the building's entrance. Beth has come to the event separately because of a desire to head back to Abe's as quickly after the conclusion of the ribbon cutting portion of the ceremony has ended.

Reggie and a crew of twelve has swept into Abe's yesterday afternoon to begin setting up for his benefit concert this evening. They have constructed a small stage in the rear, taken over Abe's former deck area and filled it with audio and video equipment. Doing all of this with absolutely no concern for Beth's ongoing business.

Beth pulls the end chair from the row out and helps Hugh position Abe and his wheelchair there. Hugh takes the chair beside of Abe which is next to where Marie sits.

"How's the setup for tonight going?" Hugh asks Beth.

"Reggie has gotten on my last nerve," Beth says to her uncle. "He seems to think that he now owns my business. If we don't come to actual physical blows before this is all over, I'll be really surprised."

"Why is he dragging in all that equipment?" Abe asks, "The last time Reggie performed at Abe's all that he had was his guitar and some kind of fancy contraption which plays backup tracks."

"From the equipment that they are setting up, I think his performance is going to be filmed," Marie says.

"Did Reggie tell you he was going to be filming or ask if it's okay?" Hugh says.

Beth shakes her head negatively before saying, "I've got to get up on the dais, it looks as if they will be starting any second."

Beth picks up the chair which she had pulled out for Abe, walks across to the back of the dais and places it there before going up the steps to assume her seat as the fourth person to the right of the governor. Beth is to be the last person to speak before the governor.

Forty minutes pass with a variety of officials offering thanks for work done plus providing stories of the obstacles, pratfalls and triumphs incurred during construction. The next five minutes are filled with the head of the Wannasea Historical society briefly describing the history of the old government center before Beth's turn arrives.

Beth strides to the podium and begins, "I am representing Alice Bailey's family today. Initially it was hoped that my grandfather, Abe, would make this presentation, but a fractured ankle has sidelined him. He has asked that I fill in. Alice was Abe's grandmother. Abe had eight years of the pleasure of Alice's company before she and his father were taken away. My Uncle Hugh and I didn't have the pleasure of meeting her. The three of us may be the last blood relatives of Alice, but as this building attests, all the residents of this island are also descendants of Alice Bailey Reginald's life."

Beth pauses for a few moments to pull a sheet of folded paper from her pocket.

"I would like now to read to you a poem which my grandfather wrote about Alice, 12 years after she and his father were assassinated.

Alice's Rule

Hugo and Alice became Wannasea legends
saved the Island without the use of weapons
defeated the villainous Nine with only a well laid plan
resulting in the overthrow of the Reginald clan

Once Wannasea's governor wrote Nine had just died
Alice's day to turn homeward finally arrived
With daughter in tow set out for Wannasea
their heart, their home and their true destiny
for eighteen long years Alice made improvements
to the island's roads, schools and political movements
with guile, compassion and vision Alice had governed
changed even the minds of the island's most stubborn

there will always be angry malevolent forces
more willing to plant explosives than engage in public discourses
Nine's cousin Sylvester was just this sort of man
capable of widespread destruction if it aided his clan
with an island distracted by the big celebration
brought on by completion of the new ferry station
a bomb was ignited in the boot of Alice's car
which exploded and extinguished Alice's bright star

for eighteen long years Alice had made improvements
to the island's roads, schools and political movements
with compassion, fairness and vision Alice had governed
changed even the minds of the island's most stubborn
always pushing to adopt stronger, fairer and better rules
moving further and further from the reign of the Reginald ghouls
Alice's legacy triumphed over the terror which Sylvester intended
making certain what had been started was not soon to be ended."

 Beth has not read the words from the lyrics which Abe and Janie had written for Reggie almost fifty years ago. Beth has read the words of the poem from which those lyrics were derived. As Beth started her reading most in the audience, 90% of whom had been out at Abe's more than once, had seemed poised to join in on the stanza of the well-known lyrics. Some expressed surprise when those stanzas did not come and they realized the words weren't about a song but about Alice.

 Once again Abe's granddaughter had surprised him. This was the place and time that poem had always been meant to be read.

Beth refolded her paper and returned to her seat.

For five minutes the island's governor described the function of the new building and how it may now better serve the island. He completed the ceremony using a large ceremonial pair of scissors to cut the sea blue ribbon at the new building's entrance.

"The new Wannasea Government Center is officially open," the Governor announced swinging open the doors.

Beth scurried down the back stairs of the dais and walked over to Abe.

"I've got to get back to 'The Place' before Reggie destroys it," Beth says.

Before she can leave, Abe takes her hand and pulls her just a little closer to him.

"That was magnificent Beth. I only wish Becca, your grandmother and mother had been here to hear it."

Abe releases Beth's hand. She and Marie quick walk to her car.

Hugh stands and stretches before pushing Abe's chair toward the receiving line at the entrance to the new building. As they clear the near corner of the dais, the head of the Wannasea Historical Society walks up to them.

"Would I be able to have a few words with you gentlemen?" the Historical Society head asks, "Let's sit over here."

He leads them back to where they had just been and pulls out one of the folding chairs, so that he is facing Abe and Hugh.

"I'm Steven DeJean, head of Wannasea's Historical society," the man says offering his hand. "I know we have all met before but I think that it has been a few years."

"At least ten," Abe says shaking the offered hand as he vaguely recalls an earlier discussion with Mr. DeJean which lead to his providing information on the early days of the Reginalds.

"Hugh Stolz," Hugh says offering his hand, "I'm Abe's son."

"I'm not certain whether or not you are aware," Mr. DeJean begins, "but the island is in the process of preparing to sell the old government center location. I also know for a fact that the Governor and most of the island council would very much like to see at least the castle portion turned into a museum."

"We were just discussing that before the ceremony," Hugh replies.

"The Historical Society is actively searching for interested parties to partner with our group to purchase the facility and turn it into the proper museum this island deserves."

"I see," Abe says. "How is it that you see us fitting into that?"

"In two ways, Mr. Stolz," DeJean continues, "You may be one of the leading experts on the history of this island during the 18th, 19th and early 20th centuries. We would very much like for you to be involved in helping to put together what would go into the museum for that period. Additionally we are wondering if you might have any interest in helping create a performing arts center on the property. We would most certainly welcome your help financially but are wondering if perhaps you might have an interest in taking on the ownership of the performing arts portion of the facility."

Abe looked at Hugh quizzically.

"It sounds like an interesting opportunity," Hugh says. "For both you and the island, Dad. On my own part, I most certainly would be willing to do something to help out financially."

"Where is it that your group stands at this point?" Abe asks of DeJean.

"We know the asking price for the property is going to be $2.88 million. Because of our plans for an actual museum, we have learned the government would sell it to us for $2.5 million. We have current commitments and funds for $1.8 million," DeJean replies. "Our real challenge is that we cannot see any way to reduce the continuing operating costs for the facility. We estimate those to be at least $12,000 per month. Then there is the approximately $500K which we believe it would cost to revamp the facility for the museum needs."

"Seems you've done a good deal of thinking about this," Abe replies. "Do you also know who you will be up against to acquire the property?"

"The Sylvester Brothers of Halifax," DeJean says. "As far as we know, there are no other interested parties."

"Do you have any idea what the Sylvester Brothers are thinking of doing with the facility once they have it?" Abe asks.

"We've heard they want to make a performance venue out of the castle area. Something like those venues which they have for large music events on the Mainland," DeJean replies. "A facility for up to 2,500 attendees. As far as a museum, what their group seem to be proposing is more theme park than museum. We've also heard that they plan to acquire another nearby property to build a hotel/resort to accommodate those attendees and the performers."

Abe looks at Hugh, who raises his eyebrows.

"Would you gentlemen have an interest in joining with us to prevent that?" DeJean asks.

"I think that I might," Abe replies, "but would you mind keeping that interest a solemn secret for the time being? I have a few things to work out within my family before we will be able to go public in joining your effort."

Reggie's Performance

After having just convinced Beth to go with Zack up to the studio to help get everything set up for tomorrow's recording session for the Zack Tillerman website, Abe takes one last look around the turmoil which Reggie has wrought. It's easy to see why Beth is ready to tear into Reggie.

There are now approximately 200 people crammed into a dining area limited by fire ordinances to 135. The wait staff is now confined behind the bar area. Only beverages and hand-held treats are now allowed to be served. Serving from the dining room counter is to stop the moment Reggie begins his first session.

There is little question that Reggie will be having the event filmed. A crew of three cameramen are set up at the table Abe has been using recently.

A group of what look to be the Sylvester Bros. thugs are dressed in black tactical outfits which have "Event Control Officer" emblazoned across the back and front pockets. Barricades have been set up all around the front of parking lot entrance as well as to the house. Reggie's group has controlled the sale of the events tickets and are making certain that anyone without such ticket is removed from the premise.

Hugh stands behind the Abe's wheelchair which is now at the entrance to the kitchen exit.

Reggie suddenly appears through the front entrance of Abe's trailed by another cameraman. Nodding and waving he moves through the crowd to the small stage area, waiting for a high sign from his audio/video engineer, Reggie walks up to the microphone.

"This is where it all began ladies and gentlemen," Reggie announces. "This is where Reggie Reginald and *The Kingdom of Wannasea* were born. This is where I struggled and sweated to become a star. This is where I first wrote and performed those song that you now love so much."

Abe laughs out loud.

An announcer, whose voice Abe recognizes from a Halifax FM radio station, approaches the microphone as Reggie steps back and begins focusing on putting on his guitar and strap, and says, "Before beginning, I need to lay out how this evening is going to go. Reggie will do five songs from this stage, then move to the stage on the back patio and do four more songs before taking a short break. Reggie will then go back on to the patio stage and perform six more songs. After a second ten-minute break, Reggie will return here and close out the night. No movement will be allowed between the dining room and patio areas. No refreshments will be available while the performance is ongoing."

The Wannasea Boys are backing Reggie up in the dining room. None of the three appear to be very happy to be doing so. They have been moved into the shadows of the stage and from what Abe can see, it does not appear their instruments are plugged into Reggie's sound system.

"It's getting too crowed in here," Abe says to Hugh. "Let's go out back."

Hugh pushes Abe through the kitchen hallway to the back patio, This area is almost as crowded as the dining room.

Hugh pushes Abe to the area of the patio on the far side of the stage.

Reggie has another band on the second stage, who are now sitting on stools.

"Thanks for your patience," comes over the loudspeaker system from the voice of the announcer. "Now without further delay, the one, the only, Reggie Reginald is going to lead you in a wonderful Wannasea evening."

"Pretty full of himself," Hugh comments to Abe as Reggie breaks into *The Kingdom of Wannasea.*

"Always has been," Abe replies as he listens carefully to the music, noting that it sounds exactly like what is on Reggie's recordings.

Reggie takes 20 minutes to go through the first four songs. Everything is from the first album. Reggie doesn't seem to be doing much to encourage audience participation while playing but. between songs, Reggie is full of animated chatter. Telling stories of his early performances at Abe's. Most of which are more fluff than fact.

As Reggie is describing how he came to make *Alice's Rule* famous, Abe turns his head toward Hugh and says, "He left out the part about your mom knocking him ass over teacups off the piano bench."

Hugh laughs as they watch Reggie, microphone in hand still bantering, come out through the kitchen hallway led by a cameraman and two Event

Control Officers. Reggie is telling about how he almost single handedly had produced his second album at this very facility.

Bouncing up the steps of the patio stage, Reggie turns to the crowd, "Now I am going to play you a few hits from that best-selling album."

Best-selling in Latvia, Abe thinks as they listen to him break into his version of *Dark Ringlets*.

Hugh leans over and whispers, "I think he's lip-syncing."

"Yep," Abe says noticing that his second band's instruments are no more live than the Wannasea Boys' had been. This second band does however seem to know how to pander to Reggie's dips and bounces.

Abe and Hugh listen through the rest of the 20-minute set, before Hugh says, "I really need to get back over to Swansea, Pop."

"I had enough about thirty minutes ago," Abe says as he releases the handbrake of his wheelchair.

Before they can go ten feet, Reggie, who has just announced a short break, has quickly come down the stage and stands in front of Abe's wheelchair.

"What do you think, Abe?" Reggie asks.

"You've got quite the crowd, Alf," Abe replies.

"This is the way this place should always be," Reggie says. "Good music. Big crowds."

"If you held another one of these tomorrow," Abe states gruffly, "you'd be lucky to fill up ten tables in the dining area. You'd also be broke in three months, because in case you haven't noticed there isn't much food and beverage being sold."

"You are underestimating the power of music, Abe," Reggie says.

"Music isn't what this is Alf," Abe says disgustedly, "and we both know it."

"If you allow my organization to make good on the generous offers which we have made to you, I believe you would find out differently," Reggie says with a little anger rising in his voice. "By the way, why haven't you been able to complete an agreement on the sale of the item which we have been requesting?"

"Alf," Abe begins, "I have told your lawyer that no decision can be made on the sale of 'The Place' until January."

"I don't think that you are listening very clearly to what we are offering, Abe," Reggie says firmly. "At a minimum you should have sold us your liquor license by now. I think you are about to find out that my associates do not have unlimited patience."

"Not until January, Alf," Abe replies as he motions Hugh to resume wheeling him toward the house.

"It's your funeral, Abe," Reggie says flatly.

Hugh pushes the wheelchair up the slight glassy incline to the rear entrance of the house's circular driveway.

"You aren't going to sell him anything," Hugh says as they move up the asphalted drive, "are you, Pop?"

"Nope," Abe replies. "I'm also going to do everything in my power to see that Reggie and the people behind him don't take over the old government center."

Hugh pushes the wheelchair thirty more feet before saying, "I don't like the looks of Reggie's associates. Next week, I'm going to send a couple of our best technicians out here to install one of our mobile surveillance systems. The systems are close to being ready for market. They are almost impossible to detect. They cover a wide area and provide an almost instantaneous response to any security breach. This would be as good a place as any for their final test run."

"I'm beginning to think that would be a good idea," Abe replies as they move onto the patio then head toward the side entrance to the brightly lit studio.

As Abe reaches out to open the sliding door, Molly motions through the glass with her finger to her mouth for Abe to be quiet.

"Seems they are recording something in there," Abe says to Hugh.

"That's okay," Hugh says, "I've already past my curfew. I think I will head back without going inside. Tell everyone in there that I said goodbye?"

"Will do," Abe replies, then pivots his chair around to face Hugh and adds, "It was really nice to spend this day with you, Hugh."

"Was for me too, Pops," Hugh says. "Let's do it more often."

Abe watches Hugh walk out to where his car is parked, then pivots his chair back around to face the sliding glass. Whatever was happening inside seems to have ended, so Abe opens the door and wheels himself inside.

"Sam and Dave got everything set up early," Molly explains, "so with Zack here, they thought they'd go ahead and start recording. They finished *Don't Blame It on the Alcohol*. They are now working on something called, *Stuck in My Mind*."

Last Monday when Zack was going through Abe's writings, he stumbled on a poem which Abe had written just as he fell into the depths of alcoholism. Abe hadn't paid much attention when Zack created a melody for it.

"What's that thing Beth is standing in front of?" Abe asks Molly.

"An electric keyboard," Molly replies. "Zack thought we need it for some of what he calls the bluesier songs, so we rented one from the music store."

I've helped to create a monster, Abe thinks to himself as he watches Beth play around with the mode settings of the keyboard while she plays a couple keys.

"That's the one," Zack tells Beth.

Zack breaks into melody which he was created for Abe's lyrics. After a dry run through the first verse, Beth joins in.

"We're ready Dave," Zack says to the young bearded guy at the audio board.

Stuck in My Mind tempo of 122BPM key of G in 4/4 time)

sailed around this bay before
in the midst of a calm blue sea
recalling all the hidden coves
special places for you and me

recalling gentle afternoons
when morning glories bloomed
all those silly songs we used to sing
bottles of red wine we consumed

remembering the way you smelled
hope to never forget
how you clung to me
our bodies warm and wet

stuck in my mind
our every loving second
miss you most at night
when sorrow starts to beckon

I've sailed this bay before
solo and headed out toward sea
hoping to forget our past
but your memory gets the better of me

you brought me peace of mind
before regret came into view
love like that is hard to find
the best I ever knew

recalling gentle afternoons
when morning glories bloomed
all those silly songs we used to sing
bottles of red wine we consumed

recall the way you smelled
hoping to never forget
how you clung to me
our bodies warm and wet

stuck in my mind
our every loving second
miss you most at night
when sorrow starts to beckon
when sorrow starts to beckon

I 've sailed this bay before
solo and headed out toward sea
hoping to forget our past
but your memory gets the better of me

    "That seems like a good one," the audio board guy says to Zack.
    "Could you play it back?" Zack asks.
    Dave presses a few keys, and a replay of what has just been recorded comes out of a set of speakers set in front of Janie's piano.
    "What do you think, Beth?" Zack asks.

"Sounds good to me," Beth replies, "but I'm no expert."

"Abe?" Zack asks turning toward Abe.

"It' got a nice sound but I'm not sure that it fits your style," Abe replies.

"Why don't we include it in our mix for the website and the music podcast," Molly suggests. "We'll let our listeners decide."

Zack nods his head in agreement.

Zack has chosen to record *Carried Away* next. They do three takes before Zack is satisfied.

"Let's take a little break," Beth suggests. "We've got cookies on the table and there's water and tea drinks in the cooler to the side."

Beth walks over to Abe and asks, "When did you write *Stuck in My Mind*?"

"Maybe a month after we gave up looking for your mom and grandma," Abe replies softly.

"Were you drinking then?"

"I was just getting started," Abe says. "I don't think I was drunk when I wrote it but I'm not entirely sure."

Beth heads to the table and brings Abe back a bottle of water, two butter almond cookies along with two pain relievers.

"What's this music podcast thing?" Abe asks Molly after downing the two pills and chasing them with a sip from the water bottle.

"Zack and Dave were talking about ways to get more audience," Molly explains, "Dave mentioned having something like doing a one set recording session once a week live on the internet. The recording would be made in podcast format and distributed for use on people's devices through a podcast service."

"Do people have to pay to view this podcast stuff?" Abe asks.

"Depends," Dave says walking up to where Beth and Molly are standing next to Abe's wheelchair. "The big thing is to first generate a pent up demand for the podcast. Once that happens the money should follow."

"Zack and I are thinking that we should buy our own recording setup to do the sessions," Molly says.

"You are planning on doing them from here?" Abe asks.

"We'd like to," Molly says.

"That okay with you, Beth?" Abe asks.

"Abe," Beth says with a wry smile, "last time I checked, you are still the person that owns this house and studio."

"We thought we'd talk about it tomorrow after we finish up the recording sessions," Molly explains.

Abe takes a bite from his cookie before rolling himself over to the back wall beside his desk.

He pulls out his tablet and begins making notes in his open notepad. Abe sits through the recording of two more songs, *Orange All Around* and *Not the Same*, being recorded in three takes each over the next hour. When Beth announces another break, Abe excuses himself and wheels himself into Marie's room.

The recording session goes on until 2 AM.

Final Offer

Monday afternoon after Reggie's Saturday night hostile takeover of Abe's. Molly has gone to town to return the rented keyboard. Zack is fiddling with a newly purchased video recorder which he is connecting to his laptop with the intent of using the device for his first podcast this evening. Abe sits at his desk with his laptop open looking over the ten songs from last Saturday and Sunday nights recording sessions which have been chosen for posting on the Zack Tillerman website. One of the songs Zack has decided to record jumps out at him, *This Side of Nowhere Blues*. Abe had penned those words in the third year of his deep dive into alcohol for the amusement of a drinking acquaintance named George Rainey. Occasionally Abe would find himself drunk and adrift in Halifax after the Wannasea ferry had stopped running for the night. In exchange for Abe buying a couple of bottles of cheap liquor, George would let Abe stay in his rented trailer which was parked in a seedy trailer park about 15 miles north of Halifax. George played a little guitar and considered himself a musician. George kept bugging Abe to write something which he could play during his busker forays in Halifax which he used to supplement his meager government allotment. Abe finally produced *This Side of Nowhere* for George. George had found the song hilarious and played it for months in his trailer, alleyways and on the streets of Halifax. Abe didn't recall if George had been able to collect much from its playing.

 That he had actually written down the song down and placed it among the papers containing his other lyrics surprised Abe. That Zack had picked it out from the Abe's writings and then actually created his own melody and recorded it, was something else again.

 Abe clicks on the MP3 file of the song. The song is only Zack and his guitar echoing a muted country twang.

This Side of Nowhere – tempo of 91BPM in the key of A flat in 4/4 time

took the Q-line bus from Pilgrim's Square
getting off just this side of nowhere
for this side of nowhere is where I reside
rented lot with a double-wide
this side of nowhere is where I now live
snarling dogs and not a shit left to give

empty bottles, empty pockets emptier soul
reaching oblivion, now my main goal
been off balance for so damned long
any other condition seems totally wrong

took the Q-line bus from Pilgrim's Square
getting off just this side of nowhere
'cause this side of nowhere is where I reside
rented lot in a double-wide

this side of nowhere is where I now live
snarling dogs with not a shit left to give
this side of nowhere is where I now roost
my expectations seriously reduced

took the Q-line bus from Pilgrim's Square
getting off just this side of nowhere
'cause this side of nowhere is where I reside
rented lot in a double-wide
this side of nowhere is where I now live
snarling dogs and not a shit left to give
this side of nowhere is where I now crash
battered and bruised without any cash

took the Q-line bus from Pilgrim's Square
getting off just this side of nowhere
this side of nowhere is where I reside

rented lot with a double-wide
empty bottles, empty pockets emptier soul
reaching oblivion, now my main goal
this side of nowhere is where I now live
snarling dogs and not a shit left to give

this side of nowhere is where I reside
rented lot with a double-wide
this side of nowhere is where I now live
snarling dogs and no shits left to give
this side of nowhere is where I now roost
my expectations seriously reduced

took that Q-line bus from Pilgrim's Square
getting off just this side of nowhere
cause this side of nowhere is where I now live

Certainly isn't how George did it, Abe thinks.

"So what do you think of it, Abe?" Zack asks from across the room.

"I'm not sure what to make of it," Abe says honestly. "I'm beginning to be more concerned that you have developed a penchant for finding my weirdest, darkest writings, setting them to music and then recording them."

"I kind of like weird and dark," Zack says as he continues to fiddle with his laptop. "They fit right into my personal history."

"Any particular reason?"

"Because I can really get into those kinds of songs. In the case of *This Side of Nowhere*, it makes me think about of my grandfather," Zack replies.

"Your grandfather?"

"He was a drunk for as long as I knew him."

Abe ponders for a few moments before asking, "What was your grandfather's name?"

"Eugene."

"Eugene Jones?"

Zack nods his head affirmatively.

Abe recalls a Eugene Jones from the seedier dives down by the docks. Eugene had been maybe ten years older than Abe but with drunks that was hard to tell. Eugene had been a flat out drunk. At least one level beyond the highest level which Abe had reached in his journey through alcohol. Eugene had been the local Wannasea west end bar fly. Unless he had money, most bars wanted him out of their establishment as soon as possible. Abe had not quite reached Eugene's status. Abe was more the go-on-a-bender after a few days of sobriety kind of drunk. Though toward the end, the time between binges was growing shorter and shorter. Abe knew that if it had not have been for his mother and Beth, he would have caught up with Eugene.

"Do you know why your grandpa drank?" Abe asks Zack.

"My dad always said that it started when he was in the military," Zack replies. "I'm not so sure though because it seemed the only thing grandpa ever really cared much about was getting his next drink."

"I don't think you ought to try that song out over at 'The Place' just yet," Abe suggests.

"Wasn't planning on it."

Abe clicks on another MP3 file named 'Hard Case.' Beth is on the electric organ and harmony on this one.

Hard Case – tempo of 122BPM key of A minor 4/4 time

just when I thought that this might be the night
you left me shrunken, reeling, not feeling right
there's no getting past your defenses today
I'm shaken, uncertain, not feeling okay

only looking for a place
in the warmth of your embrace
you're such a hard case

smoldering contempt from your eyes
overcoming advances and barroom lies
tougher than nails
too short with details
you never change pace
you're such a hard case

thought you of all people might understand
this isn't some nefarious plan
to receive what you don't want to give
only wish to be part of the life you live

so quick to rebuff
tougher than tough
you push me away
left with nothing to say

smoldering contempt in your eyes
overcoming advances and barroom lies
tougher than nails
too short with details
you never change pace
you're such a hard case

only looking for a place
in the warmth of your embrace
you're such a hard case

just when I thought that this might be the night
you left me shrunken, reeling, not feeling right
there's no getting past your defenses today
I'm shaken, uncertain, not feeling okay

smoldering contempt from your eyes
overcoming advances and barroom lies
tougher than nails
too short with details
you never change pace
you're such a hard case

this isn't a chase
I wear no false face
you're such a hard case

This was one of the first songs Abe had written for Janie. Abe had always felt the production of that song had led Janie to understand how much he cared for her. The pair had even suggested Reggie use it on his 2nd album. Reggie had thought the song was too much a lament for unrequited love. Reggie had wanted to establish himself as the romantic folk singer, not as a love-struck crooner.

"What do you think of that one?" Zack asks.

"I like it," Abe says nodding his head. "I like it quite a bit."

Just as Abe gets ready to click on another MP3 file, his cell phone rings. Seeing that display shows, "Bernard Fuller," Abe begins rolling his wheelchair toward Marie's room before answering, "Abe Stolz."

"Mr. Stolz," the lawyer begins, "Reggie Reginald has just informed me that you still refuse to consider or continue your negotiations with us."

"As I told you the last time that I spoke, I will not be in any position to make a decision on selling the business before January," Abe says as he wheels into the room and closes the door behind him.

"I am authorized to make you one final offer, the lawyer continues, that offer is $3.5 million for both parcels and the liquor license. The offer is contingent upon our coming to a signed agreement by the end of this week."

"I cannot do anything before January," Abe says tiredly.

"That's very unfortunate," the lawyer says. "My clients are beginning to feel that you are not negotiating with them in good faith. Please be aware that both my clients and myself are very proficient in dealing with people, who do not operate in good faith."

Abe has an urge to disconnect the call but overcomes it, "You don't seem to be comprehending what I am telling you. There simply isn't any way I can sell anything before January. If I sell, the only thing which will be sold is the business."

"It is you, who has the comprehension problem, Mr. Stolz," the lawyer barks. "You have two days to accept the offer which I have just made. If after those two days pass and do to unforeseen or unfortunate circumstances, you decide to take up our offer, that offer will be reduced by $100,000 each day that you fail to commit to it."

"Not until January, Mr. Fuller."

"My clients have no intention of waiting until January. Based upon my past experience, I think you will soon enough come to feel that way as well. I will be placing no further calls to you. When you wish to respond to our offer, you will need to call me."

With that the call is disconnected.

Abe shakes his head as he puts his phone into his pocket hoping that this will be the last time he has to deal with Reggie or his partners, knowing full well that it most likely won't be.

An Unwelcome Discovery

Abe has risen early this Thursday morning. Yesterday, after three weeks of itching misery, Abe's hard cast had been removed. He is now in a walking cast which may be removed for shower and sleep. Abe has also been instructed to begin doing more walking using the crutch only as necessary. The only downside, other than still being unable to drive for 4–5 more weeks, will be the two days of physical therapy per week which he has to undergo. Beth had somewhat mitigated the inconvenience of those session by scheduling the therapist to come out to the house to perform them.

Abe has also been moved out of Marie's room into the refurbished in-law suite which Janie had built for Becca. Abe was actually beginning to think that he was going to enjoy living there It is much more quiet than his old room over the business had been. The unit has a nice little kitchen and eating area which lead to the patio. Good sized bedroom and attached bath, though Abe still prefers the bathroom attached to the studio. Although there was plenty of room for Abe's desk, he had asked Beth to leave it over in the studio for use in his ongoing work with Molly and Zack. In the past few weeks, Abe had gotten used to spending most of his day working in the studio.

Abe makes himself coffee then sits down at the small table situated between the refrigerator and the sliding glass door to the patio.

His cell phone rings. Abe rises and without the crutch hobbles over to the kitchen counter to pick it up.

He notices that the caller is Beth before picking it up and saying, "Hello Kitten."

"You've got to come down here, Abe," Beth says. From the sound of her voice, it seems as if she has been upset by something.

"What's wrong?" Abe asks with concern rising.

"I can't tell you over the phone," Beth sniffles.

"Where are you down there?" Abe asks

"Outside the kitchen on the other side of the stairs going up to your old room."

Abe hops over to his new bedroom, grabs his jacket and picks up his crutch before heading out of the unit's front door. He negotiates the driveway, noticing that Beth and most of the kitchen staff seem to be standing about five feet to the left of his old stairway. The same place Reggie's stage had been this past Saturday night.

Arriving at the group, Abe sees that they are gathered around the prone body of Riley V. Something traumatic has happened to Riley's head.

"I think he must have been hit by a car and crawled back here," Beth says after coming up to her grandfather and clutching his left arm. Sallie, Josh and Ralph are staring at the dog trying to hold back tears.

Abe awkwardly bends down and places his hand on Riley chest which is cold and still.

"He's gone," Abe says, the words catching in his throat.

Riley V hadn't really been Beth's dog, any more than Riley had been Abe's dog. Riley had been 'The Place's' dog. Few workers ever took their break without spending time with Riley.

"Why don't you and Sallie go back in," Abe tells Beth. "Josh, Randy and I will handle this."

"I feel so bad Abe," Beth said. "I knew that he wasn't around last night and should have gone out looking for him."

"It's not your fault," Abe says. "Now please go inside. We'll take Riley down to Miss Vicky's and then go from there."

Reluctantly the pair turn toward the kitchen entrance.

"Randy, would you mind going in the kitchen and bringing back one of those big plastic trash bags?" Abe asks, then adds. "Josh, would you get the van and pull it around to this side?"

The pair disappears as Abe takes a closer look at Abe's bloody head.

Unless I am mistaken, Riley was hit by something other than a car and hit more than once, Abe thinks.

Abe pulls his phone out of his pocket and calls Miss Vicky's Veterinary Clinic. No one's sure how the sixty-something veterinarian, Victoria Myers, came to be called Miss Vicky but that's now how everyone on the island addresses her.

After exchanging pleasantries with the receptionist, Abe asks to speak to Miss Vicky. Two minutes pass before she comes to the phone.

"Good morning, Abe. What can I do for you?"

Abe explains what the situation with Riley asking that he be cremating but requesting a special service from the vet before the is done.

"Beth seems to think Riley was hit by a car, but I am not so certain," Abe tells the vet. "Would you be able to do a close examination and tell me in your professional opinion what you think might have happened?"

"Be glad to Abe," Miss Vicky replies. "I'm so sad to hear about Riley. I know everybody up there loved that dog."

"We did," Abe says. "Would you mind having someone give me a call when everything is finished?"

"Certainly, I'll give you a call as soon as we are done here."

Both Ralph and Josh have returned by the time that Abe says his goodbyes to the vet.

Abe holds open the bag as the boys carefully help to slide Riley's body inside. Josh opens the sliding van door and the two boys place the bag into the van.

"I've made arrangements for Miss Vicky to handle cremating Riley," Abe tells the pair. "Would you two mind driving him down there?"

"Not at all," Josh says. "We're sure going to miss that dog."

"Once we get the ashes back, we'll have a little ceremony for him out behind the storage shed where the other Rileys are buried," Abe tells them.

He watches the boys pull away in the van before again pulling out his phone and calling Hugh.

Another Unwelcome Discovery

Monday morning just a little after 9 AM, two technicians from the Defense One Surveillance company have arrived to install the new security system.

"It's a mesh network of smart cameras and multi-frequency scanners with dual control centers," Sam, the lead technician explains to Abe as they sit at one of the patio tables.

Sam shows Abe one of the camera units which are no bigger than the small bottle of ibuprofen in Abe's pocket.

"We will install four of these camera units plus a controller in the outside area, two inside your business," Sam explains. "Two more units with another controller on the light poles up at your house. Each unit has its own battery backup which is good for 2–3 hours depending upon activity. If you happen to have an emergency power source though, that will extend their coverage time."

"We do have a generator which is connected to the kitchen refrigeration units and the emergency lighting," Abe answers. "The generator and switch are on the other side of the shed."

The generator which is diesel driven had been placed behind the shed to keep fumes as far away from the patio area as possible.

"Would you mind showing us?" Sam asks.

Abe lifts himself from the chair carefully, picks up his crutch and leads the two men past the kitchen to the shed. As they pass the entrance to the garage, Abe notices that the door is ajar.

"Give me just a second," Abe asks the men as he stops to inspect where the padlock which secures the door used to be.

Abe has not used the Morris in almost four weeks now. No one else has either. Abe swings open the two garage doors to find shards of broken glass, taillights and damage to the trunk and the fenders.

"Was your car like this before?" Sam asks peering into the garage.

Abe shakes his head and begins to move toward going into the garage before Sam restrains him.

"I'd call the constabulary and allow them take a look before you do anything in there," Sam suggests.

Abe nods his head slowly in agreement and leads them around the building to the small generator.

"Will you guys be okay to get started now?" Abe asks.

"If we need anything more, we'll let you know," Abe swings his way back over to the patio table and pulls out his cell phone.

Being out of the city, Abe calls the overall island constabulary. After being transferred to the duty sergeant, Abe describes the situation. He's told an officer will be dispatched and should be there within the half hour. Abe returns to the patio table and sets down to wait. Ten minutes pass before a black late model island police vehicle pulls up the driveway leading to the garage shed. Abe recognizes the uniformed man exiting the vehicle as Jack Druce, a frequent customer of Abe's.

"Morning Abe," Jacks says. "Mind showing me what you called about?"

Abe leads the policeman to the garage and the Morris.

"Somebody really did a number on your car," Jack says after first glance at the damage. "That's a damned shame. There aren't many Morrises like this one around anymore."

After taking a good look at the lock hasp which has been pried from the garage door, the policeman asks, "When was the last time you saw the car before today?"

Abe explains, "I've not been able to use the car for almost a month due to my fractured ankle. However, as this garage is used as a storage shed, I'm sure someone would have noticed the damage and lock being broken much sooner."

"I'm going to take a look around now," Jack says. "Would you be able to try to find out who was in here last?"

"I'll do my best," Abe says as he heads back toward the patio table.

He sees Beth coming down the lawn from the house.

"What's going on, Abe?" Beth asks pointing toward the storage shed.

"Hugh's men are here to install that surveillance system he told us about," Abe says hoping to buy some time.

"I mean with the police car?"

Abe knows that his time to keep Beth in the dark about what has been going on with Reggie and the Sylvester Bros has reached its practical limit.

"Sit down," Abe instructs Beth, "this may take a while."

"Start with the police car."

"Somebody broke into the shed and smashed the bejesus out of the Morris. Taillights, headlights, all the window glass, big dents on the fenders and trunk."

"I was just in the shed yesterday morning to get some cleaning supplies for the counter area," Beth observes. "The Morris was just fine then. Who would do something like this?"

"I've got my suspicions," Abe says. "You know Reggie and those Halifax thugs have been after me to sell them the liquor license. What you don't know is that they have been after me to sell both properties. They've offered $3.5 million for them."

Beth studies Abe for a moment before asking, "So you were thinking about selling?"

"I wouldn't sell that lot the time of day," Abe says in disgust. "You know that I've been toying with the idea of selling or leasing the business if I could talk you into going back to pursuing your education," Abe said. "I have absolutely no intention of selling the house."

"You went to them?"

"I did not," Abe says firmly.

"You aren't thinking about selling out to those bastards now are you, Abe?" Beth asks with the fire rising in her eyes.

"Not unless that is what you want to do," Abe replies. "Reggie made an offer when he was out here a month or so ago. He's had his lawyer calling me about it since then. When he did his benefit, Reggie made another offer and some type of vague threat. His lawyer called me on Tuesday to reinforce it. Earlier this month, I had pretty much decided that if the business is sold, it will be strictly your decision. Didn't want to tell you about it until I figured out how to push Reggie and his backers away."

"I'd sooner burn in hell for all eternity," Beth responds. "Why did we let those lowlifes have that event out here. They must think they can push us around anyway that they want."

"The benefit was for a good cause," Abe says firmly. "It's also given us a chance to see their true colors."

"You think they had the Morris smashed?"

"Among other things," Abe replies lowering his head.

Saturday when Miss Vicky had brought Riley V's remains out to Abe's, she had told him that it was doubtful the dog had been struck by a car. Her opinion, just as Abe's had been, was that someone had struck Riley repeatedly with a metal object.

"Riley?"

Abe nods his head affirmatively.

Beth thinks over the situation for a few moments before asking, "What are we going to do?"

"Same thing our family has always done," Abe says, "fight back."

Jack Druce appears from out of the garage area. After exchanging pleasantries with Beth, he says, "Whoever damaged your car didn't leave behind any apparent evidence."

Beth relates that Morris was intact yesterday morning.

"You don't have any disgruntled employees or ex-employees, do you Miss?" the police officer asks.

Beth shakes her head before say, "Abe, I think you need to tell Mr. Druce what you just told me."

Abe relates his dealings with Reggie and the Sylvester Bros as well as Reggie V's untimely death to the police officer.

"You don't' think that what's happened to your leg has anything to do with it?" Jack Druce asks.

Abe looks at Beth and both raise their eyebrows.

"Not that I know," Abe says.

"I am going to secure your garage as a crime scene for at least the next few days," the policeman states. "If there is anything you absolutely must have out of there, I will help you get it now."

"I think we'll be okay not being able to get in there for a while," Beth says.

"Okay then," the policeman replies, "I'm going to go back to the center and file my report. There, very likely, will be a few detectives coming out here in the next few days to take a closer look."

"Thanks so much, Officer Druce," Beth says.

"Thanks Jack," Abe adds as the policeman disappears back into his vehicle.

"Could you drive me somewhere?" Abe asks Beth.

After giving her grandfather a quizzical look, she says, "Sure."

"Let me go see if Hugh's guys need anything and then we'll go," Abe says as he rises and walks toward Sam who is working on the light tower behind the storage shed.

"I've got to make a couple trips," Abe tells the technician. "Is there anything that I can get you before I go?"

"Just your WIFI access information," the technician replies, picking up a clipboard with instruction information to be filled out and pointing Abe toward it.

Abe carries the clipboard over to Beth to be filled out. Once complete, he uses the pen to write down his and Beth's cell phone numbers in the margin.

"Call me if you need anything else," Abe says, "We won't be more than ten minutes away."

"Will do," Sam says returning to his installation.

"Van or bug?" Beth asks.

"Let's take your beast," Abe decides.

Beth holds on to Abe's left arm gently as he hobbles across the patio, up the slight grassy incline on to the paved rear portion of the driveway and up to where Beth's car is parked at the rear of the house's patio.

"Where to?" Beth asks as she starts up the engine.

"The old government center," Abe says.

Beth gives him a quizzical look before steering her vehicle down the front side of the driveway and onto the road leading up to the Castle and old government center.

Only three cars are parked in the center's old parking lot. As they are parked closed to the trail up the mountain, Abe assumes they are cars of hikers.

After the takeover of the castle which had been orchestrated by Hugo and Alice, the civilian elected government had chosen to tear down the front facing area of the castle and begin building the government center on to it. The castle had been built of primarily stone slabs taken from the nearby quarry. The government buildings where primarily stone and cement. It was indeed an odd structure.

"Drive right up to the main entrance and park as close as you can get to the steps," Abe instructs Beth.

Beth positions her car as Abe has requested. She then helps Abe out and up the granite steps to the main entrance which has been chained shut. The pair spend the next thirty minutes peering through windows at empty rooms and vacant spaces. They walk completely around the building past the thick rear walls which their ancestors had constructed.

"Any particular thing you are looking for in there, Abe?" Beth asks.

"Just want us to get a feel for what shape this facility is in and how big it actually is," Abe says. "Would you mind driving up the pathway to the old quarry?"

After reentering the Beetle, Beth turns the car around and goes down what looks to be an unused, one lane gravel road for about a third of mile. She stops in front of the entrance to the quarry which is closed off by large metal barricades with large "No Trespassing" signs posted everywhere.

"Haven't been out here since I was in high school," Beth says. "The kids used to come here and throw kegger parties until the Constabulary would run us off."

The quarry is cut into the side of the mountain in opened ended rectangular formation. The sides being wider than the back end which is cut into the granite. The sides appear to be about 250 feet long with the west side slightly longer than the east. The back is probably 175 feet wide. The granite sides of the walls range from 3 to 50 feet high as the quarry goes further back into the mountain.

"How many people do you think could fit into that quarry?" Abe asks.

Beth gives him a quizzical look, before saying, "I've seen at least 400 high school kids out here and that didn't even fill a third of it."

Abe takes a mental survey of the grassy areas outside of the actual quarry before he begins to stroll back toward Beth's car.

"What are you thinking, Abe?"

Abe opens the passenger door and cautiously climbs into Beth's car. He waits for Beth to climb in before saying, "I think that we might want to consider buying this place."

Not the Same

Wednesday afternoon just a little past 11 AM. Abe sits in his desk chair in the studio just to the left of Molly, who is explaining the dashboard to the Zack Tillerman website.

"This button takes us to how many computer users have viewed our website," Molly explains. "The view also shows how many clicks have occurred on our website."

Molly points to two different rows of statistics on the display.

"I think we'll leave that all up to you for the time being," Abe says. "The only real question I have is whether or not we are starting to make any money from what we are putting up on the internet?"

"Actually we are," Molly says. "More than I thought we might at this point."

Molly makes a couple of clicks, then points to a listing of sales from the website. She and Zack had decided that the ten singles which had been recorded the weekend before last would, were priced individually at $1.29. The entire catalog of the ten songs which Zack was hesitant to call an album at this point, may be bought for $8.99.

"So far we have sold $1,643.69 worth of recordings," Molly says pointing to the total sales figure. "Costs for the bank and credit card services as well as internet bandwidth fees reduce our profit from the website to $1,344.15."

"So you've sold 83 copies of Zack's catalog?" Abe says point toward the catalogue figure.

Molly nods her head in the affirmative.

"Where do you think most of these sales are coming from?" Abe asks Molly.

"My guess would be most are coming from kids down at the Wannasea Extension," Molly replies. "Zack has become rather popular down there."

Abe also notices that *Not the Same* and *This Side of Nowhere* lead the single recording sales. *Not the Same* doesn't surprise Abe, *Nowhere* does.

"Zack is also starting to take off a little on You Tube," Molly adds. "We kind of messed up by not putting anything into the recordings to point to the website or podcast, but Dave is helping us fix that."

"Any feedback from the podcast?" Abe asks as he pushes himself over to the table where his tablet lays.

Zack had made his first podcast the past Monday. Abe had dropped in to watch Zack and Dave handle the session. After spending an hour not understanding how it was any different from one of Zack's practice sessions, Abe had bid the pair goodnight.

"Won't be able to see anything there until the first part of next year," Molly says.

Abe tries to remember how long it had taken Janie and him to see any income from Reggie's first album. The album had been four months on the market before it began taking off. The sales seemed tied to the Mainland's sudden interest in local folk music. Abe thought it might have been at least eight months to a year more before they had actually received any income at all from their work.

Abe's cell phone rings displaying a number from the Mainland. Abe has been expecting the call.

Abe clicks to answer the call and says, "Abe Stolz," into the device.

"Mr. Stolz," the voice on the other end says, "this is Bill Graham from the Swansea District CID division. We are here to have the meeting which your constabulary told you about yesterday."

Abe had received a call from Jack Druce yesterday that a group of investigators would be coming out to meet with him today.

"Where are you parked?" Abe asks.

"In the parking area right behind your house," the detective says.

"I'll be right out to get you," Abe says.

Abe disconnects the call and pulls his jacket from the back of the desk chair. Abe picks up his crutch which has been leaned at the end of the table and before going through the sliding glass door on to the patio, says to Molly, "I have to meet with some investigators about the Morris. If you need anything give me a call."

"I'll give you a text," Molly asks with a bright smile. "Don't want to interrupt investigators."

"Okay," Abe says heading out the sliding glass doors.

He makes his way across the patio to an unfamiliar dark four door sedan which is parked beside Molly's Vespa scooter.

Two rather large men dressed in knee-length all-weather raincoats exit the vehicle. The men look to be in their late thirties. Both look to be very fit.

The man, who has come from the passenger side of the vehicle walks up to him with his hand extended, "Bill Graham."

Abe shakes the man's hand before he points to the car's driver and says, "John Steadman."

Abe shakes the hand of the second, slightly larger investigator.

"Could we go somewhere to talk?" Bill Graham asks.

"Would you like to go down to Abe's?" Abe suggests. "We can get something to drink and bite to eat there if you'd like."

"We prefer something a little more private," Bill Graham responds.

"Let's go over to my in-law suite, then," Abe suggests leading the way toward the rear entrance to his new residence.

The two investigators follow Abe inside and take seats at the small dining table after Abe points toward them.

"Would you like coffee, tea or water?" Abe asks.

"Wouldn't mind a spot of tea," Bill Graham replies.

"That will work for me as well," the other man says.

Abe goes to his electric kettle fills it and switches it on. As it is heating, Abe places a selection of teas, various sweeteners, three spoons and three cups on a tray. He carries them to the table and sets them down.

"It's really nice up here," John Steadman says. "How many years have you lived out here."

After a little mental calculation, Abe replies, "Going on 62 years now."

"Don't think I have ever met anyone who has stayed that long in one place," Bill Graham says.

As he waits for the water to boil, Abe explains to the officers how his mother had come to acquire the property.

"She once told me that the only way she was going to leave this mountain was dead or someone carrying her off the island. Said she bought up here so that she could see coming whomever might be interested in assisting either possibility."

The remark draws a laugh from the investigators.

Abe knows that his mother had not been making a joke when she said it.

Abe hobbles over to get the now steaming kettle. He notices a plate of cookies which Beth had brought to him earlier and sets those on the table as well.

After the three have poured their tea, Bill Graham says, "Looking out for what might be coming up this way is why we wanted to speak with you about."

Abe gives them a curious look.

"It's somewhat unusual for the Mainland CID to get involved out here," Abe comments, "isn't it?"

Bill Graham nods his head before saying, "These are unusual circumstances, we believe."

"We have heard that you have reason to believe that the Sylvester Bros. are behind the vandalism of your vehicle as well as several other possible incidents," John Steadman says.

"I cannot be certain," Abe replies, "but it seems oddly coincidental that bad things have begun to happen since they first became frustrated with my refusal to jump at their offer to buy this place."

"That's what we've heard," Bill Graham says. "The Sylvesters are not people to be trifled with. Is your intention to continue negotiating with them on the sale of this property?"

"My intention has never been to sell the property to them," Abe says. "I figured if I gave them a date out in the future, they'd eventually go away."

"But they haven't," John Steadman says, "have they?"

"Sadly no," Abe says, "Additionally I have begun to explore the possibility of joining with the Wannasea Historical Trust in the purchase of the old government center. My understanding is the Sylvester Bros. are actively working on trying to acquire that property as well."

The agents exchange glances before John Steadman says, "Does anyone associated with the Sylvesters know about your interest in that property?"

"The only people, who I have spoken to about such a possibility are Steven DeJean, my son, Hugh, and my granddaughter."

"How serious is your interest in that property?" Bill Graham asks.

"I am certain that I will work with the Historical Society at a minimum to help them acquire the property to serve as a museum," Abe says. "Lately we have also begun to think about Beth and I taking an active role in helping to create a performance arts center there."

"Our understanding is that bids for the property will not begin to be accepted until Jan. 21," Bill Graham states. "That's a little more than eight weeks off, so I assume you are thinking of formally having a plan and bid put together?"

"Was hoping to talk with the Historical Society about it this week," Abe says.

"Would you mind holding off on that effort until we get back to you," John Steadman says. "At this point, if the Sylvester Bros are indeed behind the incident in your garage and they find out about your interest in the old government center, it may drive them to even more rash actions."

"Okay," Abe says somewhat tentatively.

"I promise you that we will get back to you on this before Wednesday," Steadman states firmly.

"Both of us have been on the trail of the Sylvester Bros. for the past seven years," Bill Graham begins. "Recently we've put quite dent into their drug importing operation. We believe their interest in both your property and the former Wannasea Government Center may have something to do with that situation."

Abe looks at the two men curiously.

"We are not at liberty to discuss why we believe these two conditions are linked," Bill Graham continues. "Suffice it say that the fact this island remains a protectorate of the Mainland and beyond the normal bounds of the Mainland's law enforcement is a key part of their interest in moving out here?"

"Seems the Sylvesters have come to believe that if they move most of their operation out here," John Steadman says, "they will be able to operate with impunity."

"What more would you like from us?" Abe asks.

"First, we'd like to take steps to ensure that no one out here is in mortal danger," John Steadman says. "Secondly we'd like you to help us plant an CID agent at your business to keep an eye on things."

Abe thinks for a moment, before saying, "You've cleared this with the island government?"

"We have direct approval from the Governor," John Steadman says, "but only the Governor and two of his assistants are aware of this effort."

"I see," Abe says. "The only issue that I have here is that I really no longer have much of a hand in running the business. My granddaughter Beth handles almost everything down there."

"Would it be possible for us to speak with her?" John Steadman asks.

"Let's see," Abe says pulling the cell phone from his pocket.

"Would you mind coming up to the suite?" Abe asks Beth right after she answers. "I think it is rather important."

"Be up in a few minutes," Beth responds.

Abe disconnects the call and relates that Beth will be there shortly.

The men sip tea and begin crunching cookies.

"We understand that you have just had a new surveillance system installed," John Steadman remarks.

Abe explains that the system has been installed at Hugh's insistence.

"One of our best ex-electronics guys is part of the management team at Defense One," Bill Graham says. The conversation is cut short when Beth arrives through Abe's the sliding glass door.

After Abe makes the introductions, the two investigators explain their concern over physical safety leaving out the fact that they are from Mainland CID and have been on the trail of the Sylvester Bros. for seven years.

"Our agent would need to work in the dining area," John Steadman says.

"Most of our waitresses are from high school or the first few years of college," Beth says.

"The agent we are thinking of sending out here can certainly pass for being in that age group," John Steadman says.

Beth explains how many of the waitresses are also residents in the house.

"Most don't have good situations in their own homes," Beth adds.

The two investigators exchange looks, before Bill Graham says to the other investigator, "This may work out better than planned. We can have Jill come up with some type of cover story. Being out here full-time will certainly make things easier for her."

"She can move into Marie's room," Beth says. "How soon can I expect her?"

"My guess would be Monday," Bill Graham replies. "Will have her give you a call to confirm. Would you mind passing us your cell number?"

Beth rises and goes into kitchen to pull a sheet of paper off the notepad hung on the refrigerator. John Steadman pulls out two business cards and a pen. He writes an additional number on each card.

"The handwritten number is the number from which our agent will be calling you," Steadman says. "The printed numbers are how to contact us directly at any time, day or night."

"Speaking of cell phones," John Steadman asks, "would you be able to give us a list of times and dates of calls from Bernie Fuller?"

Abe pulls out his cell phone and brings up his recent calls, before handing the device over to the agent, who pulls out a tablet and begins entering information as he goes through the call list.

"If you receive any more calls from Mr. Fuller or anyone else associated with the Sylvesters," Bill Graham says, "please don't answer. Either call us or bring it to the attention of the agent, who will be placed here."

"One other not so minor consideration," Bill Graham says, "we have found that in addition to your car being smashed in the garage, someone has injected toxic substances into at least two of the bags of sugar and flour which were stored there."

"What should we do about it?" Beth asks with genuine concern rising in her voice.

"Nothing at the moment," Graham says. "We have removed the two bags which we know are contaminated. Once we have released the garage back to you, we'd suggest destroying everything you've stored there."

"Additionally," John Steadman adds, "we suggest you find somewhere more secure inside your business to try to store such supplies. We would also very much encourage you to make certain that only your staff has access to your supplies. We also very strongly suggest that you take great care to make certain that all areas of your business and this house are locked whenever that is possible."

"If you have anything else come up which you think may interest us in regard to the Sylvesters, please call me," Bill Graham says rising from the chair and beginning to move toward the sliding glass door.

"Thanks so much for your help and your hospitality," John Steadman adds as the pair leave.

"That was somewhat frightening," Beth says to her grandfather.

Abe takes Beth's hand and squeezes it, before saying, "We are going to need to be very careful."

Losing Power

Friday evening, 7:15 PM. Abe sits at the in-law suites kitchen table looking over drawings of the layout of the old Wannasea Government Center which he has been able to pull from the Wannasea Island government website. Abe's particular focus is the small auditorium which will seat up to 150 people. Historically the auditorium had been used for public meetings.

Wish it wasn't so small, Abe thinks. *If we could expand it by a hundred seats or see, it would be a nice venue for plays, music and whatever else will make enough to keep the place running.*

The lights flicker for a moment and go out. Realizing that he does not know where candles or other such supplies might be in his new residence, Abe fishes for is cell phone on top of the table in the darkness. Finding it, he slides his finger to open the device then uses it as a light to guide him out the sliding door. Abe goes around the corner of his suite and sees that except for the emergency lighting, the lights down at 'The Place' are out also.

Except in the most severe storms, power outages are rare on the island. Wiring is underground. The electrical source from the lakes and generators located there have been stable for at least the past twenty years.

Abe hobbles up the rise at the back of the house to the road leading up toward the government center and down toward the village. He looks down toward the village. He can see lights at a distance he estimates to be a mile down road. Everything back up the mountain is dark.

Abe hobbles back down to the patio and sits in the aluminum chair which gives him the best view toward the mountain. The night is essentially cloudless. Abe leans back and studies the stars which glide by. Abe drifts into a half-sleep, half astronomical observance mode for the next 30 minutes until his cell phone rings. It's Beth.

"What's up, Kitten?"

"I've called the electric company," Beth says. "They are saying, they think a transformer down by West Road intersection has gone out. They won't know for at least two hours if it can be fixed. If it has to be replaced, we may be without power for a couple days."

"Would you be able to tell me where I can find some candles?" Abe asks.

"Forget candles," Beth advises. "We are going to start closing up down here and sending everyone home. As soon as I have that organized, I will come up and bring you a couple battery powered lanterns."

"Sounds good," Abe says.

"Maybe you ought to give our investigator friends a call about this?" Beth suggests.

"Will do," Abe replies. "See you when you get here."

Abe pulls his wallet out of his pocket, locates the card which John Steadman has given him and using the bright moonlight dials the off-hours number.

A voice which Abe doesn't think is John Steadman's answers, "CID Special Investigations."

"This is Abe Stolz," Abe says into his phone. "John Steadman asked me to call this number if anything unusual came up out here."

"I'll try my best to help you if I can Mr. Stolz," the voice on the other end of the call says. "What seems to be the issue?"

"We've lost power out here," Abe says. "It may be nothing but as we were instructed to call about anything unusual, I thought it best to let you know."

"How long has the power been out?"

"About 40 minutes now," Abe relates. "We are being told it may be anywhere from two hours to two days until it is able to be restored."

"Are power outages rare there?"

"I cannot remember one happening for the past ten years and that was during a hurricane," Abe says.

"I see," said the voice. "I think it was a good idea for you to call. We will investigate to see if it has anything to do with our investigation. If anything else odds happens, please don't hesitate to call us back."

"Thanks," Abe says as the call is disconnected from the other end.

Abe sits in silence for another few minutes until he hears Beth pulling up the driveway in her Beetle. Abe rises and walks toward the car. Beth, who is carrying two battery powered lanterns intersects Abe and the pair walk into Abe's suite.

As Beth turns on one of the lanterns, Abe sits back down at the table where Beth joins him after turning on the other lantern and setting it on the side table in the front room.

"Pretty much cleared out down there?" Abe asks.

"Most customers left after the first twenty minutes without power," Beth replies. "It will probably be another 45 minutes or so until everything is cleaned up so that I can go back down to lock up. Did you call our friends?"

"I did," Abe said. "Wasn't either one of the agents which was out here, who answered. They said they'd look into the power outage."

"Let's hope this is just a power company glitch," Beth comments.

"If you aren't really needed down there," Abe asks of Beth, "why don't you sit with me a little bit and I'll explain about my interest in the old government center."

"Marie and Sally pretty much have things under control," Beth says. "What are you thinking?"

Abe relates the discussions that he and Hugh had with Steven DeJean in addition to the instructions from the CID agents.

"Your interest is now more than just in the museum?" Beth asks.

"I'd like it to be," Abe says, "but I also might be willing to help my granddaughter turn the place into a first-class entertainment venue for this island."

Beth wrinkles her brow and says, "What would we do with Abe's?"

"Don't know," Abe says. "Whoever ends up owning that building if they turn it into a performing arts center, will, at a very minimum, cut into Abe's business."

"Fair point."

"I think if it can be expanded in size, the auditorium would make a cozy little venue," Abe says. "There is also plenty of other areas for a great kitchen and eating space."

"Actually might be too much space. Are you just thinking of doing this because you are pissed off at Reggie and the Sylvesters?"

"Won't say that isn't what drove my first reaction," Abe says, "but the more I have thought about it, the more sense it's beginning to make to me."

Beth fiddles with the lantern and thinks for a moment before saying, "We are getting awfully crowded in the summers at Abe's. If the crowds keep coming out to hear Zack, like they were on Wednesday and Thursday, I'm not sure we will be able to accommodate them for long. 'The Place' also isn't really set up well to be able to deal with cover charges as we learned from the Reggie fiasco. Fairly certain cover charge is where we are headed with Zack."

"The only variable there is how long Zack is going to be willing to stay with us."

"I'm not sure Zack is a big worry in that regard," Beth says. "Any idea what it might cost for us to purchase the whole facility up there?"

"If we go in with the Historical Society," Abe says, "I'm thinking that I'm going to have to come up with $1.5 million for the real estate and updates plus another $500k as a cushion for operating expenses."

"Have you got that much?"

"I do and I can afford to put it at risk," Abe says. "There is another option however that's gradually been creeping into my mind."

"What's that."

"Buying the entire property, selling the castle portion to the Historical Society," Abe relates. "We would still use the old government center for a food, beverage as well as an entertainment venue."

"You can afford what that would cost?"

"Not only can't I afford to do that on my own," Abe says, "at my age, there isn't one chance in a trillion that I have the energy to pull it together."

"So, who were you thinking might be able to help make all this happen?"

"You."

Mindy

Sunday afternoon, 3:05 PM. Abe and Beth are sitting at the table in Abe's suite awaiting the arrival of the CID agent, who had phoned Beth just after lunch to coordinate the start of her assignment at 'The Place.' Power had finally been restored at a little after 10 this morning. 'The Place' had essentially been closed since Friday evening. Beth and the staff had made the best of the unexpected down time, having decorated both 'The Place' and the house for the holiday. Beth had made a trip to the Halifax and purchased both new decorations and lights. All of the girls, who lived and the house plus Zack and Marie's two brothers had spent the past two days making both properties more festive than they have been in the years since Janie and Julia disappeared.

"Have you decided what to do about the Morris?" Beth asks her grandfather.

Saturday morning, after having been given the all clear by Jack Druce to return to use of the garage, Abe had taken some pictures, swept up all the glass metal and plastic, taken some more pictures then with Beth's help had sent those images off to a specialty auto body repair shop in Swansea which Hugh had recommended. Abe had been somewhat surprised when the shop had told him that their estimate was between $10,000–12,000 for full restoration. The shop couldn't make a full determination on cost until the Morris was at their shop. As Abe had not bothered to carry anything other than liability and personal injury insurance on the vehicle since he downgraded his coverage almost thirty-five years back, he was on the hook for the entire amount.

"I'm kind of torn," Abe replies. "On one hand, I am so used to that car, it is almost like a part of my body. On the other, I know that it is old, hard to keep running and no longer is really safe."

"Why don't you just have it fixed up and keep it as collectible," Beth suggests. "You can buy yourself another car for normal use once you are out of your walking cast. You could even buy that red convertible if you wanted."

Abe laughs before saying, "I've got a few days to think on it because that repair shop is so backed up with work, they can't take on anything before the week after next."

A light wrap on the sliding glass door interrupts them. Beth opens the door to young lady in a motorcycle helmet and black leather jacket with silver stripes. She is carrying a large leather duffle bag.

As the young woman removes her helmet, Abe thinks, *Those CID agents certainly weren't exaggerating when they said the agent could pass for someone in their late teens.*

The agent unzips her jacket and hands it to Beth, who places it upon the kitchen table. As she does so, Abe gets another surprise. The agent looks very much like Julia. This unsettles Abe.

Beth offers the woman a seat at the table and introduces her grandfather. Abe takes a moment to clear the connection with his memory of Julia from his mind and stretching out his hand, says "Abe Stolz."

"Very glad to meet you Mr. Stolz," the agent says taking his hand and shaking it firmly. "While I'm on this assignment, I will be known as Mindy Prosser. As I have discussed with Beth, the cover story for my being here is a serious falling out with my family over in North Halifax. Beth will say that she has known me from previous meetings at the SuperMax over on the Mainland. After I unburdened myself to Beth, she offered me a job and a place to stay out here."

Such an arrangement would not be abnormal. What the agent has just described was close to being the prime reason for many of the people working or living at 'The Place.' It was a tradition which Abe's mother had started.

"Seems easy enough for us to remember," Beth says. "Doesn't it Abe?"

Abe nods his head in agreement.

"I will try to blend in as normally as I can here and at your place of business," Mindy says. "There will however need to be some considerations which will allow me to fulfill my actual mission. I will need somewhere to store for my use a few communications and surveillance devices which I have brought along with me. I'd also like part of my role to be something which gets me away from the business whenever needed."

Beth thinks for a moment before suggesting, "In addition to waitressing, why don't you take over the role as our van driver? Sallie, our cook, has been saying that she's spending too much time running errands. You can also use it to drive Abe around, who still likely will not be able to drive for the next month or so."

"Sounds good," the agent agrees.

"Could Mindy store what she needs to use up in upstairs space here, Abe?" Beth asks.

In the suite's front room, there is stairway to a second floor which has remained untouched since being refinished for Becca. Becca had used the space as an office and storage area. All of Becca's old furniture was still up there.

"Works for me," Abe replies.

"Good," the agent says. "The ground rules are that none of the three of us are to discuss anything related to this investigation anywhere other than here and only when just the three of us are present."

Abe and Beth nod their heads.

"When something comes up, I'll arrange some excuse for us to meet," the agent continues. "When I need to go somewhere on CID business, I will ask Beth to make an excuse for my absence. Other than that, please try to forget that I am an agent and treat me just as you would any other person living or working here."

"We will," Beth promises.

The agent unzips her duffle bag and pulls out a smaller gym sized bag with a lock on it.

"This is what I need to store here," the agent says.

"Follow me," Beth instructs Mindy as she heads for the front room and the stairs to the attic area.

Abe hobbles over to the kitchen sink area, fills up the electric kettle and switches it on. He stands by the counter waiting for it to boil as the two young women come back down the stairs.

"Would you like some tea or coffee?" Abe asks Mindy.

"Tea would be great," Mindy replies. "Originally we were planning on starting this assignment on Monday. Due to the results of the findings on your power problem, I was instructed, just before I spoke with Beth, to get out here as soon as I could. As I had to come from about 30 miles west of Swansea, haven't had time for anything but the trip."

"I can fix you something if you'd like," Abe offers impulsively. "I can do eggs, waffles, bacon or a sandwich if you'd like?"

"Anything that's easy," Mindy says.

"Why don't you let me do the cooking, Gramps?" Beth instructs as she moves to the refrigerator. "You can do the tea, this time."

As Beth closes the door with supplies in hand, she asks the agent, "What were your findings from the power problem?"

"Someone blew up the transformer located at the first intersection going toward Wannasea village," Mindy replies taking a seat at the table.

"Blew it up?" Abe says with raised eyebrows.

"Blew it up with a small M112 demolition block," Mindy says.

"What's that?" Abe asks.

"Not something anyone is going to buy at their local hardware store," Mindy replies.

Reggie Unsolicited

Wednesday afternoon, 6:57 PM. The dining tables at 'The Place' are full. Zack is getting ready for his first set. Quite a few people wait in line at the counter. Abe sits alone at the table at the far end of the stage, fiddling with his tablet. Abe hears a commotion coming from the direction of the entrance.

"I'm just going to sit with my good friend," Reggie Reginald announces to Marie, who is trying to push Reggie back into the queue but is prevented from doing so by the two burly men which Reggie has with him.

Reggie marches across the dining room area and pulls an empty chair out from the end of Abe's table.

"Why don't you guys go get yourself something to drink," Reggie tells his two companions. "Then go out and keep an eye out on my car. I've heard bad things are happening to cars out here."

"Don't remember sending you an invite, Alf," Abe says as Reggie sits down in the chair.

"Abe," Reggie says with a broad smile, "we are old friends. Do old friends ever need invites?"

Abe shakes his head more to himself than Reggie as Mindy approaches the table.

"Is there something I can get for you or your friend?" Mindy asks.

"You certainly have improved the quality of your wait staff," Reggie says to Abe as he performs a visual assessment of Mindy. "I'd like a decaf latte with almond milk. If it's not too much bother."

"Anything for you Mr. Stolz?" Mindy asks.

Abe shakes his head negatively as Mindy disappears back toward the bar.

"I'm surprised that you haven't called Bernie," Reggie says to Abe.

"Not until January, Alf."

"That's going to cost you money, Abe."

"I'll deal with that when the time comes."

Abe rises to go to the stage to do the introduction for Zack but Reggie leaps from his chair and puts a hand on Abe's right forearm attempting to stop Abe from going forward.

"Let me do the intro," Reggie says. "You look like you could use a rest."

Abe, who is at least four inches taller and thirty pounds heavier than Reggie, knows that even with a bum leg, he can force Reggie out of his path. Deciding that he'd rather find out exactly what it is that Reggie is up to, Abe sits back down in his seat.

Reggie marches toward the stage. Says something to Zack, then moves to the microphone, "Welcome, Welcome friends. I'm going to give you a special treat tonight by doing a few vocals with our young singer/songwriter here."

Reggie pulls the microphone up on the stage before continuing, "We are going to start off with *The Kingdom of Wannasea*."

Polite applause. Abe does a quick survey and estimates that most of the crowd is Zack's age. The Reggiephiles are few and far between this evening.

Zack breaks into the song. Reggie sings along on the stanzas. Abe doesn't think Reggie's singing adds anything to the quality. Zack follows that up with *Hugo Flies*. Reggie seems a little better when he comes in on the stanzas but it is marginal. Zack then goes into *Not the Same*. To Abe utter amazement, Reggie tries to harmonize the song with Zack. Abe won't say that it is a total failure but it certainly isn't as good as having Zack perform the song by himself. At the end of the song, Reggie says a few words to Zack then comes back to Abe's table.

Reggie takes a few sips of the coffee which Mindy has delivered, as Zack breaks into a solo rendition of the song. The crowd now begins singing along. Zack does *Hard Rain* and *Sundown* as the audience continues to pick up their applause level. He finishes out the set with *Hard Case*.

"Your kid is pretty good," Reggie says downing the last of his coffee.

Reggie rises from his chair and says to Abe as he walks toward the stage, "Don't wait long to call Bernie, Abe. My associates are getting very, very impatient."

"January, Alf."

Reggie has a brief conversation with Zack before he signaling to one of his large companions to escort him out the door. Reggie stops and tries to chat at few of the tables, but most of this crowd has no interest in him. Abe watches Reggie sign one autograph for a lady, who appears to be in her sixties. Unable to find anymore takers, Reggie and his escort head out the large main entrance doors.

As Reggie is making his exit, Mindy swoops to the table takes Reggie's coffee cup into her possession then calmly walks back past the stage and out the exit by the kitchen.

Abe watches Zack finishing up taking requests. Zack is only able to get through half the cue before he tells them that he has enough for this set. Before Zack starts again, he comes off the stage and walks over to Abe's table.

"Your friend just offered me the opportunity to be his opening act for a tour that he is going to be doing next month in Eastern Europe," Zack tells Abe.

"Are you going to think about doing it?"

"No," Zack says. "I told him that he'd have to talk to my partners. When I told him who my two partners are, he didn't seem very happy with the answer."

Different Direction

Monday, 11:40 AM. Abe is seated at his desk in the studio with Molly in front of the new All-in-1 computer which they had purchased for Zack Tillerman LLC last Thursday. Zack is on the piano bench leafing through one of Abe's oldest journals.

"We are up to almost $2,400 of net profit from our website," Molly tells Abe. "Of course, our company is still a little over $3,000 in the red if we factor in what we have spent so far in start-up costs."

"I'm hoping we can begin showing a profit soon," Zack comments from across the room. "I'd really like to increase the money that I'm paying Abe back for my car. Don't like owing anyone money. Not even Abe."

"When can we take the money out of the website and put it into our bank account?" Abe asks.

"The money is frozen for six days by the credit card companies, banks and internet service firms," Molly advises. "Anything that's been in there for more than six days we can take out."

"Shouldn't we do that?" Abe suggests.

"It probably would be a good idea to start," Molly replies.

"Why don't we set a day each week for doing that?" Abe suggests.

"I vote Monday," Zack says, "because all three of us are usually here on Mondays."

"Sounds good to me," Molly agrees as Abe nods his head.

Zack rises from the piano bench and carries the journal over to Abe. He points to a set of lyrics which Janie and Abe had turned into a song more than forty-five years ago.

"What's this, Abe?" Zack asks.

"It's a set of lyrics which I wrote thinking they might be used for Reggie's second album," Abe explains. "Reggie didn't like them so they never really went anywhere."

"Do they belong to Reggie?" Zack asks.

"Fortunately, none of the songwriting which Janie and I wrote belongs to Reggie," Abe says. "We have an agent over on the Mainland, who handles the copyrighted songs which we produced during that period."

"Was this one copyrighted?" Zack asks.

Abe looks at a page entitled, 'The Pilot' with a lot of scribbles in the margins. He goes to the rear of the journal, thumbs through a grouping of pages of finished songs, finds the right one and hands it to Zack.

"Nope," Abe says. "I don't think Reggie did more than glance at this one."

"It looks like a sea song," Zack says.

"More or less," Abe replies somewhat surprised Zack knows about sea songs. "Janie and I felt that what made Reggie's first album sell was his audience's ability to easily remember the lyrics and sing along. Sea songs are pretty much a natural for that sort of thing. How do you know about sea songs?"

"It's the first songs that I learned with Dad and my uncle," Zack replies. "First songs that I could sing. First songs that my dad taught me to play on the fiddle."

"You are thinking that you may want to do this one?" Abe asks.

"If you could kind of change it around so it would be about the tillerman instead of the pilot, I think it would be worth a try," Zack suggests.

Abe studies what's written on the page in his journal for a few minutes. It's a song about impressed sailors. Many of this island's original residents had been impressed sailors at some point in their lives. Abe's study of those lives had driven the writing of the words.

"I can give it a try," Abe says to Zack.

Abe rolls himself away from the desk to the table then swipes on his tablet. Abe spreads out the journal and begins typing.

"What about our accounting review?" Molly asks Abe.

"We trust you," Abe says. "Just go on by yourself and pretend I'm paying attention."

"You'll trust me until I run off with all your money," Molly mutters.

"We know you wouldn't do that," Zack interjects.

Molly shakes her head as Abe returns to his work on the lyrics. After 30 minutes, he prints out what he has and hands it to Zack.

"See if you can put music to this," Abe says.

Zack takes the printed sheets, picks up his guitar, goes back to the piano bench. Referencing the song as originally written by Janie and Abe which he has also placed on the piano stand, Zack begins strumming his guitar. Zack stops and writes musical notes above the words on the printed pages which Abe has given him. Zack continues to play and write various notes in increasingly faster increments.

Abe remains at the table going through the journal and the finished songs at the back, placing notes into his tablet as he goes. After 40 minutes, Zack rises and says, "Listen to this."

Comes the Tillerman – 97BPM tempo – Emajor key – 2/2 time
(Sea song)

totally against me own accord
knocked me out and placed me aboard
a ship headed straight to sea
a ship called 'Wrath of the Marquis'

liquored me up, took me down
pull me 'pressed boy, pull
soon the tillerman will bring us rum
and steer us off to kingdom come

unbound eight miles from shore
I'll do me share or live no more
cursed the fate as an oath I swore
to bring these brigands down

soon the tillerman will bring us rum
and steer us away to kingdom come
beyond slippery decks and toward the sun
we'll pull our weight 'til the day be done

three long years their yolk I wore
learning every trick doing every chore
doing what I could but nothing more
joining the crew when they drank and sang

pull me 'pressed boy, pull
soon the tillerman will bring us rum
and steer us off to kingdom come
beyond slippery decks and toward the sun
we'll pull our weight till the day be done

was no dimming of desire to be free
as we sailed upon e'er changing sea
in the press gang of 'Wrath of the Marquis'
was fifteen of the King's ships we took down

pull me 'pressed boy, pull
soon the tillerman will bring us rum
and steer us off to kingdom come
beyond slippery decks and toward the sun
we'll pull our weight 'til the day is done

totally against me own accord
knocked me out and placed me aboard
a ship headed straight to sea
a ship called 'The Wrath of the Marquis'

liquored me up, they took me down
pull me 'pressed boy, pull
soon the tillerman will bring us rum
and steer us off to kingdom come

for three long days and four terrible nights
we rode the storm of the century's heights
six men lost fightin' their very last fights
even that wretched cap'n could be heard to sing

pull me 'pressed boy, pull
soon the tillerman will bring us rum
and steer us straight to kingdom come
beyond slippery decks and toward the sun

we'll pull our weight till the day be done

sixty foot wave came up and we went down
down into the depths below Neptune's crown
down to where humans all drown
past any attempt at rising
pull me 'pressed boy, pull

soon the tillerman will bring us rum
and steer us off to kingdom come
beyond slippery decks and toward the sun
we'll pull our weight til that day has come

was drug "board a ship put out to sea"
a ship called 'Wrath of the Marquis'
liquored me up, they took me down
pull me 'pressed boys, pull
soon the tillerman will bring us rum
and steer us off to kingdom come
beyond slippery decks and toward the sun
we'll pull our weight till the day be done

pull me 'pressed boy, pull
soon the tillerman will bring us rum
and steer us off to kingdom come
beyond slippery decks and toward the sun
we pulled our weight till that day has come

 Zack has sung the song injecting a Wannasea accent into its flow full force. By the second stanza, Zack sounds as if he's been singing the song his entire life. Even Molly turns around from her accounting to listen.
 "What do you think?" Zack asks putting his guitar down.
 "It's a damn good sea song," Abe says. "Likely it will be a hit down at 'The Place,' but does anybody buy sea songs these days."
 "Only one way to find out," Molly says, "let's get it recorded and put up on the web."

Zack fishes through the recording equipment stacked in the corner and begins setting up the video recorder. Once complete, he plugs the noise cancelling microphone in front of the piano into it, sets the recorder on top of the piano and says to Molly, "Could you come over and get the recorder started when I tell you?"

"Give me a second," Molly requests, as she finishes up scanning in the printed sheets from 'Comes the Tillerman' in order to have them copyrighted.

Abe rises from his desk chair and hobbles over to the piano, "I'll do it."

Zack fiddles with guitar and the microphone height before nodding to Abe. Seeing the red record light is lit, Zack begins to play.

Zack and Abe are in the process of doing the third recording when Beth enters through the sliding glass door. As quietly as possible, Beth goes over to Abe's vacated chair and sits down to listen.

Once Zack has finished, Beth asks, "What was that?"

"That was my sea song," Zack says with obvious pride. "You like it?"

"It's very catchy," Beth says before switching subjects. "Abe, we need to have a little meeting over at your suite."

"You guys okay if I go?" Abe asks Zack and Molly.

"We'll hold down the fort, Abe," Molly replies as Zack returns to the process of judging the recordings on his tablet.

"We shouldn't be more than 45 minutes," Beth says leading the way out of the glass doors.

Once the glass door is closed and they are out of earshot of the studio, Abe asks, "We're meeting with Mindy?"

Beth nods her head, before adding "Plus another gentlemen. It's about our interest in buying the old government center."

"You guys just might be on to something with that song Zack just played," Beth says as she pulls back the sliding glass door to Abe's suite. "If nothing else, it will be a terrific singalong for down at 'The Place.'"

Abe follows Beth inside to see Mindy and a dark-skinned professionally dressed man, who looks to be in his fifties sitting on the couch. The man rises and extends his hand.

"Mr. Stolz," Mindy begins, "this is Eston Wright. Mr. Wright will be assisting in being both a cover for your interest in purchasing Wannasea's old government center as well as what we hope will be a distraction causing the Sylvester Bros to move their focus away from you for the time being. Mr.

Wright has a reputation as one of the top lawyers for development companies in the Swansea district."

Abe shakes the man's hand and goes over to office chair of his newly purchased desk.

"Our plan is to structure everything that you will do in regard to possible purchase of that property as having come from a group of investors in Dubai. I have a long history of working with such investors," Mr. Wright says. "I have spoken with both the Wannasea Historical Society and your son Hugh as interested parties. I would like to proceed with the both of you being so far in the background of the negotiations that no one will have any opportunity to know of your involvement."

"We are also going to start a very active campaign," Mindy injects, "of spreading the word both here and throughout the Mainland of the interest in the government center property by Mr. Wright and his investors. Is there anything which we have said so far which concerns you?"

"My grandfather and I have decided that we would like to be the primary purchasers of the old center," Beth says. "We hope to either sell back or lease the castle to the Historical Society. Currently we are in a position of being able to allocate at least $4 million between us to that effort."

"Excellent," Mr. Wright comments. "We can begin by working out how we will be able to move forward."

"I want to caution you," Mindy interjects, "I would like this to be the last time that you have any direct contact with Mr. Wright for the time being. I prefer that your discussion with him now be by phone when you are alone and in this suite. No email. No texts. Just voice."

"May I offer an alternative?" Abe suggests. "Might we be able to make Hugh our primary contact for negotiations and then work everything through Hugh making certain that no one else gains knowledge of our involvement?"

"It's possible," Mindy replies, "but I am going to have to clear it through CID first. Would you have any issues with that, Mr. Wright?"

"I cannot think of any," the lawyer replies. "I already have some other dealings with Hugh, so meeting with him wouldn't be seen as out of the ordinary."

"I should have an answer on this way of working in a few days," Mindy says. "Is there anything pressing in this matter which you'd like Mr. Wright to address in the interim while you have him in person?"

"My first concern would be to have architectural review done to determine whether or not it would be possible to expand the auditorium to hold anywhere between 400–500," Beth begins. "As the auditorium abuts that portion of the castle, which was used as second floor office space, would like to see if the expansion could be done in that direction offering 2–3 balconies. We would also like some information as to exactly what the government expects us to be submitted as far as plans. Finally, we would like clarification on whether or not the property which the old quarry resides is part of the package. Lastly, who will be paying for Mr. Wright's services?"

"Anything done by Mr. Wright will be paid by CID," Mindy replies. "As far as your other requests, let's wait until CID approves how this arrangement will work out in the future before Mr. Wright gives you that information."

Mindy waits a few moments, before saying, "So we are all good at this point?"

Abe, Beth and the lawyer nod their heads affirmatively.

"Beth, would you mind walking Mr. Wright out to his car?" Mindy asks.

"Not at all," Beth says rising from seat in the armchair on the other side of the couch.

Beth leads the lawyer out the sliding glass door toward his car which is parked just off the patio.

Mindy rises from the couch, walks across the room and goes up the stairs to place the call to CID.

Results

Thursday, 12:57 PM. Abe is seated at the table working on his tablet. Molly is at the desk in front of the new computer.

"Wow," Molly exclaims. "Abe, you've got to come see this."

Abe slides his chair over toward the desk and looks at a news article from the island's lone newspaper. The headline reads, "New star in the making at 'The Place'?" Abe scans through the five-paragraph article which is primarily about how Zack is catching the musical interests of those on the island under thirty. The review is full of superlatives about Zack performances, the new songs which he is doing and his practice of spending the last two sets mainly doing requests from the patrons.

"Wonder if Zack has seen it?" Abe asks.

"I just texted him the link," Molly replies. "That's got to be good for Zack's career, right?"

"Wouldn't see why not," Abe says. "Would you mind texting that link to Beth?"

"No problem," Molly replies reaching for her phone to fulfill the request.

Abe returns to working on re-writing another of the songs which had been rejected during Janie and his work on Reggie's 2nd album. Zack has performed "Comes the Tillerman" the last two evenings down at Abe's. The crowd has quickly gotten into singing along with the refrains. After a comment by Zack that he would like to begin doing less of Reggie's song, Abe is hoping sea songs can be created to fill that gap. Abe's s increasingly becoming convinced that the less Reggie Reginald there is on this island, the better it will be for everyone.

Mindy enters the sliding glass door carrying a tray filled with food. Zack is right behind her toting drinks and mail. Mail which he places on the table to the left of Abe.

Noticing the sun is out and it's warmer than normal, Abe suggests eating on the patio.

The four move out of the studio and to the aluminum table and chairs. Zack helps Mindy place the food and drinks and then pulls out her chair and seats himself in the chair to the left. Abe notices that this does not seem to be met with Molly's approval.

"Seems you've become a local star," Abe says to Zack as he begins unwrapping his sandwich.

"What's this?" Mindy asks.

"Zack has had a review in our local newspaper," Molly replies. "It's a quite good review."

"I'll text it to you," Zack tells Mindy which results in another disapproving look from Molly.

Once Zack has completed his transmission, Mindy picks up her cell phone and begins reading the review while munching on a BLT with avocado on thick grain bread.

"The review is quite good," Mindy says Zack putting her phone down. "I'm glad to see that they recognize your talent, Zack."

For the next fifteen minutes, the three younger participants engage in chatter about the goings on of the rest of Abe's employees. Abe is somewhat surprised that Mindy actually seems to be in the know about these things. Having finished his lunch, Abe puts his empty cup and plate back on the tray.

"Come see me before you go," Abe tells Zack, "I think I may have found another sea song for you."

Abe, his hobble now much less noticeable, rises and makes his way back into the studio. As he sits down in his chair, he notices that the mail which Zack has just delivered contains a large envelope from the DNA research company to which he had mailed the samples five weeks ago. Ignoring the rest of the mail, Abe opens the envelop to find instructions on how to examine the result online.

"You said you have another sea song for me," Zack says from behind Abe's chair.

Abe quickly pushes the instructions back into the envelop and hands Zack the three-sheet printout of the song he has renamed as *Shan't deceive her*. The original words had been written by Abe after he reviewed letters written by his grandfather during the war to his grandmother. Becca had granted him permission to study the letters as part of his historical research. What had struck Abe in reading the letters was how much Hugo, despite his love of flying, missed Alice.

After a quick perusal of what Abe has given him, Zack heads toward the door saying, "I'll take a look. We'll discuss before tonight's performance."

Abe waits until Zack is out the door before rising and pulling the large envelop from the table.

"I have a little personal business to which I need to attend," Abe informs Molly, who is still sitting at the patio table.

Molly nods her head as she continues texting.

Abe unlocks the sliding door to his suite, then goes over to the newly purchased small desk upon which his laptop resides. The laptop had been restored to his possession after Molly had completed extracting and cataloguing all the files it contained.

Abe pulls the instructions from the envelope. He creates his username and inputs the required information before he is able to go to the chart for Zack's information. Abe quickly reviews "the related by generations columns" and finds nothing related to Beth. Uncertain of how these matches work, Abe opens his own profile. Hugh and Beth are the first two entries listed as related directly by DNA. Abe opens Beth's results, above Hugh and his own name is the name Ephraim Cox.

Abe searches his memory. Ephraim Cox was the name of Reggie's younger brother. Abe had met him a couple times but did not think Eph ever been out here or anywhere near Julia. The last Abe had heard of Ephraim, he was making a career out of the Navy.

Suddenly Abe's blood begins to build toward a murderous boil.

"Reggie," Abe says aloud. "That damned Reggie!"

Suddenly Abe clearly understands why Julia refused to reveal who the father of her child was.

"Something wrong, Mr. Stolz?" Abe hears Mindy say from the bottom of the stairs.

"Family problems," Abe says feigning a weak smile.

"So Reggie Reginald is actually part of your family?" Mindy asks noticing the DNA envelop and screen which Abe had been viewing.

Abe stumbles for a few moments before responding, "It seems Reggie may very well be Beth's father."

Mindy walks to the chair at the other side of the desk and sits down.

"Are you absolutely certain, Mr. Stolz?" Mindy asks. "Claiming paternity is very serious business."

Abe explains to her what he is seeing on the screen and why he has deduced Reggie is Beth's father.

"That's still not one hundred percent certain," Mindy says. "I just so happen to have a DNA sample from Reggie Reginald which I collected last week as part of my investigation. Why don't you allow our DNA experts to do a more thorough research for you?"

"What information do you want?"

"Give me a minute," Mindy says as she disappears up the stairs and returns in less than 30 seconds carrying a device which Abe judges to be a laptop.

Mindy goes to Abe's computer and begins printing out documents to PDF which she transfers to the device.

"Promise me you won't do anything about your findings until you discussed it with me, Mr. Stolz," Mindy requests.

"If you'll promise me that you won't say a word about this to Beth."

"Deal."

Emma Receives a Visitor

Friday, 10:47 AM. Abe has been able to think of little else than his anger at Reggie since receipt of the DNA results. The only other emotion Abe has been able to entertain during this period is an aching remorse over having pushed Julia's best friend and her husband out of Julia's life after arbitrarily deciding Hank Jones had impregnated his daughter without evidence, Abe had forced Janie to no longer book 'the Tillers.' At the time, the dropping of the booking had not really been all that much of a surprise to the band. Along with the rest of island, Abe's main music fare had turned toward country and pop rock and away from the folk music bands like the Tiller's played. Abe had also requested his mother not to offer Prisha her old job back in the kitchen after she returned from giving birth to Zack's sister.

Yesterday evening, after discreetly telling Mindy that he'd like to talk with Prisha and receiving her approval, Abe had asked Zack to check with his mother whether she might agree to talk with him about Julia. After receiving Prisha's okay, Abe had called this morning to set a meeting time around 11.

Mindy, who was making a supply trip to the Mainland, offered to drop Abe off on the way to the ferry. Going so far as to suggest that Abe stop off to buy some flowers before Abe presented himself.

Mindy steers the van up the winding road and parks in front of the Jones's townhome.

"If it is after one, call me and I'll pick you up for the trip back to Abe's," Mindy says as Abe exits the van and walks up the two cement steps.

Abe is nervous as he uses the knocker in the center of the door to announce himself.

Prisha answers the door with her usual bright flashing eyes and wide smile, "Come in Mr. Stolz. We've been expecting you."

Abe hands Prisha the flowers then walks over the open threshold and has his right hand immediately seized by Zack's grandmother, Emma.

"You've come home, Eugene," the slight woman in the printed dress who looks to be in her eighties tells Abe. "I told her that you would."

Abe allows the old woman to lead him to a table in the dining room, where Prisha has set out tea.

"Zack said that you would like to talk with me about Julia," Prisha comments as Abe takes a chair with Emma seated right beside him. The old woman does not release Abe's hand.

"First I have something of a confession to make," Abe says.

Prisha looks at Abe curiously.

"After Julia became pregnant," Abe says, "I jumped to the incorrect conclusion that your husband was responsible. I had Janie no longer book your husband's band. When you returned from having your first child, I asked my mother not to rehire you. I cannot express to you how sorry I now am for those actions."

"Why on earth would you think Hank was responsible for Julia being pregnant?" Prisha asks.

"He always seemed to be around her at that time," Abe said.

"He was around her because I asked him to keep an eye on Julia to make sure she didn't do anything rash," Prisha says with an edge in her voice. "Julia was extremely emotional at the time and I was worried that she might harm herself or the baby. We had moved over to Halifax at the time and I was not able to be there to help her."

"I jumped to a conclusion to which I should not have jumped," Abe replies. "I should have come to you as I am doing now instead of reaching that unfounded conclusion."

Prisha studies Abe for a long minute. Emma still continuing to tightly hold on to Abe's hand.

"As a parent I can understand how you might overreact," Prisha finally says. "Why is it that you have decided at this time to talk with me about it."

"I learned through a DNA test earlier this week, that your husband could not be Beth's father."

"Mr. Stolz," Prisha begins, "in all honesty, you did not really push us away from Julia or cause much of anything to change. Hank and I had already moved to Halifax. Hank had decided that he was going to have to drop out of his brother's band due to his work requirements on the Mainland. I did not ask your mother for my old job back because I had decided it was just too much time away from the family to go out to Wannasea."

Abe remains silent with the old women continuing to cling to his hand and occasionally mumble, "Eugene, you've come home."

"I also saw Julia quite a bit back then," Prisha continues. "She used to come out and visit with me often. When the baby came, Julia usually brought her along."

"Did Julia ever confide in you, who Beth's father might be?"

"She did not," Prisha states. "From what I knew or gathered from watching Julia before she became pregnant, you likely were on the right track in thinking it was someone from one of the bands which were out there at the time. Which one however, I have no idea."

"Do you know why Julia was so insistent in not revealing Beth's father?"

"She simply wouldn't talk about it, other than to say that she had made a mistake and was going to try to make the best of it."

"I also have one other thing which I'd like to request," Abe says. "We usually have a party for the staff a day after Christmas. Along with current staff, we have an open invitation to all who have worked at 'The Place' over the years. Would you like to come if I can somehow arrange help with care of your mother-in-law?"

"I will need to discuss it with Hank."

"Does your husband still play the fiddle?"

Prisha looks at Abe curiously, then replies, "He does occasionally, though he isn't as good as he once was."

"Then I have a special request of your husband," Abe says. "Recently Zack has added some sea songs to his repertoire. He says playing sea songs with your husband and his uncle is how he learned to sing, play the fiddle and fall in love with music. I'm wondering if I send the sheet music for these new songs out to your husband, whether he might be interested in coming out and playing them with Zack as a Christmas treat. He can bring along his brother if he wants."

Prisha's eyes return to the normal brightness, "I'll talk with Hank about it tonight."

"Would you happen to have a sheet of paper so that I can leave my contact information so your husband can get in touch with me to confirm and send the music?"

"Give me a second," Prisha says as she disappears into the kitchen.

She returns with a sticky pad and pen.

As Abe writes down his phone number and email address, Prisha comments, "I haven't seen Emma this quiet for at least the past eighteen months."

"So, she's usually not this sedate?"

"Heavens no," Prisha says, "She's usually trying to run around the house and turn things upside down. That is when she isn't screaming about Eugene."

Abe rises, the old woman still holding on to his hand with him. She goes with him to the door.

"I have to go work now, Emma," Abe says as pries his hand from her clutch.

"You'll be back soon?" the old woman asks.

"As soon as I can," Abe says and waves to Prisha as he opens the door and goes out.

For the first time in 20 years, Abe suddenly has a burning desire for alcohol. Abe decides to walk. He walks down the hill along West Road until it runs into Main Street. He crosses the street and walks toward the ferry. Unable to control himself, Abe strides into Archie's and sits down at the far end of the bar. Abe's right leg is now aching. Archie's is deserted, which is not all that unusual on the island during this portion of the holiday season.

"What will it be?" the bartender walks down to Abe and asks.

"Double of Johnnie Red," Abe says. Then after fishing in this pocket for his bottle of ibuprofen adds, "May I have a glass of water, too?"

Abe sets the bottle of pain reliever on the bar before opening it. He pulls out two tablets holding them in his left hand until the bartender returns with his order. Abe picks up the glass of water with his right hand, places the pills in his mouth with his left then takes a large sip from the water glass. His ankle is now thumping.

After placing the glass of water back on the bar, Abe studies the shot glass which is almost full to the brim with amber liquid. As he reaches his right hand toward the drink, his hand shakes. Abe pulls his hand back a few inches from the shot glass and sets it atop the bar.

Abe knows full well where the alcohol in the shot glass leads. Abe also knows that he is the primary cause for Reggie being out at 'The Place' when he impregnated Julia. The thought turns Abe's stomach.

Straight toward oblivion, Abe thinks as he studies the alcohol for the better part of two minutes.

The only thing holding Abe back from oblivion at this moment is his wish to bring physical harm to Reggie. Abe has promised himself that the minute that he has concrete DNA confirmation that Reggie is Beth's father, no matter the consequences, Abe is going to track Reggie down.

Once again Abe moves his right hand to the shot glass, this time he grips it and begins to lift it. He handshakes badly enough that some of the alcohol spills on to the bar and his hand. Abe sets the glass back on the counter and moves himself closer to bar. Just as he's ready to lift the glass again, his cell phone rings. Abe releases his hold on the shot glass and fishes in his right pocket.

"Abe Stolz," he says into the speaker when the phone is brought up to his face.

"I'm just pulling into the Wannasea ferry dock," Abe hears Mindy tell him through his device's speaker. "Would you like me to come pick you up."

"I'm not at Zack grandma's anymore," Abe says swinging around on the barstool toward the front window. "I've come down to Archie's. If you'd like to come join me, I'll buy you some fish and chips."

"Sounds good to me but I'm not familiar with Archie's," Mindy says.

"They have the best fish and chips on the island for my money," Abe says. "When you come off the ferry, take the first turn off the roundabout then come up Main Street a half block, there is a parking garage. Pull the van in there. Archie's is right across the street."

"Should be there in five minutes or less."

Abe disconnects the call and places the cell phone back into his pocket. His ankle still throbs but it has now begun to throb a little less. He looks out the front window of Archie's into the almost deserted street. A few people walking toward the ferry. Hardly any cars pulling into or out of the parking lot. Abe continues watching the activity on the street until he sees the white panel van marked 'The Place' turn into the parking garage. He turns back around on his stool, picks up the shot glass of alcohol then walks halfway down the bar where he knows the sink resides. Abe dumps the alcohol into the sink before walking to the other end of the bar where the bartender has his back turned to him watching the replay of a football match on the overhead television.

"May I get a table?" Abe asks.

"Pick anyone you like," the bartender says. "I'll be over as soon you get settled."

"There's someone else joining me," Abe advises.

"I'll wait until you are both settled," the bartender announces without turning toward Abe.

Abe carries the shot glass back down to the other end of the bar and sits it back in the same position from which it came. As he turns to pick out a table, Mindy walks through the front door.

"Bartender says that we can have any table we want," Abe tells Mindy.

"Let's take that booth back in the corner," Mindy suggests.

They sit across from each other in the last booth on the left.

"How'd your talk with Zack's mom go?" Mindy asks as she unwinds a scarf around her neck and pulls off her knit hat.

"Not really sure at this point," Abe says honestly.

"Do you feel better having talked with her?"

Abe thinks for a moment before responding, "I guess that I do in regards to the Jones family but as for the other part, I now know that I'm directly responsible."

"You are tangentially responsible," Mindy replies. "You had no way of knowing Reggie could be such an unprincipled bastard."

"Other than the ten years that I'd come to know him," Abe says with a grimace.

The bartender comes up and takes their order for fish and chips. Mindy orders iced tea, so Abe follows suite.

"Did you learn anything?" Mindy asks.

"Julia didn't tell Prisha who Beth's father is," Abe says. "She was rather put out that I thought it was her husband all these years."

"Maybe she has right to be?"

Abe nods his head in agreement.

"Do you think that your wife knew who Beth's father is?" Mindy asks.

"I'm not sure," Abe says. "She and Julia were really close, but I suspect that if Janie knew that Reggie was the father, she would have gone ballistic. Janie had little use for Reggie. I also believe that she would have told me."

The bartender delivers the ice teas. Abe picks his up and takes a sip.

"What happened to your wife and daughter?"

Abe describes the Saturday when Janie and Julia had gone out sailing. He describes the next three months of almost constant searching for some sign of them or their sailboat. He even includes the spat over the Morris and that he and his wife weren't talking.

"No sign of the boat or them has ever been found?" Mindy asks.

Abe shakes his head negatively.

"Do you know specifically where they went sailing that day?"

"Janie was tuning up for a race which was to be held the following month," Abe relates. "I have always thought that they went out to the west end where the course had already been set up to practice."

"Then a storm came up?"

Abe nods his head, beginning to grow uncertain that he wants to continue this particular line of conversation. Along with the dull throb in his leg, the words are renewing the dull ache in his heart.

"Was it a bad storm?"

"Not terribly bad," Abe says. "There were wind gusts up to 25 knots out of the southeast with three-foot seas."

"Was your wife a good sailor?"

"She was."

"Why was your daughter with your wife?"

"They were a team," Abe says. "Julia probably liked to sail more than my wife."

"Was your daughter a good sailor?"

"Almost as good as Janie."

The kitchen staff delivers their fish and chips.

"Did you ever go sailing with them?" Mindy asks Abe.

"Often," Abe replies as he douses his plate with vinegar.

"Were you a good sailor?"

"I used to be."

"You don't sail anymore?"

Abe shakes his head.

The pair munch on the fish and chips for the next few minutes.

"What would you have done if you were out sailing and a storm came up?"

"It would depend where I was," Abe says. "If the wind was right and I was close enough to a good spot on the shore, I'd head there."

"And if you weren't close enough shore?"

"I'd probably tack real hard and head for the little south islands. There are a lot of sheltered coves there that are pretty safe no matter how bad it gets."

"When you went looking for them, you looked around all those islands?"

"At least three times each island."

"The day that they disappeared," Mindy asks after finishing with a piece of fish, "do you recall if there where powerboats out on the water?"

"Only those bigger than twenty feet," Abe says. "The swells were too big for the smaller craft."

"Did you or anyone else actually see your wife and daughter go out sailing that day?"

"I didn't personally," Abe replies, "but the people who managed the docks where she kept her boat said they saw the boat head out using the electric motor and turn toward the west."

"Did anyone report seeing them sailing out on the course?"

"No," Abe says, "their last sighting was motoring away from the dock."

Mindy finishes her last piece of beer-battered cod before continuing, "How old was you daughter when she had Beth?"

"One month shy of her 18th birthday."

"How old was Reggie Reginald then?"

"44, I think," Abe replies using his fork to pick through his mostly uneaten food. "Is there anything which he could have been charged with in relation to Julia?"

Mindy thinks for a moment, "Unless there he had sexual relations with your daughter prior to her getting pregnant when she was 16, it's unlikely. Seventeen is when children stop being a minor."

Abe takes a long sip of his iced tea.

"There is one other possibility," Mindy offers. "If Reginald had forced sexual relations on your daughter."

"You mean rape?"

"I mean rape," Mindy says firmly. "Would you mind telling me a little about your wife and her history?"

Abe fiddles with his now empty drink glass before beginning, "Janie was from South Halifax. She was an only child. Her mother died of cancer when she was thirteen. Her father began sexually abusing her shortly thereafter. She ran away from home at 15 and came out to the island."

"I see," Mindy said. "How did you meet her?"

"There's more to coming out to the island before we get to that," Abe says avoiding Mindy's eyes which remind him too much of Julia's. He looks out toward the street. "Janie was probably fully physically developed by the time she was 14. At 14 she could probably have passed for 20. Back then out here in the summer, business didn't ask questions about people's age or bother with running them through payroll. Janie worked at a bar about four blocks from here on the east side. She was beginning to have problems with one of the bartenders. My mother, who had a habit of collecting strays, found her crying in the market one day. She brought her out to Abe's to work and live. At the time, what is now my in-law suite was kind of dormitory where 6–8 girls might live at any given time. By the time Janie was 18, she was running the dining area at Abe's. My mother helped her finish high school and take classes at the Wannasea extension. I guess you could say, I met Janie the first day she went to work for my mother. Once I saw her, I never really had eyes for anyone else. It took me the better part of two years to get her to notice me. three years on, we started writing songs together. First for Janie herself, then for Reggie. I'm still not sure how or why, but by the time she was 22, we were having a torrid affair. We ran away and got married about six months after."

"Did your wife have a temper?" Mindy asks.

Abe tells Mindy about the incident with Reggie and the piano bench before adding, "Abe's was a bar at that time. I'm not going to say that our clientele was usually much trouble, but when they were Janie would deal with them. We didn't have a bouncer."

"I think I would have liked your wife a lot," Mindy says.

The bartender comes to the table and Abe asks him for the check.

"I notice that you still wear your wedding ring," Mindy says looking at the ring on his left hand.

Abe smiles a sad smile, "I cannot be certain that Janie is not out there somewhere."

Full Disclosure

Sunday, 3:37 PM. Abe and Beth are seated in front of the desk in Abe's in-law suite. Beth in a chair which she has brought over from the kitchen area. Abe in the desk chair. Abe is using his tablet and following along with what Beth is doing on her laptop which she has brought along. Hugh is providing instructions though the speaker on Beth's cell phone.

"Do you both have the VPN Access app on your cell phones?" Hugh asks.

"I've put them on both phones and checked to see that they are providing access numbers," Beth replies.

"Good," Hugh says. "Now click on the link which I just sent to each of your email accounts to access the secure area which has been set up for communications with Mr. Wright's team."

Abe watches Beth click on the link from her email account and follows her lead. He notices when she enters a new password for her account, she types in "JuliaJane87." Abe goes through the same procedure and decides to make his password "79Morris." Abe watches as Julia begins going through the information Hugh has placed there.

"You will not be able to upload or download any information from the site," Hugh informs. "You will notice that Mr. Wright's team has provided a good deal of information about the layout of the center. Right now I would suggest focusing on the file marked 'archs.pdf.' You have been given the names and background of three firms which Wright's team believes have the best skills to at least do the preliminary work."

"Do you have any experience with any of those firms," Beth asks.

"Unfortunately no," Hugh replies. "Wright's firm has a solid reputation, though. We used them for the acquisition and buildout of our facility here in Swansea."

"Have you decided how you'd like to be involved in this effort?" Abe asks his son.

"I've pretty much reached my investment limit with what I have put into Defense One," Hugh replies. "I do however intend to give the Wannasea Historical Society $250K as well as whatever help I can give them in setting up a library when the museum is up and running."

"Is there anything else Mr. Wright has asked us to focus upon?" Beth asks.

"He told me that thanks to the Sylvester Bros. strongarming and buying off three of the seven members of the island council, there will very likely be no other bidders but the two of us," Hugh passes along. "As far as the funds which will be required for the bid, plan on as much as $3million to close on the government center with another $500K in bid expenses which includes architectural planning. Based on his experience, he suggested that you may be looking at anywhere from $2 million to $5 million to get the place the facilities where you want them. Almost forgot that Wright indicated the quarry is not part of the government center parcel. If you want it, it's likely going to cost another $1.5million. That's all I can think of at the moment. Why don't you guys go through everything and give me a call if you don't understand something or are ready to communicate a response to Wright?"

Beth is still furiously writing down the figures, so Abe answers, "I think we've got enough to go on for now. Thanks for doing this for us, Hugh."

"It's the least that I can do," Hugh replies. "You guys be careful. From what I've learned, these Sylvester Bros are dangerous."

"As we are beginning to find out," Abe says. "See you."

Hugh disconnects the call just as Beth finishes her calculations.

"We could be looking at needing as much as $10 million if we are going to do this right," Beth says. "How much did you say that you can put in, Abe?"

"I can do at least $2 million without really hurting myself," Abe replies. "If I want to take on more risk, I could probably go up to $3million. Are you actually in a position to deal with the rest?"

"I am," Beth said. "Becca left me a serious trust fund which was set up to be used for just this sort of thing. Why don't you work on getting $2 million ready to be liquid? I'll handle the rest."

"You are now all in on buying the old government center?"

"The more I think about it," Beth says, "the better I think it will fit my long-term goals."

"What are your long-term goals, Beth?"

"How about we discuss it later?" Beth says. "I have a dinner date at 5. I'll start looking over the documents on Hugh's site when I get back."

"Is your date with anyone I know?"

"Probably," Beth says as she logs out the site which Hugh has set up, closes her laptop, puts it under her arm and goes out Abe's front door.

Abe spends the next 90 minutes looking over the drawings and stipulation which the government has placed on the property and bidding process. Finally, unable to absorb more, Abe rises from his chair, goes into the kitchen and starts up his electric water kettle. He makes himself a cup of tea and goes over to the table by the sliding glass door and sets down. As he does so, Mindy opens the sliding glass door behind him and scurries in.

Abe is used to Mindy coming in and out of his new place. Even at strange hours of the night. The normally goes up the stairs and spends 20–30 minutes doing whatever she does up there.

"I've got to rush," Mindy says on her way past Abe, "but don't go anywhere I got some things we need to talk over when I'm done."

"Okay," Abe says. "Do you want tea or something to eat when you come back down?"

"Only tea," Mindy says as she hurries up the stairs.

Abe prepares the tea tray and takes it over to the table. When the kettle has boiled, he pours water and prepares a cup of tea for himself before taking the kettle back over to the sink and filing it from the tap. He sits sipping his tea and thinking about the government until Mindy comes back down the stairs.

"Switch the kettle on," Abe requests of her.

Mindy switches the device on as she goes by then pulls out the chair beside Abe and sits down.

"I've gotten the lab results back on Reginald," Mindy says. "He is Beth's biological father without any doubt. Seems he's also the father of at least five other kids scattered across the Mainland."

Abe's anger rises enough that Mindy can sense it. She takes hold on his hand which is on the table, squeezes it and doesn't let go.

"I know you are mad, Abe," Mindy says. "You have every right in this world to be angry. You are also want to believe that you are the cause of Julia becoming pregnant. You anger is justified. Blaming yourself isn't."

The kettle whistles but Mindy ignores it, still holding on to Abe's left hand.

"I am going to do something which I have never before done on one my assignments," Mindy says. "I'm going to tell you exactly what is going on here but before I do, I need you to promise me that you will hear me out when I ask you to forget about any actions which you are thinking about taking against Reginald in the near future. Are you willing to do that?"

Abe remains motionless, his eyes avoiding Mindy's.

"Although protecting you and your business from the Sylvester Bros. is part of this mission," Mindy says, "it is a small part. I've been involved in trying to bring down their drug operation for the better part of the past 18 months. A big part of their drug operation is Reggie Reginald."

"Reggie is a drug kingpin?" Abe asks in amazement.

Mindy shakes her head and says, "You know those two goons, who are always with Reggie and wear those tactical uniforms?"

"I've noticed them."

"They are Reggie's minders," Mindy says. "For the past 35 years or so, the Sylvester Bros have been using Reggie as a drug mule. When he goes to Eastern Europe for a concert tour, Reggie brings back the Sylvester's drug supply with him. He used to do it on a leased jet. Up until six months ago, he was doing it on a private jet. We closed down their ability to land that jet anywhere within the Mainland unless it undergoes a full importation search. Due to that restriction, the Sylvesters have switched to using their large private yacht to run drugs and guns. Reggie made one concert trip in August. He's planning another in January. What that yacht brings back isn't coming directly into the Mainland however. It's now making a stop out here somewhere first. The new drug running practice is one of the bigger reasons why the Sylvester Bros have decided to purchase your old government center. They are planning to make this island their new base of operation."

"The only reason they want to buy this place is to transfer their liquor license up there?"

"It's slightly more complicated," Mindy says. "The Sylvester Bros would prefer not to have anyone else operating at our near the facility they are planning. In addition, there is a little-known perk of that liquor license your establishment holds."

Mindy releases Abe's hand, rises and goes over to the electric kettle, picks it up and carries it back to the table. She fills her cup with water and places a tea bag along with a packet of sweetener.

"Perk?"

"That license was issued almost 90 years ago," Mindy says. "At that time, it was common practice to include a gaming license in with the permit. Most of the resorts out here, which have gambling, operate from those same grants."

"Hugh mentioned something like this," Abe says, "but we weren't sure it applied to our license."

"You need to actually read the grant if you have it with the rest of the ownership papers for this property," Mindy states. "If you don't have it, it may be pulled from the island's records. Which happens to be where we ran across it."

"So gambling is high on the Sylvesters Bros. list of priorities?" Abe asks.

"It's probably pretty high but I think the money laundering aspect of a gambling operation on this Island would greatly simplify and enhance their operation."

Mindy finishes preparing her tea and takes a small sip.

"Early last year, we could have taken Reggie down," Mindy says. "We busted one of his roadies, who was in the know about the drug operation. Getting Reggie however, won't bring down the Sylvester Bros. Since the two brothers took over the operation from their father and uncles, they have become very cautious and very well advised legally. Until we busted that roadie, we hadn't been able to come close to laying a finger on them. The roadie had worked with one of the Sylvester's worst goons, a guy called Cecil. Cecil likes to talk. Cecil, in addition to being a running mate of the two brothers when they were the muscle rather the brains of Sylvester Bros., is their explosives guy. Cecil is also wanted by Interpol for a bombing he helped pulled off three years ago in Minsk. Cecil has been in deep hiding since the bombing, trying to avoid extradition. Based on the handiwork we saw in the transformer bombing on West Road, we now have reason to believe Cecil is holed up out here somewhere. Considering that we have managed to place a tracking device on the van which Reggie's two minders use, we are now very optimistic about nabbing him. If we can get Cecil to talk, the Sylvesters will be going down along with Reggie."

"I'm not all that surprised in Reggie's case that he's involved with these guys," Abe says, "but that still doesn't lessen my anger toward him."

"I promise you that the before Reggie is due to head off for his next Eastern European tour, he will be arrested," Mindy says. "Based on what we have on him, he will spend the rest of his life in prison."

"Cannot happen soon enough for my taste," Abe says.

Mindy once again takes hold of Abe's hand.

"Don't mess this up, Abe. Don't put you or your family at any further risk than you already have. It may have escaped your attention that a whole bunch of people, starting with your granddaughter need you."

"Julia and Janie needed me too and I wasn't there."

"You have no real idea that you could have changed your wife and daughter's fate," Mindy says. "No matter what their fate actually was. Right now, you can best help protect those around you by keeping as far away from Reggie as possible. Until we have either blown this case open or taken Reggie down, I'd like you to stop going down to 'The Place.' That will reduce the chances of running into him. If Reggie calls, do not answer. I will do whatever I can to make sure Reggie cannot come out here to see you."

Abe takes a sip of his tea and looks up at Mindy.

"Promise me, you'll do this," Mindy says squeezing Abe's hand.

"I will promise you that I will do everything I can to avoid Reggie until a week before he's due to leave for Eastern Europe. After that point, I won't promise anything."

Cha-ching

Thursday, 10:35 AM. Abe sits at the table in the studio looking over two new videos which Zack had made last evening. Zack had decided to have both video/audio recordings made of the two sea songs which were starting to really catch on down at Abe's. Molly had arranged to have Dave come in and do the recordings. The video was shot during Zack's last set. After Abe's had been closed for the evening, Dave did the audio recordings. This morning, Molly had put the videos up on You Tube and added the new MP3 recordings to Zack's catalogue on the website.

Abe plays the video marked *Shan't deceive her*. Zack is using his acoustic guitar, which he also bangs to the rhythm. Zack sings in full Wannasea tenor.

Shan't deceive her (Sea Song) 127BPM tempo – D major key – 2/2 time

thought it wouldn't end this way
but leaving is what shall now occur
one more anchors aweigh
the going not what I'd prefer
but going away, we must endure
of that I shan't deceive her

the time to go is growing neigh
leaving is what must occur
the words will fly, our passions high
forsaking all we hoped to deter
our remaining moments slipping by
going not what I'd prefer
but going away, we must endure
of that I shan't deceive her

the time to go is growing neigh
of that I shan't deceive her

I rue the very life I live
but leaving is what must occur
my time no longer mine to give
of that I shan't deceive her
going not what I'd prefer
but going away, we must endure
of that I shan't deceive her

thought it wouldn't end this way
but leaving is what must occur
one more anchors aweigh
going not what I'd prefer
but going away, we must endure
of that I shan't deceive her

my return uncertain and far away
of that I shan't deceive her
leaving now my orders say
my going not what I'd prefer
I'll do my best come what may
the waiting now is up to her

thought it would not end this way
not what either of us prefer
but going away is what shall occur
of that I shan't deceive her

what is to be is not what either prefer
but going away, we must endure
of that I shan't deceive her
what is to be is not what either prefer
but going away, we must endure
of that I shan't deceive her

The video has a lot of singing along from the crowd in the background. Not loud enough to really have any impact on Zack's performance. Just loud enough to really sound like a sea song. Dave had done a really good job on this recording.

Looks like it was a hell of a performance, Abe thinks, beginning to be more certain that the Reggie Revival at 'The Place' is finally on its way out.

"Look at this Abe," Molly requests from her chair at the desk.

Abe rolls his office chair over beside Molly and looks to where she is pointing on the screen. The screen shows the sales and income summary from the Zack Tillerman website. In the total column after all the deductions it shows a total of $53,427.70.

Abe looks through the sales figures. Almost 5,500 purchases of Zack's catalogue have occurred. *Not the Same, This Side of Nowhere and Hard Case* are the leading single song sales.

"I've got to call the payment people to see if this can possibly right," Molly says after clicking the print icon on the screen dashboard.

"When did you last look at these sales totals?" Abe asks.

"I've been tied up with the new recordings and my finals and haven't glanced at them since Monday," Molly answers. "On Monday they weren't anything like this."

Molly opens the right desk draw and pulls out a file marked "Website Payment Company." She picks up her cell phone and calls the service number. After eight additional phone keypad entries Molly finally talks with an account rep, who tells her the number is in fact correct.

Molly looks at Abe in amazement.

"Merry Christmas to us," Abe says with a big smile as he pulls his cell phone from the desk and dials Beth.

"What's up, Gramps?" comes from his cell phone speaker.

"Is there any way that Zack and you can break free to come up and have a talk with Molly and I?"

"It's not very busy at the moment, so I don't see any problem being able to do that," Beth says. "We'll be up in a couple minutes."

"With what we took out Monday, that leaves us with over $50,000 in profit," Molly says in disbelief. "That's even throwing in what Zack spent on Dave last night. Did you expect anything like this Abe?"

"Maybe in a year or so," Abe says shaking his head in wonder. "Certainly not now."

"What do we do now?" Molly asks.

"I'm not sure," Abe says. "This isn't how things worked when I broke into the music business."

Molly prints out three more copies of the website income summary, then does four print outs of the sales screen for each recording and the catalogue.

Beth and Zack come through the sliding glass door. Molly hands each one of the four a print out of each screen. Beth takes hers to the piano bench and sets down. Zack pulls up the chair at the front side of piano.

"Is this real?" Beth asks.

"That's pretty much the same reaction Molly just had," Abe says. "It is in fact accurate."

As Zack looks at the figures, he looks up at Abe quizzically, "What does this means, Abe?"

"It means, if I'm not mistaken," Abe says, "that you have already had more success in the music recording industry as many have had their entire careers."

"But I've just gotten started," Zack says shaking his head.

Molly has gone back to looking over the dashboard for the website.

"We have 300 plus messages in the website comments section," Molly says. "Two of them are from Mainland recording studios."

"Let's all take a deep breath," Beth says. "There's no need to be in a big hurry to do anything at this point."

"I was just looking to make enough extra money to hire someone to look after my grandmother so mom and Saanvi can have a break," Zack says more to himself than anyone else in the room.

"Beth is right," Abe says. "We need to take a step back. Right now all we can be certain is that this is one big change in sales. We can't be certain how long it will last or if it will last."

"Let's try to define what this changes," Molly suggests, "as well as trying to figure out why it has changed."

"I will start by suggesting that Zack cannot continue to perform the same way that he has been for the past few weeks," Beth says. "At a minimum, there should be a cover charge, two performances per week and he should only do two sets a night."

"But I like playing out here," Zack says. "I'd play every night without any cover charge if you let me."

"That isn't how supply and demand works," Molly says. "You can play all you want, but if you want to continue and make serious money from it, you need to limit what you give out for free."

"When we got this thing rolling," Zack says, "I told you guys that the music and having fun was what I wanted. I'm hoping that no matter how much money comes in, we will keep it that way. Playing down at 'The Place' has been the most fun that I've had in my entire life. That I've now earned enough to pay off my car and get some help for grandma is really all that I'm looking for."

"Zack is the primary money maker here," Beth states. "He probably…"

"It wouldn't have happened if Abe hadn't worked with me to write those songs," Zack interjects. "Without those songs, the only extra money that I would have is what they put in my guitar case on show nights."

"You would be fine playing out here as much as Beth lets you?" Abe asks.

"I would," Zack replies.

"As Beth's grandfather and your creative adviser," Abe says, "I don't think that's a good idea."

"The good news as far as performances here," Beth says, "is after next Wednesday, we will be closed until the following Tuesday for the holidays. I have already talked with Zack about switching to doing Wednesdays, Fridays and Saturdays. I'd suggest after the holidays that we trim that into just Fridays and Saturdays only with a cover charge."

The room goes silent for a full thirty seconds.

"I'd also suggest that it's not a good idea for Zack to continue working the counter for at least the time being," Beth says. "I seriously doubt that sales bump is a glitch, but if it is, he can go back to it whenever he wants."

"What do I do with the rest of my time?" Zack asks.

"I'm sure you can work with Abe in the studio to create new songs and work on improving your podcast," Beth says.

"I'm willing to work on songs with you anytime Monday through Friday," Abe says. "As long as you aren't planning on doing it 24 hours a day."

"If it's okay with you guys," Zack says, "I'd still like to do Wednesday nights for at least a short period of time. I don't think you understand how much playing down there makes me better."

"I'm fine with that," Beth says, "but only two sets a night. Start at 8, be done by 10."

Zack nods his head in agreement.

"I think that I may have discovered at least part of the reason for this sudden surge in sales!" Molly exclaims. "Yesterday afternoon, the London Tribune had an article in their Living section which reviewed our podcast, videos and website. The review is very positive going as far as to say, 'Zack Tillerman is an emerging force in the folk-rock arena.'"

Zack rises and walks behind Molly, looking over her shoulder to view the article.

"I'm surprised no one called us to talk about specifics," Abe says.

"I don't think that is how these reviews work, Gramps," Beth says. "The internet is a venue of its own. What shows up there becomes its own reality after a while."

"What do we do about the website requests from those music producers?" Molly asks.

"Send their contact information to me," Abe says. "I will try to figure out if it makes sense to speak with them."

Explosions

Sunday, 12:22 AM. Abe has just glanced at the display of the clock radio on his bed stand. About fifteen minutes ago, he had heard, who he assumes to have been Mindy come in the sliding door and go quickly up the stairs. This was not all that unusual an occurrence in the past few weeks. Less than two minutes later, Mindy had come running back down those stairs and out the front door.

Abe rubs sleep from his eyes, sits up and turns on the lamp beside the clock/radio. He picks up the book on his bed stands and resumes reading where he had left off a few hours ago. He reads for approximately three minutes.

"Whomp!"

The sound of an explosion in the direction of the front of the house.

"WHOMP!!"

The sound of a larger explosion from the same area just one second later.

"WHOMP!"

An even bigger explosion just a moment later.

Abe puts down his book. Dressed in his pajamas, he wraps the blanket from his bed around himself and fishes under on floor for his slippers. Finding them, he rises goes into the living area and switches on the overhead lights.

Abe goes to the cabinet under the stairs and pulls out one of the battery powered lanterns which Beth had provided him. He turns it on. Abe then walks across the front room and goes out the front door. Only the emergency lampposts are lit down at 'The Place' There is a great deal of commotion and a couple flashing police lights coming from the parking lot in front of the building. Abe hears the sounds of men shouting. There seems to be a small fire burning where he used to feed Riley V. The part of the building from there back is unrecognizable.

Abe makes his way to rear portion of the driveway and walks toward 'The Place.' As he crosses the road, a figure comes out of the shadows near the back area of the rear patio.

"Mindy?"

The figure walks up to Abe. Abe notices that she seems to be shaking. She's also holding her left arm. She is wearing what appears to be some type of tactical uniform complete with a face shield. The left side of the shield is shattered. Abe takes off the blanket and wraps it around Mindy. As he does, Abe notices that she is bleeding from the hand which she is holding.

"What happened?" Abe asks.

"I got a little too close to my work," Mindy says in a shaky voice.

Abe tears off a strip of the lower part of his pajama top and wraps it around Mindy's hand.

"I think we need to get you down to the clinic," Abe says.

"Please just help me get up to the house," Mindy says. "I'll work out what comes after that."

Abe takes hold of Mindy's shoulders and helps guide her up the path and through the front door of his suite. Once Mindy removes the helmet and shield, Abe sees that most of the blood has drained from Mindy's face.

"Mindy," Abe says forcefully, "you really need to have your hand attended to."

"Just give me a couple minutes," Mindy says shaking free of Abe's arms and moving to the stairs, then up.

Abe goes into the kitchen, grabs two clean hand towels, a glass of water and what is left of his prescription for Percocet. Hobbling as he goes, Abe carries the load up the steps to where Mindy is seated in an old wooden chair, using her right hand to enter keystrokes on the device Abe takes to be a laptop. Beside it is some form of camera connected with a cable to the laptop.

After setting the towels and glass of water down on Becca's old dresser. Abe opens the container of pain killers, pulls out a tablet and offers it to Mindy.

"What is it?"

"Percocet," Abe says. "I have it left over from my ankle fracture."

Mindy opens her mouth. Abe pops the pill onto her outstretched tongue. Abe lifts the glass of water from the dresser and puts it to Mindy's lips. Abe stands watching for another five minutes as Mindy continues to communicate through her keyboard. Finally Mindy closes the laptop cover.

"Someone will be here in no more than ten minutes to get me," Mindy says.

Mindy starts to rise from the chair but is somewhat unstable. Abe notices that there is blood on his blanket near the upper area of Mindy's left arm.

"Would you mind helping me put everything here in my bag?" Mindy asks.

"You sit there," Abe says. "I'll get it."

Abe takes the devices and places them in the gym sized bag then lifts the bag using his left hand. Returning to Mindy, Abe offers her his right forearm to lean on as she rises. Mindy still grasping Abe's forearm, exits the upstairs room and goes down the stairs in tandem with Abe. Abe supports Mindy across the room and over to the kitchen table chair closest to the sliding door. He helps her to sit down, then removes the blanket from around her to inspect her left arm. There is a nasty gash on the side of her bicep area. Abe goes to the kitchen and pulls out two more clean towels. "Abe switches on the electric kettle before returning to Mindy and wrapping the towels tightly around her upper arm before once again covering her back with the blanket."

"Two steps closer and I would have been a goner," Mindy says.

Abe isn't sure if Mindy is saying it to him or herself.

Abe pulls the chair next to Mindy up beside her and holds takes her hand.

"Did I ever tell you how much you look like Julia," Abe tells Mindy.

Through her fog Mindy replies, "No, you haven't."

"You look so much like her that I couldn't believe it when I first laid eyes on you. You aren't another one of Reggie Reginald's kids, are you?"

Mindy emits a small laugh before saying, "No, Abe, I'm not one of Reginald's kids. In fact, my dad served with your son Hugh in West Asia about fifteen years back."

As the kettle boils, Abe rises and says, "Tell me about it while I fix your tea."

"My dad is five or six years older than your son," Mindy begins. "I think Dad was Hugh's squadron leader when they were out there."

Mindy continues telling Abe about her father as he rises and walks through the kitchen. Abe goes into his room, to the end of his bed and opens the chest which resides there. For the first time in twenty years, Abe pulls out the picture album from the far corner. He carries it into the kitchen and sets it down on the table in front of Mindy. He opens it to pictures of Julia working on her sailboat right after she had Beth. As Mindy looks through the pictures, Abe goes into the kitchen and fixes her a mug of strong tea.

"You really weren't exaggerating," Mindy says looking over the photos. "Julia and I could have been sisters."

"Drink a little of this," Abe instructs putting mug down beside Mindy.

Mindy takes two long sips of the tea before a light wrap comes on the sliding glass door. Abe unlocks it and slides it back to allow John Steadman to enter.

"What happened, Jill?" the CID agents asks with concern immediately upon entering the room.

"I was taking photos of the guys planting the explosives, keep taking those photos when those two took off for the front of the parking lot. I was too close when the propane tanks when up."

"We've got to get you to the clinic," John Steadman says.

"Would you mind grabbing our bag," Mindy instructs John. "Abe will help me out to your car."

Abe once again holds out his right forearm which Mindy uses to pull herself up, then helps her walk out the sliding door, across the patio and into the car in which John Steadman has come.

After helping to buckle Mindy in place, she says to him with a smile, "Please don't go around offering Percocet to anymore CID agents tonight, Abe."

Abe gently closes the door and watches until the car drives out sight before re-entering his suite. He immediately goes into his room and changes into his standard, for this time of year, khaki pants and flannel shirt. He switches off the bedroom light before moving through the living room area and out the front door.

Now there are two fire engines and at least two more police cars down at Abe's.

Abe turns right, then traverses the eighty feet or so to the front entrance of the house. He knocks loudly four times. Beth opens the door almost immediately. Abe sees all of the other house residents, save Mindy, seated in the various couches and soft chairs in the front room.

"Jack Druce told us to we need to stay in the house until they can sort things out down there," Beth says. "I was wondering where you got to or if you might not have slept through the whole thing."

"The explosions woke me," Abe says.

"Have you seen Mindy?" Beth asks.

"Saw her a little after 11," Abe lies. "She told me that she was going to go out with some friends down in the village and probably would spend the night there."

Assessment

Sunday, 2:35 PM. Jack Druce had come up to the house a few minutes ago and informed Beth that it would be okay to come down and assess the situation at 'The Place' other than in areas which are marked off by police tape. Beth and Abe stand at the rear of Abe's surveying the damage. The deck area leading to Abe's old room has crumbled. Most of the composite planking has fallen on to the patio below. The supports are small, charred reminders of their former function. The stone and mortar of the wall is blackened from the top to the bottom.

Moving past the rear entrance and toward what used to be storage garage, the pair finds that the back third of the cement block kitchen wall has been turned to rubble. The van, which had been parked in the garage driveway to the west side of the building is in shambles. The upper half is blown off. The rest of the van is melted mess. Police tape encircles the entire area from the van back to where the kitchen wall used to be. Where a pair of propane tanks had been is now a hole about four feet in diameter and two feet deep. The shredded backs of the refrigeration units can be seen just beyond the remnants of the wall. The front third of the garage is gone. The Morris is now in much the same shape as the van.

Beth and Abe walk around the outer perimeter of the police tape to the front parking lot. Aside from debris scattered everywhere the parking lot and front of the building do not look to be impacted. Beth walks to the front entrance and uses her key to open access door to the electronic keylock. She enters the code, then swings back the two heavy front doors before entering the dining area and disarming the alarm on the right side.

At first glance, the dining area doesn't look all that bad. The tables and chairs are in place. There were no sign of fire or wall penetration. Beth begins taking pictures with her cellphone's camera.

"We've lost the mirror," Abe informs Beth, after he notices that the century old mirror which had run across the back length of the bar cabinet area was now shattered and laying in pieces on the floor. Beth carefully walks over the glass to find that most of the cups, saucers and mugs also lay in ruin on the floor. She swings back around the cash register area and heads toward the rear hallway. Abe pops in the restrooms which seems to be undamaged. There is now a large crack along the supporting wall in the kitchen hallway. The pair go through the swinging doors into the kitchen. The kitchen is a war zone. The two refrigeration units in the rear have been shredded. The stoves are in multiple pieces scattered throughout the room. The metal counters have been turned into curved metal sculptures.

"There isn't much to be saved here," Beth comments.

Abe walks back out of what used to be the kitchen and goes the first table out of the door and sets down. After two or three minutes, Beth does the same.

"Where do we go from here, Gramps?" Beth asks.

"That's entirely up to you," Abe says. "If you want to call it quits, I'm certainly fine with that. If you want to rebuild, I help however I can. If you want to do something else within reason, I'll help out there too."

Beth rises from the chair, walks up on the stage and goes to the piano. She begins softly playing Simon and Garfunkel's *Bridge over Troubled Waters*. She plays it through twice before walking back to the table where Abe sits.

"How many years has it been since Becca started running this place?" Beth asks.

"Going on 62 now," Abe says.

Beth runs her right hand over her face.

"One thing I know," Beth says fiercely, "we aren't giving into Reggie Reginald and his thugs. We'll put this place back together. We'll also make sure that there is no chance his cartel takes over the old government center."

"I'd suggest the first thing that we need to do is get our insurance company out here to assess the damages and tell us what they can and cannot do," Abe says.

"Probably a good idea," Beth replies.

They sit in silence studying what is now left of the foundation of both of their lives.

"When you started talking about buying the old government center," Beth says unprompted, "my thinking was that we would keep this place running until got things going up there. After that, I was thinking about possibly turning what we have down here into a youth retreat."

"You mean something like a hotel? Abe asks."

"Not exactly," Beth says, "more like a place where kids who are having problems can come and get help working on moving forward with their lives."

"Isn't that the sort of thing which you are now doing up at the house?" Abe asks.

"In a sense," Beth says. "but I'd also like to have a fitness facility plus a space where health and educational seminars can be held. That sort of thing. I also want to provide a lower cost alternative for people with limited means to come out and enjoy the island. Now though, I'm going to have to figure out how to get this place back in some kind of working order so the kids will still have jobs."

"You'll need to get creative," Abe suggests.

"That's one way to put it," Beth laughs.

"Any ideas on what you are going to do with your staff until you can get back up and running?" Abe asks.

"I'll just bite the bullet and keep paying them," Beth says. "There will be plenty of cleanup work for a while. The big problem for the kids will be that most of them rely on their tips as much as their pay."

"There's also the matter of what to do about our after-Christmas Party," Abe says.

Beth thinks for a few moments, before saying, "Maybe we can rent someplace and still have it. I will start working on that tomorrow."

They remain in silent thought for a few minutes until hearing a voice call through the main entrance, "Hello anybody in there?"

"Sorry," Beth calls back, "we are closed. Very likely we will remain closed for quite some time."

Bill Graham walks through the door. After his eyes adjust to the dimness, says, "Good. You are just the two that I am looking for."

Jack Druce, who is accompanying the CID agent, walks in behind him. The pair come across the dining room floor to the table where Beth and Abe sit.

"Pull up chairs," Beth says. "I'd offer you tea or coffee but I'm fresh out of china."

"Along with power, water and a few other niceties, I'd imagine," Jack Druce says as the two men pull out the remaining chairs from the table.

"How is Mindy?" Abe asks.

"She's doing fine," the CID agent says. "She had to have stitches in the cuts on her hand and arm. The real problem is the blow she took to the side of her face shield. Seems it gave her a grade three concussion. We really want to thank you for taking care of her last night. Jill would be much worse off if you hadn't tended to her as well as you did. She'll have to rest up for a few days, but will be back out here Tuesday to pack up and say goodbye to everyone."

"That's finally some good news," Beth says.

"Thanks to Jill's efforts," Graham says, "we have been able to tie the Sylvester Brothers directly to what happened here last night. We have taken into custody a long-time linchpin to most of their illegal activities. There is a very good chance, we are going to be able to bring down their entire operation."

"Couldn't happen to a more deserving bunch," Abe says.

"Before I get into specifics," the agent says, "there is one thing Jill asked me tell you. She said that before you do anything else, you need to get yourself a lawyer and begin the process of suing the Sylvester Bros in civil court. As we have been able to tie everything that has been done back to them, Jill suggests you start your lawsuit at $50 million."

"Don't criminal cases have to be tried first?" Beth asks.

"Not the way that we think this case is going to play out," the CID agent says. "The Sylvesters very likely will try to get a plea agreement for what they've done here in the next week to try to avoid everything else which is going to be coming at them."

"I'll talk to my cousin Herbert later to see if he can take on handling a civil suit for us," Abe informs Beth.

"Beyond the news from Jill," the agent continues. "I want to assure you that you no longer have anything to fear from the Sylvester Brothers. We placed both brothers and four of their associates under arrest earlier this morning. In addition to what they have done here over the past month, there are a few other atrocities which they perpetuated which are now coming back to haunt them. We will not be at liberty to discuss those charges with you until later in the week. I want to make certain that you are aware that we may need your help in that area, Mr. Stolz."

"My help," Abe says, "other than what I've told you about my dealings with Reggie and his lawyer over the past month, I'm not sure how else I can help you."

"We will make that clear when the time comes," Graham says. "I just want to make certain that you will be available to assist us if that becomes necessary. It will be no later than Thursday. Can we count on you being available?"

Abe nods his head affirmatively.

"Finally, we believe that you are now free to do whatever it is that you would like to do in regard to the old government center in the open," Graham says. "Please contact Eston Wright to either have him continue his work for you or transfer it to another firm."

"You really believe that we are now in the clear?" Abe asks. "What about Reggie Reginald?"

"We are confident that danger has also passed. Mr. Reginald will be in custody very soon," Jack Druce says. "We have no reason to believe that Reginald on his own is capable of causing harm to anyone. Reggie Reginald very likely has no future beyond spending the rest of his days at the Seward Prison."

"One last item," Bill Graham says, "the security system which your son had installed here has been aces. The system helped us crack our case against the Sylvesters wide open. It allowed us to track exactly what was happening out here, second by second and prevented the damage from becoming even worse. If you want a play-by-play of what went on last night, Defense One can give it to you. One caution however, there is to be no discussion of any CID involvement with anyone. Either last night or previous to that. Understood?"

Abe nods his head in agreement. The two men rise, walk across the dining area and out into the parking lot.

"Why would Reggie be going to prison?" Beth asks her grandfather. "Was he part of the plot to try to get us to sell or burn us out?"

"I'm not sure how deep Reggie was involved in trying to strong arm us," Abe says. "I think we'll have to wait a little bit to find that out."

"Whatever they get that guy on," Beth says, "won't surprise me."

Abe thinks for a long moment before saying to Beth, "There is something else related to Reggie that you probably need to know."

Abe starts by explaining his worry that Zack's father might also be Beth's father, moves on to arranging the DNA tests and stops just short of describing the results.

"I'm not following you, Abe. What's this got to do with Reggie?"

"The results of the DNA tests show that Reggie is your biological father," Abe says.

Beth says nothing for the better part of two minutes.

"How long have you known this, Abe?"

"Less than two weeks."

"When were you planning on letting me know?" Beth asks.

"Until just a few moments ago," Abe says, "I wasn't planning on telling you."

"How old was he when my mom got pregnant?" Beth asks.

"44."

Beth shakes her head, before saying, "Shouldn't he have been brought up on child endangerment charges or something?"

"Your mom was 17 which means in this jurisdiction, she was not a minor. As far as I know, your mother never told anyone who the father was," Abe says. "Until these DNA tests, nobody, except maybe Reggie or your mom, knew who your father might be."

Beth rises from her chair and walks back over to the piano. She starts playing Dylan's *Hard Rain Gonna Fall* loud and raw. She plays it for ten minutes. Stops abruptly in the middle of the song and comes back to the table.

"Abe," Beth says forcefully, "the only family that I have ever had was you, Becca, Uncle Hugh and to a much lesser extent Grandma Jane and my mom."

"That's true."

"Other than starting my own family," Beth says solemnly, "it is the only family which I am ever going to have."

The News

Monday, 6:07 PM. Abe has pushed his rolling office chair against the back wall of the studio. This has been his busiest day in recent memory. After spending an hour and half with his insurance company having them outline what they can and cannot do for him, Abe finally gave up and told them to get back to him immediately after they had completed their assessment and investigation. Shortly thereafter his cousin Herbert had arrived with his two lawyer daughters to discuss options in regard to civil lawsuits and their needs to progress with purchase of old government center. On Sunday night, mainly because of Beth's insistence that whatever was done by them at the government center needed to be a local product, Abe had agreed to Beth calling Eston Wright and transferring all of his work done on the sale to Herbert's law firm. Cousin Herb, after agreeing to personally handle the civil suite, had assigned his oldest daughter to handle the government center purchase endeavor. Herb's interest in the civil suit, much like Abe's own, stemmed from a joint desire to see the Sylvesters put out of business permanently. Nathan's assassination had neither been forgotten or forgiven by his extended family. All of this had been accomplished while trying to put off constant badgering from both local and Mainland reporters about the destruction and arrests at 'The Place' early Sunday morning.

The reporter situation had gotten so bad, that no one inside the house could set one foot outside without being accosted. Beth had enlisted Marie and Sallie to help with planning regarding what was to be done at the business. Marie additionally had decided to take on the task of trying to control the reporters coming on house property. Two hours ago, she had given up on that effort.

Right after lunch, Abe called both of the record producers which had contacted the website. The story was basically the same for each. They wanted Zack to sign an exclusive recording contract which would provide them with essentially full control of Zack's output. Molly and Zack, who had been in the studio since 10 this morning, wanted nothing to do with such an agreement. Abe had recused himself from the decision process on the recording contract offers.

Zack Tillerson LLC had moved on from that decision to a review of finances and purchases. The website had generated another $28K in income since last Thursday. Additionally, there were signs that Zack's podcasts would soon be profitable. Zack had suggested that they purchase some serious sound equipment, the bulk of which is to be portable. Abe had gotten a break when Molly and Zack had spent the better part of two hours deciding what was to be purchased. The total for the equipment sums up to almost $18k. Molly had just moved on to noting that something was going to have to be done to compensate Beth from her performances on Zack's recordings.

"I'll speak to her about it," Abe offered, "but right now I think that might be the least of Beth's concerns."

That brought them to the point of having to address the main consideration which had been facing them since early Sunday morning. How to deal with what had happened down at 'The Place' from the perspective of Zack's musical career.

"When do you think we'll have some idea when 'The Place' will be going again?" Zack asks.

"Beth told me an hour ago," Abe relates, "that Sallie is looking to bring in what she is calling a 'Mobile Kitchen' solution. There's a company up in Sheffield which provides them. The earliest that they could get one out here is the middle of next week. That's assuming that all the rubble can be cleared and the building inspector gives Abe's a permit for occupancy. The other issue will be sorting out the power and water down there. Where the explosion occurred, is where both came into the building. I doubt that we are going to know anything about that until later in the week, if then."

"Seems as if we may be looking at a month without performances?" Zack calculates.

Abe shrugs his shoulders, before asking Zack, "Do you want me to look around to see if I can find other places where you can play? Being out of season, it will probably be hard to find anything on the island but there ought to be venues over on the Mainland which we can book."

Zack thinks for a few moments, before replying, "I'm not interested in playing anywhere off this island".

"Zack," Abe begins, "I'm 70 years old. If I said something like that, they'd write it down as me being a senile old fool. You are 23. Wanting to limit your options is not a good look for a 23-year-old."

"I'm serious. Abe," Zack says. "Over the past month or so, I've come to realize that I only make good music on this island. The island feeds me the power to perform. Off this island, I suck."

Both Molly and Abe look at Zack dumbstruck.

"I'm serious," Zack repeats. "Maybe I can do two or three podcasts a week until 'The Place' is back in business. It's not the same as having an audience but it may be enough to get by until then."

"You don't want to over-expose yourself," Abe says, "that's as sure a route to killing off what you've managed to get going as anything."

"I'll do three podcasts," Zack says. "I have to do something."

"Would you consider performing down at the extension," Molly asks, "if I can figure out some way to arrange it? The extension has an on-going concert program. You are fairly popular down there. I'm fairly certain that if I go to the right people, it can be arranged."

"I'd play there," Zack says.

"They aren't going to be able to pay much," Molly says, "if anything."

"It will just be good to play in front of an audience," Zack says.

Beth comes into the room and announces, "You guys need to come out and see this."

The three follow Beth back out to the living room area where Sallie and Marie sit in armchairs looking at the tv. Usually the tv isn't turned on until late in the evening when everyone returns from work.

"Can you play it back?" Beth asks Marie.

Marie uses the remote to replay the 6 PM news broadcast from the island's one local tv station.

"WKWS evening news," comes along with the image of the male and female news anchors.

"In today's top story," the female anchor announces, "local folk music legend, Reggie Reginald, has been taken into custody by island authorities and charged with drug smuggling, extortion and other mob related activities. Reginald was arrested earlier this morning by island authorities. Due to the seriousness of the crimes, Reginald is currently being held in Wannasea Island holding facility without bond."

The screen switches to a video only recording from the benefit performance Reggie had performed at 'Abe's.' The recording seems to be from Reggie's first set inside the dining area.

"Reginald recently performed a benefit concert for the Wannasea Island Hurricane Relief Fund," the male news anchor continues. "An undercover island investigation alleges that Reginald has been smuggling drugs through Wannasea for the past eight months. Additional charges are pending against Reginald in the Hanover District on the Mainland."

The screen switches to still image of 'The Place' which appears to have been made yesterday afternoon.

"Early Sunday morning," the female anchor states, "a fire and resulting explosion decimated the popular local music venue and coffee house known as 'The Place.' This is the same facility where Reggie Reginald recently held his benefit concert. The facility will be closed for the near future according to business spokesperson, Marie Ault. The cause of the fire is being investigated as possible arson according to the Wannasea Island Constabulary."

An Ending

Tuesday, 11:11 AM. Beth and Abe are standing on the patio outside of the studio. The sun is shining brightly. It's exceptional weather for Wannasea Island just four days before Christmas. The pair are waiting for Mindy to arrive. Mindy had phoned Beth a few minutes earlier and said that the ferry had just docked. They watch as a late model BMW528i pulls up to the patio. A young man exits the rear seat, then swings open the passenger door, Mindy climbs out. Her left arm is in a sling. A fifty-something distinguishing looking gentlemen comes out of the drivers' side.

Mindy hugs Beth and then Abe before gesturing toward the older man, who is with her.

"This is my father," Mindy says, "Charles Paul."

Abe and Beth shake the man's outstretched hand.

"This is my younger brother, Steven," Mindy explains, "he's come along to drive my motorcycle back home."

"To drive her motorcycle back home," Mindy's father says, "very carefully. Right son?"

Steven frowns at his father as he shakes Beth and Abe's hands.

"I hate to run," the younger man says, "but I'm hoping to grab the turnaround from ferry."

"No problem," Beth says as the young man goes back to the car, pulls out a helmet from the back seat and goes to Mindy's bike. He starts it and is off toward Wannasea in an instant.

"I'm just going to grab my stuff and say goodbye to everybody," Mindy says heading toward the studio.

"Would you like to come in?" Beth asks Mr. Paul.

"Better not," he says. "Jill doesn't need to completely blow her cover."

Abe gently takes hold of Beth's arm, "Are Hugh and Helen still inside?"

Hugh and his wife had decided to come to the island for the holidays.

"Yes," Beth replies curiously. "Why?"

"I believe Mr. Paul and Hugh are old acquaintances," Abe says. "Would you mind asking him to come out?"

"Will do," Beth says heading toward the studio.

"It's really beautiful, out here," Charles Paul says. "Jill told me how nice it was."

"It certainly is today," Abe replies. "Did you have far to come to get here?"

"We live about 40 miles north of Swansea in a little town called Killery," Mr. Paul relates. "It's where I grew up."

Hugh comes out through the sliding glass door.

"Colonel Paul," Hugh says giving his old squadron leader a hearty handshake, "you are certainly taking good care of yourself."

"You as well," Mr. Paul says. "I hear you've now gotten yourself into the surveillance business."

As Hugh and Mr. Paul catch up, Abe excuses himself to go back inside the studio. He had promised to give Zack a copy of the music Janie had written for two poems that he wanted to research turning into songs.

Beth is carrying Mindy/Jill's bag as she is hugging Molly and Zack goodbye. Abe goes a folder of papers which he placed in this lower right hand desk drawer and pulls out the handwritten scores. Abe takes them to the front of the piano and sets them on top, near the chair wear Zack usually resides.

He follows Beth and Mindy/Jill out to the patio, where Hugh is still reminiscing with her father.

All five walk to Mr. Paul's car. Beth inserts Jill's large black leather bag inside the trunk after it is popped by the remote.

"Guess this is it," Jill says, "I can't express to you how much I've enjoyed being a part of what you have going on out here or how much you've helped me."

Jill hugs Beth, then says, "I know you'll have 'The Place' going again in no time. What you've made here is very special."

Jill moves to Abe and hugs him firmly.

"I've never become more attached to anyone on any my assignments," Jill tells Abe. "You've become the grandfather I never had."

"Promise me," Abe says, "that you will stop getting too close to your work."

"Deal," Jill says before Abe swings her door closed.

She waves goodbye through the car window.

Light Blue Sailboat

Thursday, 9:51 AM. Abe is seated in the cabin of a Wannasea Island Constabulary patrol boat which has just rounded the east end of the island along with Hugh, Jack Druce, and John Steadman. The CID agent and sergeant are engaged in a discussion of jurisdictions. Hugh has been using his cell phone to show Abe the composite recordings from the surveillance system at 'The Place' which were taken early last Sunday morning. Abe has been surprised by not only the video quality of the recording but the audio as well. Even though taken in the dark of night at a distance of more than forty feet, the recordings look and sound as if they were made within feet of the two figures clothed in black, who could be seen setting fires and placing explosives. The final stunning aspect of the Defense System One recording is that only a few moments prior to the placing of an explosive at the base of the propane tank, both of the perpetuators cell phones had gone off with an emergency type warning saying, "Illegal activities have occurred during which you are being recorded." This announcement seemed to send both individuals into fits of panic.

"How did they manage to do that?" Abe asks his son.

"When the system determined that some form of unwanted activity was occurring, in addition to using directional algorithms to home in on those individuals, a scan of any cellular devices in the nearby area was made. Each of the individuals were carrying burner cell phones. As their devices had registered with the cell tower up at the Castle, the system was able to determine the numbers for each of those phones. By the point that the first fire was set, our operator was able to monitor every move those two made. At that point, we notified the island authorities. After the fire was set, our operator placed the emergency warning call to their phones."

"The authorities certainly responded quickly," Abe comments.

"I think they were tailing those guys," Hugh says. "Based upon some other scanning results, we think the van that they were in had a tracking device installed on it."

"Is it all legal?" Abe asks.

"If you look at the signs which we posted down at Abe's," Hugh says, "anyone who sets foot upon the property becomes subject to surveillance."

"What about in court?" Abe asks.

"The prosecutor says everything will be admissible," Hugh says. "It makes it virtually impossible for the Sylvesters' two men to claim that they were anywhere else. To make matters worse, one of them tried to make a call back to the younger Sylvester brother."

Jack Druce walks up to Abe and Hugh holding two sets of waders.

"Would you mind putting these on?" the policeman asks. "You are going to need them in a few minutes."

Abe and Hugh comply. It takes Abe a little longer to get the waders on as he still has the walking cast on his right lower leg.

Abe and Hugh have been asked to come on this boat trip around the eastern end of the island to see if they may be able to identify something related to CID's Sylvester Bros. investigation. Both officials have been extremely vague about what it is exactly Hugh and Abe will be asked to identify.

The boat goes between two of the small islands and slows as it come up to an outcrop of four loosely connected lava spires and one large lava dome structure which are known locally as the Four Spires.

About ten feet from the first two spires, the boat is brought to a stop. The pilot gently uses the engine to position the craft so that its aft is facing the outcrops then swings the boat through a hidden seven foot wide arch which is only visible at low tide. Cautiously the pilot then moves the boat within five feet of the right outcrop. He then lowers both anchors. The sea is almost at low tide but because of the structure of the spires and the basin between them, the water level here does not usually vary more than a few inches from high tide to low tide.

"Follow me," John Steadman says as he uses the ladder and railing to go over the back end of the boat into a little over three feet of water.

Hugh goes down first, then Abe. The bottom feels like sand. John Druce comes down the boat's ladder right after Abe.

John Steadman leads the pair through the first two spires which are separated by about fifteen feet. The second set of spires are twenty feet to the rear but at an angle of 270 degrees from the first spire. The opening between these two spires is almost forty feet. The depth of the brownish-green water is approximately two and a half feet. In front of them is a large lava dome. Its sides covered in seaweed and kelp. Hugh gives Abe a what-are-we-here-for look.

Jack Druce goes to the corner where the left-hand spire meets domed lava structure. He spends more than a few moments reaching into the crevice at the juncture of the two outcrops. He comes out holding both sides of a rusty brown chain which seems to be connected to the crevice in some manner.

Druce pulls the chain downward. As he pulls the kelp and seaward part to a distance of about six feet revealing a small sand covered beach. The beach is approximately thirty-five foot in length. On the right side of the beach, a good-sized wooden platform has been built to which both an inflatable raft and small boat are attached. A pallet, three crates, two lounge chairs and a desk are on the deck. The deck is strung with lights with wires which lead from the rear of the platform into what seems to be a cave.

It is what is on the left-hand side of the beach which has caught Abe's attention. As if pulled by its force, Abe wades through the gradually diminishing water to the light blue sailboat which is tilted on its side on the far side of the beach.

For the first time in over twenty-three years, Abe runs his hand over the boats mildewed port side. The mast is broken and hanging. There is no sign of the sails. As he nears the bow, he notices three small holes just above the waterline about a foot down from the railing.

"Is there anything here which you recognize?" John Steadman asks.

"This is my wife's boat," Abe says, his voice shaking.

"Is there anything which you can see which will verify that for us?" Steadman asks.

Abe goes around to the leeward side which is beached. Hugh is now right behind him.

"Would you mind holding on to her while I climb in?" Abe asks his son.

Silently Hugh grabs the railing and braces himself.

Abe lifts himself over the rail then drops the short distance on to the deck landing on his left knee first. Abe uses the sides of the boat to crawl into the cabin. The first thing which catches his eye is a badly burned section of the couch on the right side. He then notices dark brownish-red stains on the fiberglass floor near the wheel. Forcing himself to ignore those stains, Abe crawls to the access door on the right side of the wheel which leads into the hull. Abe squeezes himself through the hole. He then reaches up into the webbing just behind and above the door. He pulls out a 6" × 8" plastic case which is four inches deep.

Abe, still holding the plastic case tightly in his right hand, crawls back out of the opening, carefully turns himself around, crawls out of the small cabin across the graying deck and lifts himself over the side which Hugh is still steadying. Jack Druce stands a little further to the rear and has just completed videoing Abe's entry into the boat and return with the container.

Hugh and Abe walk around the small beach to the platform. John Steadman is seated on the old wooden desk chair. With some difficulty, Abe is able to unclasp the cover of the plastic container. Janie's wallet is on top. Julia's is beneath it. Under that are the sailboats registration papers. Abe hands them to John Steadman.

Steadman lays the papers on his desk and takes out a small audio recording device.

"Please state your full name, your address, your current location and today's date," Steadman instructs Abe.

"Abraham Hugo Stolz," Abe begins. "I reside at 111 Mountain way on the Island of Wannasea. Currently I am in a hidden cove at the Four Spires portion of the South Islands. Today is Dec. 21."

"Please provide to me a brief statement about the plastic box and how you have come to possess it," Steadman requests.

"After discovering my wife's sailboat, I climbed into the hull and retrieved the case from the upper hull space where we always used to contain our personal documents. Do you need anything more than that?"

"That should be fine," Steadman says. "Hugh, would you mind coming over and giving me your statement."

Hugh goes to the desk, as Abe walks back off the platform and goes back over to the sailboat. Jack Druce is now filming the outside of the sailboat. Abe leans against the side. He can't seem to bring himself to take his hands off Janie's boat.

"Is this the first time you've been out here, Jack," Abe asks the policeman.

"Third time since Monday," Jack Druce replies.

"So you are aware of the stains under the wheel and the burns in the cushion?"

"I am," Druce says, "There are also stains on the cushions on the other side. We are awaiting the results of those stains analysis. Would you mind holding the boat, I want to climb in and get one more set of interior videos."

Abe holds the railing of the boat. In approximately two minutes, he is joined by Hugh.

"John says as soon you've got all the videos you need," Hugh calls into the boat, "we can go."

Abe doesn't know how he feels about going. At the moment, all that he wants to do is to hold Janie's boat.

Jack Druce finishes the video and climbs back on to the beach. Abe is still holding on to the boat's railing.

"Come on, Pop," Hugh says to his father, gently taking his father's arm and pulling him away from the sailboat.

Reluctantly Abe follows Hugh around the stern of the boat and out of the cove. They watch as Jack Druce pulls the chain up and closes the curtain. After the curtain is closed, John Steadman pulls three-pointed wire clasps out of his pocket and uses them to ensure the curtain cannot be reopened without great difficulty.

Back aboard the boat, Abe and Hugh remain in their waders, waiting for John Steadman and Jack Druce to return. The moment the pair are in the boat, Abe asks, "Do you know how my wife's boat ended up in there?"

"We believe that we do," Steadman says. "Two days prior to your wife's disappearance, she had confronted Reggie Reginald about not only having forced himself on your granddaughter but doing the same thing to a 15-year-old waitress at your place. Allegedly after a rather physical argument erupted between your wife and Reginald, she informed him that not only was she going to the police over the matter, she was going to the press and would do everything in her power to destroy Reginald's career. Reginald told the Sylvesters about your wife's threat. The Sylvesters immediately became worried that your wife's actions were going to wreck their drug smuggling and other illicit operations into/out of Eastern Europe. On the day of your wife's disappearance, after your wife and daughter went into the sailboat, the two current heads of the Sylvester mob came from another area of the dock and jumped in the sailboat after your wife and daughter had gone into the cabin. The pair unmoored the sailboat and began using the electric motor to get out of the marina zone and head toward where two of their crew had moored their power boat. We are unclear what the actual intentions of the Sylvesters were at the point, but what follows is rather grim, are you sure that you want to hear it?"

"I need to hear it," Abe says with conviction. "Hugh, how do you feel about it?"

"I need to hear it too," Hugh says firmly.

"We are told that you wife grabbed a fire extinguisher and hit the younger Sylvester on the side of the head with it," John Steadman continues. "Somehow your daughter also got hold of knife, which she managed to stick in the older Sylvester's left thigh. The younger Sylvester pulled out his .38, using it to shoot and kill your daughter."

Steadman stops for a moment as the boat's pilot pulls up anchor and slowly moves away from the spires.

"Meanwhile, your wife managed to get her hands on the boat's flare gun," Steadman continues. "She fired a flare at the younger Sylvester but hit the couch when the boat lurched. The younger Sylvester then shot and killed your wife. The Sylvesters used the motor to get the sailboat out to their powerboat. They tied the sailboat to the powerboat and towed it out here to the Four Spires. Seems the Sylvesters have been using this cove as a hideout for as long as anyone remembers. After getting two of their crew to help them wrap your wife and daughter in the sails and weighted each down with an anchor, they used the powerboat to go ten miles beyond the edge of the southern reef and dump their bodies into the sea. They decided to put the sailboat into their hidden cove, thinking that's where it would be least likely to be found. The sailboat has been there ever since."

"How do you know all this?" Abe asks.

"One of the people who we arrested at your place on Sunday," Steadman goes on, "was the Sylvesters' explosives guy. A cousin of theirs named Cecil, who was on the powerboat the day that you wife and daughter were murdered. About three years ago, Cecil made the mistake of blowing up three competitors of the Sylvester Bros. in Minsk. Those competitors happened to be related to the longtime head of the nation's security services. Cecil has a very serious aversion to extradition to Minsk. Here, Cecil might face the rest of his life in prison. In Minsk, Cecil would face the rest of his life being tortured. We've been trying to get our hands on Cecil for quite some time. Seems he's been living in that hidden cove for at least the past 18 months. He only came out to do the odd piece of explosives work for the Sylvesters, handle drug shipments or collect supplies. Cecil also likes to talk. Seems he talked a lot to another Sylvester cousin, Danny, who we pinched about four months back as part of drug smuggling sting at the Halifax airport. As Danny is a Sylvester, we immediately started pressuring him to give us something. He kept going on about Cecil and a sailboat. Most of the people in CID didn't know anything about a missing sailboat. Danny didn't know where the sailboat was from or who had been on it. Danny had most of the people in CID wandering around the office saying 'Sailboat, sailboat?' to each other. Danny kept telling us that the sailboat was about two women, who were trying to blackmail the Sylvesters. The only other thing of value which Danny gave us was that he knew Cecil was hiding out on Wannasea island."

Steadman pauses for moment. Abe stares at the wall. Hugh at the floor.

"You know this sailboat thing which Danny was first trying to use as bargaining chip, didn't mean a thing to us," Steadman continues, "That is until a few days ago when Jill told us who that sailboat probably belonged to."

Abe remains silent trying to fully process what he has just heard.

"Once we nabbed Cecil on Sunday, everything basically fell into place. We squeezed Cecil using extradition to Minsk until he not only told us about the sailboat but took us to it. Once we arrested Reginald, it really didn't take all that long to get him talking about everything and anything. He didn't know anything about the sailboat, but he did know that where Cecil had been hiding is where they've been storing the drugs which he helped the Sylvesters bring in and the guns which they ship out. What Cecil & Reginald have provided along with the documents from your wife's sailboat will bring an end to the Sylvesters."

The Party

Wednesday, 7:38 PM. Outside of Zack's grandmother's townhouse, Abe sits in the back of a Geely TX4 cab which he has hired for the evening. Abe plans to wait until exactly 7:45 to go to the door and pick up Emma and Saanvi.

Thanks to herculean effort on the part of Abe's staff and many and varied customers and friends, 'The Place' had been able to be put back together enough to receive an occupancy permit earlier this morning. The rubble had been cleared out. Power and water had been restored. Two island construction companies had finished shoring up the kitchen walls on Friday afternoon, leaving the area where the explosion had occurred as a garage type opening where a Mobile kitchen was scheduled to arrive on Thursday. Two new refrigeration units had been brought in this morning. The back wall, where the mirror had been, was now painted over with a mural of the island done by Alexandra and Stefanie. Beth had bought a new van and then gone off to the Mainland to purchase replacements for all the ruined items. The current plan was for 'The Place' to reopen one week from this coming Wednesday. 'The Place' will be on a new schedule however, open only Wednesday through Saturday.

Through her boyfriend, Sally had arranged catering from one of the island's premier resorts. The dinner portion of the party had actually begun at 6:30. Abe had eaten quickly and had the cab driver pick him up at 7:20. When Abe arranged with Saanvi to bring Emma out to the party, Saanvi insisted that she not go until after the meal. They had then agreed to meet at 7:45 tonight at Emma's townhouse.

Abe sits in silence with his thoughts as the sixty-something cab driver turns the taxis radio in search of soothing music. Since learning of Julia and Janie's fate, time spent alone was time spent in torment for Abe. After Hugh and Abe returned from the Four Spires and told Beth what they had learned. Abe had spent a long evening and Christmas Eve essentially strapped to Beth's hip. Late on Friday, Abe was finally able to convince Beth that he was not going to go off the deep end.

Abe knew that he would spend the rest of his life feeling guilt for having brought Reggie into Julia and Janie's lives. Just as he knew that he would spend the rest of his life harboring burning hatred against Reggie and the Sylvester Brothers. Abe had decided, however, that his primary focus for whatever remained of his life would be spent assisting Beth to do whatever it is that she decides to do. Secondarily, Abe will focus as much as he is able on his partnership with Zack and Molly. Anger and remorse will be forced to take a back seat.

"7:45, Boss," the taxi driver announces to Abe.

Abe climbs out of the cab and walks up the two cement steps. He uses the knocker to announce himself.

Saanvi pulls the door back and says, "Come in for a minute, I just need to get Grandma's coat on."

Two seconds after Abe has come in the door, Emma has taken his left hand in both of her frail wrinkled hands.

"Eugene, you've come back," the old lady says to him.

Abe helps Saavi get the coat on Emma. The waits a moment as Saanvi grabs her jacket and puts it on.

Emma continues to hold Abe's left hand with both of hers but refuses to budge through the doorway.

"We have to go, Grandma," Saanvi says. "Zack, Mom and Dad are waiting for us."

Emma won't budge.

Abe moves in front of the old lady and says, "Emma, don't you remember, I promised to take you dancing tonight."

A brief glimmer of recognition passes through the old lady's eyes.

"Eugene is taking me dancing," Emma announces and finally moves through the door.

Saanvi enters the cab first, then Emma followed by Abe.

"I expected her to throw a fit over getting into the cab," Saavi says to Abe.

"Guess she likes to dance," Abe says with the old lady still grasping his hand as they climb inside.

Saanvi sits in contented silence as the cab makes the short seven-minute trip up to 'The Place.'

"I wouldn't have believed this if I hadn't just seen it," Saanvi whispers to Abe as she steps past him exiting the cab. "I expected to have a complete catastrophe and get no more than a block from the house until Emma turned the cab upside down."

Emma is still holding tightly to Abe's hand as he tells the cab driver, "I don't know how long we'll be in there, but it won't be any longer than 10. There's food and music if you'd like to come in and join us."

"I just might do that after I listen to the match," the taxi driver says.

Emma still clutching his hand, Abe walks through the familiar front door which Saanvi is holding open. They make their way to Abe's table by the corner of the stage. Zack is currently up on stage getting prepared for his performance. Zack's mother is sitting at Abe's table. Abe slides into the chair beside her and seats Emma, who continues to clutch his hand. Saanvi greets her mother then moves to a nearby table to sit with Beth and Marie.

There are a little more than 50 people present. All are past or current employees plus their significant others.

"I'm going to play some music for you, Grandma," Zack says after stepping off the stage and coming over to Abe's table.

"Eugene has come home," Emma says.

"That's great Grandma," Zack says. "I hope you'll like the music."

Zack returns to the stage. Just as he is preparing to step to the mic, Molly leads Zack's father and his fiddle plus Zack's uncle with his base out of the kitchen doors and up to the stage.

"We thought you might want a little help," Zack's father tells him.

Zack hugs his father then his uncle and helps them set up. Molly pulls two music stands with sheet music on them out from behind the piano as well as two microphones.

"We are going to start out with a few sea songs, tonight," Zack announces. "I have the great pleasure of having my father and uncle helping me to do them. These songs are meant to be sung along to, so as soon as you catch on, sing them with us."

Zack adjusts his microphone and pulls his stool up toward it.

"We are going to start off with a new song which Beth and I put together Friday night. It's called 'The Place.'"

Around six on Friday evening, after most of the day spent running around with Beth organizing things, Abe and Beth had gone into the studio to see if

Zack was serious about doing a podcast. Zack was insistent a podcast would be done whether or not anyone tuned into it. After a heated discussion between Molly, Beth and Zack, Molly and Beth had been able to convince Zack that if he was going to do multiple podcasts in a week, each one of the podcasts needed to have a different, well-defined theme.

Zack had insisted that he was going to do sea songs which had brought on another fifteen-minute squabble. Both Molly and Beth felt sea songs didn't belong on podcasts. Zack persisted. Beth finally got him to agree that if he was going to do sea songs, they would be done with an introduction and description of where this song had originated and how they were to be played. Zack pushed Beth to make the introduction. Beth pushed back and said Zack needed to have a song which would be the focus for the podcast session. Although Zack liked the sea songs which he had been playing, none of them seemed to be an anchor song. Beth and Zack began discussing what kind of song that might be. In the next forty minutes, they came up with 'The Place.'

In addition to the creation of the song, Abe had been impressed with Beth's introduction of Zack's session. Beth had begun by explaining where Zack usually played his sea songs, gave a brief history of 'The Place' and also threw in a plug for the Wannasea Historical Society, if any listener wanted to learn more about the island. Although Zack had been over an hour and half late starting the podcast, it had quickly become number 4 on his list of most viewed.

The Place (Sea Song) 127BPM tempo – D Major key – 2/2 time

built upon memories of determined women and a flying ace
please make yourself welcome to what we call 'The Place'
half-way up a mountain road
guests arrive by the carload
violins, fiddles and strings are bowed
here, island music has always flowed

yo ho ho and cups of java
on an island built of erupting lava
ye he he and Wannasea teas
playing songs from past centuries
made from memories none wish to erase

we welcome you now to our favorite place
built upon the memory of determined women and a flying ace
please make yourself welcome to what we call 'The Place'

mortar and brick, cement and stones
omelets, quiches, blueberry scones
join in our songs, we don't like to sing alone
we hope your worries, you choose to postpone
we'll sing tunes which time has not erased
be welcome now to our favorite place

ya ha, ha and bundles of spices
put away your worries and cellular devices
yoo hoo hoo and lemon cake slices
recreating tales of real sacrifices
made from memories none wish to erase
be welcome now to our favorite place
built upon the memory of determined women and a flying ace
please make yourself welcome to what's called 'The Place'

mortar and brick, cement and stones
omelets, quiches, blueberry scones
join in our songs, we don't like to sing alone
we hope your worries, you choose to postpone

where musical threads are often sewed
violins and fiddles and strings are bowed
where island song has always flowed
we'll chart a course for sensory overload
singing tunes which time did not erase
be welcome now to our favorite place

be welcome now
to "The Place"

Zack follows it up with *Comes the Tillerman, Shan't deceive her, Blow the Man Down, Randy Dandy Oh, Barrett's Privateers* and *Haul Away Joe*.

At this point, Annette and Josephine, two waitresses from a decade back, call out for Zack to do 'The Place' again. Zack, his father and uncle play it through twice with everyone in the crowd but Emma singing along. Emma is still tightly gripping Abe hands and smiling broadly.

"We are going to take a short break in just a few minutes," Zack advises, "after which I will take requests for anything you would like to hear played. Before that however, Beth is going to play a song for us. It isn't a sea song but I think that it is something which needs to be heard."

"This next song has been taken from a poem which my grandfather wrote three years after my mother and grandmother disappeared," Beth says. "In honor of them, I've used the poem to produce this song. Only the words to the a few of the stanzas were my creation. All the words represent what Abe has been feeling for the past twenty years."

Beth rises, walks across the stage to her piano. With Zack accompanying on guitar, Beth begins to play.

Julia, Janie and July – Tempo of 145BPM Key of G Major in 2/2 time

Julia, Janie and July
Julia, Janie and July
gone in the blink of an eye
gone without saying goodbye

westerly winds prevailing
where did they go sailing
what was the failing
that twenty-first of July?

three dreadful long days
four much longer nights
searched all West Bay
without setting sight
on their blue monohull boat
with dual sails of white

soon cast afloat
in the depths of their plight
despite all the best wishes
the sea often becomes vicious
raising hungry waves and threatening skies
and all that's left to do is to cry

Julia, Janie and July
gone in the blink of an eye
westerly winds prevailing
disappeared before saying goodbye
where did they go sailing
that twenty-first of July?

unbearable days
follow long sleepless nights
life a gray haze
full of worry and frights

a blue monohull boat
with dual sails of white
cast all of us afloat
lost in the depths of their plight

Julia, Janie and July
gone in the blink of an eye
Julia, Janie and July
their destinies unfulfilled
years slowly flow by
we long for them still

despite the best wishes
the sea often becomes vicious
raising hungry waves and threatening skies
with little now left but the tears in our eyes
for Julia, Janie and July

twenty-three years on
we learn what went down
two courageous, strong women
brought down by lowlife vermin
executed by Reginald thugs
for posing a threat to their running of drugs

a wife and a mother
years and years of wondering why
Julia and Janie gone in the blink of an eye
all we could do was to cry
Julia and Janie, may they rest in peace
our grief now finding a bit of release

westerly winds prevailing
disappeared before saying goodbye
disappeared before
having the chance to say goodbye

Julia, Janie and July
Julia, Janie and July
gone in the blink of an eye
gone without saying goodbye

***